MotherLess

GABRIEL HORN

WHITE DEER OF AUTUMN

Lisa Hagan Books

Powered by ShadowTeams

Cover art by Carises Horn "Bleeding Black"
Designers Kimberley Heurlin & Katherine Phelps

ISBN-13 :9780996968607

ISBN-10: 0996968601

Library of Congress Control Number: 2015956217

For my wife Amy
And daughter, Calusa

And thank you, Arianna Smith

MOTHERLESS

A NOVEL
GABRIEL HORN

AWARDS

2016 INTERNATIONAL BOOK AWARD
MULTI-CULTURAL FICTION

2016 NATIONAL INDIE EXCELLENCE BOOK
AWARD - VISIONARY FICTION

2016 PARIS BOOK FESTIVAL
HONORABLE MENTION - SPIRITUAL

2016 AWARD OF LITERARY EXCELLENCE
- FRIENDS OF FLORIDA MID-COUNTY
REGIONAL LIBRARY

2016 NEXT GENERATION INDIE AWARD
FINALIST BEST OVERALL COVER DESIGN
- FICTION

2015 FLORIDA BOOK AWARD BRONZE
MEDAL - YOUNG ADULT LITERATURE

SELECTED BY DEPARTMENT OF
EDUCATION FOR TALKING BOOK LIBRARY
FOR THE BLIND

CONTENTS

Prologue:

There and Not There

The little girl with long brown and sun streaked hair, who was just learning to speak, stood on the shore, holding her mother's hand as the Ocean lapped around their bare feet. Their ankles shared similar strands of pink and white shells buried in the soft sand as colorful coquinas wriggled around their toes. The wet hems of their floral sun dresses flowed back and forth with the water.

"Mommy! Mommy!" she called, the child's outstretched arm and fingers pointing, reaching, at something she was seeing, almost touching, across the water. "Look!"

The woman strained her eyes. "What is it, Sweetheart? I don't see it ...."

"Look!" the little girl called out again, her entire body energized and moving.

The woman squatted, her focus following her child's raised arm and tiny fingers, her mind stretching beyond the waves and the sand bar, and then at the moment she wondered if it must be her excited daughter's imagination, she caught a glimpse of a silver dorsal glistening in the sunlight. "A dolphin!"

"No, Mommy. Look!"

The woman held her breath. Beyond the silver dorsal, an island appeared wavering in the sunlight, white sand, palm trees, and tall sea oats rising from the dunes, everything undulating and dream-like, and then—not there....

"See it, Mommy?"

At first, the woman couldn't answer. "Yes.... Yes, I did see it.... I did."

The child finally dropped her arm and squeezed her mother's hand. Still looking across the water at the island her mother could no longer see, she smiled.

... love knows not its own depth until the hour of separation.

KHALIL GIBRAN

THE OPENING:

MEETING DESTINY AT THE BUS STOP

(Destiny: the power determining the course of events that can be fulfilled or missed depending on the individual's response)

The semi-frantic bus driver gripped his long dreadlocks, pulled them tight behind his shoulders, and fastened them with a thick stretch band. He looked down at his watch, then into his cracked side view mirror.

"Come on, Little Girl!" he hollered at the kindergartener with long sun-streaked auburn hair. She was still standing near the back of the bus staring into the ditch that ran the length of the road into a channel that emptied into the Gulf.

"Dat be de Indian kid," he said to himself in a Jamaican whisper.

The other children at the bus stop, and the ones retching in their seats inside the bus, held their noses and gagged as the ones outside squeezed through the slim opening of the jammed door; some bigger and older kids pushing behind and passing the slower and smaller kids up the steps; each with an acute sense of urgency trying to escape the stench coming from the ditch where the kindergartner appeared oblivious to the stink and to the bedlam.

Across the narrow two lane street, a heavy first grader who really should have been in second grade, wrestled with his nylon Nike backpack out the back seat of a shiny gold car with dark tinted windows, which sped away almost simultaneously as the heavy kid's new

2 Sketchers hit the asphalt.

In what appeared like a hurried waddle across the intersection, the boy paused on the faded yellow line in the middle, not because the weight of his 200 dollar iPod (a gift from his mother for being a good boy during the divorce), and those extra packs of cream-filled cupcakes he began carrying since the first day of school that year, were weighing him down, but because the putrid cloud of stink he had ambled into had triggered the mechanism in his half asleep brain to suddenly stop and pinch his nose shut.

"What the hell?" he bawled, scrunching his face behind his hand in a distortion almost as ugly as the stench. "Who farted?"

Unlike other mornings, he didn't cause any of the girls to cringe at his crudeness because they were already wincing from the stench. And the boys, given other circumstances would have laughed, but not now.

"Oh Mon!" the bus driver gasped, bravely poking his head out the window and turning to look at the little girl still standing by the ditch. "Come on, Child! Get in de bus, Mon!" he shouted. Then he grumbled to himself, the new influences on his language mixing with the old. "Dey ain't paying mi to breed dis shit."

"Leave her!" a tall fifth grader demanded, then held his breath, slamming the nearest windows, and then shouted again for the bus driver to leave the girl. He was leaning over the boy in front of him with the Nike backpack whose head was pressed against the grimy glass, watching the kindergartner.

"Please, Bus Driver!" the children shouted in a whiny, gut wrenching, out of sync chorus. "Let's go! Let's go before we die in here!"

The driver sounded the horn two times,

but it was as if the little girl at the edge of the ditch didn't hear it or didn't think about hearing it. He glanced at his watch. They were running late for the second time that week, and he would hear from the principal about it. He sounded the horn again, and again. The small kindergartener just stood there like the stink had somehow gotten herself frozen stuck. She wasn't moving.

Reaching under his seat, the driver had grabbed an old red rag, tied it into a bandana so that it covered his nose and mouth, and sort of slid down the bus steps, prying himself through the jammed door, and then moving as fast as he could to the rear of the bus.

In an instant that seemed to him and everyone else – a much longer time, he was reaching down and had taken hold of the kindergartner's hand, but, immediately, he could feel the resistance in her little arm, her doe brown eyes desperate as she gazed up at him, like hope before it dies.

"We can't leave her there," she said. His thick brows rose up his forehead as his own eyes went wide open at the very idea that there might be someone down there, maybe even a kid from the bus stop. He peered over the rag, down at the two grungy barrels that had been illegally dumped overnight.

"Leave who, Child?" the bus driver's muffled plea under the rag was near to panic, his eyes now squinted and wildly searching where the lid on one of the rusty barrels had popped open, spilling noxious gunk he recognized as too awful for him to even imagine who could do such a thing. "I don't see no one!" he said, as he scoured down the ditch at the corroded drums' deadly swath to the shallow stream where the water had changed colors.

4   He pressed the bandana to his face, his eyes blurry and still straining, they probed passed the other barrel that had a crack running the length of it, leaking used motor oil and diesel and what appeared like antifreeze from car radiators, and rancid smelling used power steering and brake fluids. Now desperate, he continued scanning around the barrels where several torn up tires and cracked and seeping car batteries had also been discarded into the ravine that was a little creek and supposed to be a runoff for rain water during big storms.

"Oh, dis be bad, bad!" he cried.... "Where? I can't see no one. Show me, Mon!"

He had always tried never to curse around a child, even his own, and he didn't allow it on his school bus, and he didn't mean to now, but the kids were pounding on the windows, and the smell was truly getting to him too, and he knew that if he didn't leave soon, he could wind up possibly suspended without pay along with losing in a very unpleasant way his breakfast: two cups of tea and a bowl of fruit. No milk. No meat. No fish too big. "Little One..." the bus driver begged, not hardly being able to catch his breath without feeling the urge to puke, eyes red veined and narrowed, still scanning over the frayed bandana down into the ditch. "I don't see who in de Lord's name yuh lookin` at!"

Then, the kindergartner with that long dark and sun-streaked auburn hair hanging past her shoulders, falling down her back, pointed; her stare fixed beyond the tip of her forefinger to a spot on the cracked drum just above the grimy liquid surface.

And, in that pool of oil chemicals and colored smelly slime, the driver did finally catch sight of a tiny body. Shaking his head slow,

he stared and gasped at what appeared like
something holy in a most unholy sight. "Ahh,...
Ain't dat too unreal!" he said soft and low in his
exhaled breath, humbled at what he was seeing,
and puzzled at his own feelings that for an instant
had distracted him from the smell.

A green tree frog that could sit in the
palm of your hand was lying lifeless on the side
of the cracked drum illuminated in a suddenly
appearing single beam of morning sunlight
shining through a jungle-like myriad of trees.

"Yuh make dat light happen, Child? Dat
some Indian magic yuh duh`?"

She looked up at him and blinked, like
the eyes of a doll, closing and opening, and he
felt embarrassed for asking.

"Listen, Sweet Child...," he said, trying
to clear his mind, gasping, and doing his best to
sound caring.

Any spark of hope that showed when she
looked up at him again was disappearing along
with the last lingering stars of the morning.

"Ain't notten' gonna bring God's little
creature back," he said. "It's dead. It got stuck
tryin` to hop itself outta dat—" and he couldn't
think of a word that wasn't swearing to describe
what he was seeing and smelling in that ditch.
"Wi don't know why sum'ady done dat.... Oh
Mon, I am so sick ah dis. Now, come on, Sweet
child, it ain't good wi breedin' dis shit."

"But we can't just leave her," she said
again, her voice cracking and coarse and pleading,
her stare, without hope's spark flickering any
longer, returning to the petrified image of the
tiny frog's long and powerful back legs bent in
the position to jump, now glued to the dark sticky
goo leaking from the drum, the tips of her once
orange colored feet soiled black and immobile.

Her big ebony eyes staring through a thread of opening at a world they will never see again. Her white throat smudged in black.

The girl had never heard the word innocent, but she recognized what it was. And though she did not know the word dignity, she understood its absence.

The bus driver had pulled the rag from his face so that it hung under his chin. And he stood with a pitiful gaze, looking down at the little girl.

"Wi can't know it be female," he said.

But she did know. The frog's white throat, the circles around her ears, the fact that she was larger than a male would have been.

"Please, Child, wi gotta go. How I say yuhs late for school because of de dead frog? Wi can't do notten' now."

"But what if she has babies?"

"Oh Mon, dead be dead.... Wi can't know it had babies." Then he coughed, the toxic smell irritating the back of his throat. "Hell, dey be probably all dead too. Or, maybe dey get out sum'how." He coughed again, yanking the bandana up. "I don't know, Child," his despair and desperation muffled in the words under the red rag covering his mouth and nose. "It's total contamination, so we can't even touch de ding."

Dead is dead, the bus driver had said. And she knew he was right; the tiny tree frog was dead, and a little girl was learning that death means never coming back. The pretty frog would not be listening to the singing of the male tree frogs that night as an angry off-shore storm, responding to their mourning songs, would bring a deluge of rain that would fall and finally free the dead frog from the corroded barrel, and in the little girl's mind she could see in that instance of pouring rain, the small stiffened body sliding down the ugly drum into the once purified water that all her life had sustained her. The little girl could even see beyond the dump site, the tiny lifeless form carried in the night songs of the other tree frogs with the rushing water on towards the womb of the great mother of all life, the Ocean.

Somewhere, at the very edge of the kindergartner's life experience, she understood, dead is dead, and yet, somewhere deep inside, she also understood that in some primal way, her death deserved more than this, more than dying in toxic waste she had no part of creating, more than dying without purpose. Death should have meaning. Death should have dignity.

She worried about the babies, waiting for a mother who will never return.

The bus driver looked at his watch again. "Come on, Little One," he implored, tugging her hand towards the front of the bus. "Dey get dis cleaned up soon," he assured her, but more himself.

"But the babies," she pleaded.

"I gotta get yuh kids to school. Heaven's sake, Mon, wi can hear the principal already.... Now come on," he repeated, as he helped her up the first step. Then, suddenly, he grasped her arm, and she turned as he let go. "Memba mi tell yuh dis," he said, talking over the red bandana, pronouncing his words as clear and serious as he could. "Everydey buck-it go a well....Wan day de battam drap out...."

She gazed at him with curious contemplation.

"Notten lasts forever, Child."

As she climbed the steps, he said, "I'm sorry," his words reaching out to her small saddened form as she headed down the aisle to find a seat amongst the commotion of grumbling and retching students.

The bus driver shook his head, and glanced again at his wrist, sad himself for the death of something so delicate and for the little girl who cared, and exasperated at the idea of a watch and an inflexible schedule holding him captive. Whether in natural time or the time ticking on his wrist, he knew that maybe we were all ...runnin' outta it.

His gaze shifted up through the half opened door across the bus stop and across the two lane road and focused on the tall palms and pines and wild oaks shimmering in the early sunlight, and then he thought outside his mind, a prayer of some kind, a dreadful prayer to God.

"It's bad, bad, Jah," he said, "such disrespect tuh nature, is disrespect tuh yuh."

He turned, pulled himself up the steps, and slid into his seat behind the wheel, the raucous in the bus, becoming a dull almost muted muttering in his head. As he pushed the ignition switch, the noisy engine started.

But, just about ready to finally leave the scene of horror, something made him glance again into the cracked rearview mirror at the ditch where the little Indian girl had been standing. Something had caught his immediate attention. Something with the color of sunlight in the eyes looking at him, looking through him, and into his soul. Something too extraordinary to imagine in this place....

The erect ears, the black nose twitching, assessing; the strong tall and powerful legs and body of golden tan and black, a white belly and paws, and a bushy black tail with a white tip that brushed the ground. Something that resembled a dog, but was not a dog at all. An animal so rare, he might've stepped in from a dream. Sacred and fearful all at once. Shocking. Captivating. The bus driver blinked. And the animal was gone.

You have noticed that everything an Indian
does is in a circle,
and that is because the Power of the World
always works in circles,
and everything tries to be round.....
The Sky is round...
the earth is round like a ball,
and so are all the stars.
The wind, in its greatest power, whirls.
Birds make their nest in circles,
for theirs is the same religion as ours....
Even the seasons form a great circle
in their changing, and always
come back again to where they were.
The life of a man is a circle
from childhood to childhood,
and so it is in everything where power moves.

BLACK ELK

CHAPTER ONE

THIS THING CALLED ... TIME

The beautiful young woman sat on a bench in the sun, staring up across the concrete walkway at the large, old clock high on the wall of the Science Building. She laughed quietly to herself, thinking that her grandfather would have also found humor in such irony, for the dictionary defines science as the study of the natural world using information gathered from the natural world, and the mechanical clock hanging from the Science Building wall is defined as a man-made device that has little or nothing to do with natural time, nor is an aspect of the natural world.

Still smiling, she remembered her grandfather saying once, that when he was a small boy, the last elder of his mother's people had told him that of all the ancient Native American languages he knew of, "None had a word for time." In front of the University Conference Room where the young woman sat, and waited, its imposing metal door remained closed. When you're waiting for something you want, this thing we've learned to call time seems to slow down. When you're awaiting something you don't want, this thing called time seems to speed up. Sitting on the bench in the warm sunlight, with the big clock just off in the distance, she shifted her attention to the east, where across the bay, storm clouds were gathering, and she was remembering her grandfather again, recalling a moment one sorrowful morning many years ago. She was a little girl, and she was scared and she was sad and she was angry, and she was sitting on the top step of the front porch waiting for something then too, only at that moment she was waiting for this something called time to turn back.

>>••<< >>••<< >>••<<

"Time is of the Mystery, Granddaughter," he said. He had seated himself on the porch step alongside of her. "One day," he said, "you'll be able to remember those ye loved that you've lost, and ye won't feel so bad. You'll feel the slant of warm sunlight streamin' through a window touchin' your skin, or you'll wake up deeply moved after seein' who you loved in a dream, or you'll be walkin' home from the bus stop and you'll smell the beach at low tide recallin' when you strolled on the sandbars together, searchin' for shells, and that tingling feelin' of warmth, or in that brief instant after a special dream, or embracin' that salt water scent of memory on your way home will fill you up, and may cause ye to close your eyes and put you in a different state of mind, and ye may even smile, and you'll feel better about havin' loved at all."

>>••<< >>••<< >>••<<

The gaze of the young woman with eyes the color of a young deer, lifted up again to the old clock, and she was smiling, still halfway in the feelings of that long ago memory crouched on the edge of the porch steps, when she and Grandpa, like always, were trying to make sense of things.

>>••<< >>••<< >>••<<

"Time is, indeed, of the Mystery, Granddaughter," he said again, raising his head, breathing in the ocean air, looking in the direction of the water that he could not see beyond the front yard and the trees and dunes.

"It is of this moment," he said. "And yet, it ebbs and flows like the tide. It circles the earth like the Moon. It circles the Sun like the earth. Time can move slower than the sap of an oak tree in winter, and faster than the speed of light through a galaxy. It can disappear into a black hole. Time does not run in a straight line, beginnin' here, and endin' there. Not time. Our lives and everything we're connected to move in circles and cycles," he said, "and one day, Granddaughter, this cycle of your life will be over, and a new one will begin."

Even now, in her mind's eye, as she sat on the bench in the warm sun, she can still see him next to her through the enchantment of memory, nearer to her than the metal door of the conference room, where she is scheduled to enter soon, and clearer to her than the hands of the old clock on the Science Building wall.

Sitting on that bench at the university in the sun on such a pretty day with the big clock just ahead hanging high up on the wall like an ornament of modern civilization, caused this very consciously aware young woman to reflect more on what she had learned about this thing called time.

>>·<< >>·<< >>·<<

They stood together on those very dark nights when the sky was absent of any light from the Moon, and on those special other nights when the Moon was full, the girl's small hand held in the security of her grandfather's, together, standing at the edge of each other's shadows, looking up at the exquisite bright being he had always called, Grandmother.

"I love you," she would hear him say to the Moon. "You are beautiful." The words as soft as the night air from a child to his grandmother, his eyes and heart in sacred wonder, gazing up, the resonance of his voice reaching across the space between them.

"Don't forget natural time, Granddaughter," she could hear him now, even as she sat quietly on a bench at a university, waiting for the hands of the large old clock on the Science Building wall to reach 3:15. And still, she could see him too, there again, in her mind's eye, her grandfather, now leaning against the porch post, the wolf Koda nearest her, standing alongside the sad little girl that she was then... so many years ago.

>>·<< >>·<< >>·<<

"No, Granddaughter," he repeated, "don't forget natural time, even though we must live in a world that is also run by the clocks of man-made time.... To forget the passage and cycles of natural time would also be to forget your kinship with the Earth, the Sun, the Moon, and the Stars. And that would be awful, Granddaughter. For nothin' can make us feel so empty than separation from our kin."

The child she was then gazed up at him, the feeling of that kind of separation connecting them.

The world she had known was changing into something else, something unknown, something new. And she was afraid.

"So," he said into the quiet of afterthought, "despite the goings on of civilized folks with appointments, time clocks, and rush hours, and regardless of what human bein's like us have gained or have lost, the sun still rises and sets. The moon waxes and wanes. The earth rotates on her axis, circlin' the great star we call our sun. Stars move with their galaxies. The galaxies move. Everything spinnin' and spiralin' in circles and cycles. All movin'... together. And us movin' right along with 'em."

>>•<< >>•<< >>•<<

Still, this young captivating woman, who knew all this because it is the foundation of her ancestral way of being human, who was aware of the nature of natural time, found herself staring up at the mechanical hands of an old time piece suspended in technological time on a university building; 3 o'clock, it read. Fifteen minutes, she thinks. Fifteen minutes and she will be judged.

In this man-made world of time, she has learned to function... in which we all learned to function. But for her, it became a symbol of the struggle she always faced, seeing the world in the ways of her ancestors, living in the ways of civilized men.

She does not give herself fully to the clock of artificial time, as Grandpa had said, for that would mean a disconnection from nature, and her ancestors, and even her celestial kin. So, she told herself, "Stop it," and turned her attention, instead, to natural time, focusing on those great mountain clouds piling high in the east, just beginning their trek across the bay.

She knows that, soon, over the churning waters, the wind will send them, the Thunder Beings and the rain. They will arrive about the time the sun moves behind the Science Building wall where the big clock hangs, and then, she imagines, the purpose and the cycle of her being in this place and time will be complete, and her life path from the time of her birth until now will

16   have reached its destination, and a new cycle will have begun.

Taking a deep breath from the depths of her abdomen, and releasing it slowly, she feels relief. Now she was back to thinking in natural time.

How fitting it would be, she thought, to rain on such a special day, making it seem all that more amazing, like another rebirth for her in the same lifespan. For now, though, while she waited with the patience she had spent her life learning, Father Sky covered the world above her in blue, and the mighty Sun shined on everything, and warmed her face in his light.

Her perfect lips forming a contented smile once again, she sighed, brushing away strands of her long chestnut hair, delicately touching the eagle feather fastened to her single sun-streaked braid lifting in the cool early autumn air. What a journey this has been, she thinks, to be here in this moment and place and to see it all opening in her mind's eye, like an ancient Mayan codex, the stories of the stars and of the earth and of her life unfolding, like so many stories, and she scanning these painted pages of her mind, looking back into this thing we call Time....

CHAPTER TWO

BURIAL IN THE TREMBLING EARTH

For several months the unusual tremors had shaken their small homes in the middle of the night. Now in the middle of the morning the trembling Earth was shaking again beneath the boots and covered shoes of the people gathered in the old cemetery. Snowflakes floated silently, landing on the snow covered and frozen South Dakota ground, even as it shook. The snowflakes fell on the many gray headstones, and on the feathers and colorful ribbons decorating the coup sticks leaning on them. The snowflakes fell on the dream catchers and hickory medicine wheels and other sacred objects, suspended from the bare boughs of the sleeping trees, lingering there and turning them white. They fell on the many crosses spread out on the snowy hill. They fell into the two deep rectangular holes dug side by side, and on the two pine boxes being lowered into the graves.

They fell on the people's teary faces as their cold breath drifted like smoke into a slate colored sky, the Earth beneath them trembling again. They fell on the men beating on a drum who sang a song that the child she was then did not understand, but the feeling of the words made her sense the strength and the sorrow of her own heart beating. The snowflakes fell and shivered on the drum. They fell on her grandfather's uncovered head and heavy coat, and on his arm that was wrapped around her little shoulders the whole time, holding her tight. They fell on the silvery white hair of the ancient woman standing otherworldly behind them who had held her in the classroom when the news of death arrived.

CHAPTER THREE

TIME WILL GIVE THE WORDS MEANING

Another strong gust, nearer to the last one, had caused Grandpa to rise out of bed early and pay closer notice to the way the fronds of the palms were scratching against his bedroom window. He and his granddaughter were it seemed to him half a world away from where they'd been....

Standing on the wood porch of his small cinder block house, looking further into the horizon, Grandpa studied the sky some more. Then he looked down. His granddaughter and Koda were at his side. After all, it was the ritual now.

"Thanks for cleanin' Koda's bowl and getting' him fresh water," he said.

She nodded, and half-tried a smile.

It had been weeks since the last storm had provided a good cleansing rain over the Florida coast where they lived. Now, another one was approaching. Perhaps a little stronger. But it was the ending of winter and the beginning of spring, and the storms this time of year tended to carry stronger winds.

She'll be starting school right after spring break, and the thought sent a quiver through his body.

Maybe before that time came, he would perceive some semblance of acceptance in her new life with him, and even small expressions of her being happy. It hurt to see his only granddaughter so gloomy, but it was her right,

for everyone needs time to grieve. Even him.
Still, it was heartbreaking, observing her little
form on occasion, gazing through the screen
door, her brown eyes following the trail past the
front yard that snaked toward the mailbox where
the pink lilies were getting ready to bloom. She
was looking at them now....

"You know, when you were still forming
in your mother's belly, she planted those flowers."

She shook her head, but kept her eye on
the lilies. "They're pretty."

"In a few days, they'll be stunning and
yet so subtle...."

He explained that the lady who owns
the beach shop, Irene Glassman, had given them
to her mom. "They were so small and kinda sad
lookin' in these big pots. Didn't have flowers. I
remember your mom carrying those pots up
to the mailbox. One at a time. There must've
been six of 'em. 'Maggie,' I said, 'let me help you
carry those pots.' But she just shook her head,
face sweatin' and all, and instead, insisted she
do it alone. It was a hot day and she worked for
hours plantin' those flowers, digging holes along
that ditch...."

The young girl's eyes strained.

"Ye can't see the ditch because the
flowers are tall now."

She glanced up at her grandfather, then
again looked up the driveway at the lilies.

"Can't ever forget how she cut herself
while plantin' the last lily."

"How'd she do that?"

"She'd told me that she knelt down
heavy on a shard of sharp shell. She was wearin'
a sundress at the time. The shell cut her knee
open pretty good. She bled a lot. Needed stitches
as I recall.... wound up with a small scar."

The young girl with long hair like her mother's, but auburn brown, not black, stared up at the road, and half a world away from where she'd been, still expecting, still wanting, someone to appear.

What could be sadder than a child's grief?

Even weeks later, standing alongside him and Koda, she seemed sullen and serious – too much, Grandpa thought, for someone as young. She appeared so small to him, especially now, so vulnerable, more than even the little beings that sheltered all around them, and the world too suddenly had become so much bigger to Grandpa, that even he felt small.

"The trees are feelin' it," he said, diverting his attention, and hers, to the wide rubbery leaves of the avocado, glistening in anticipation of the rain, branches heavy with fruit swaying ever-so-slightly. He gestured in contemplation at the palms as the wind grew to be less persistent, but with the occasional gusts becoming stronger. Then he cast an eye further out from the yard where palmettos were scattered along the forest floor and trees not native to this place, and susceptible to greater winds, grew near or around the indigenous huge oaks that rose from the sandy ground, the lengthy tendrils of grey leaved Spanish moss hanging from their long twisting limbs.

"Some trees must fall because they're old," he said, "and it's their time, and some are too young and their roots too shallow, maybe got seeded in places not good for their growin', or they simply fulfilled their growin', and it's their time. Birds build strong nests and care for their young, but even they can be blown away. Know that a storm can change things, Granddaughter. Sometimes for the worse. But," he said, "with its destruction, there's always some kind of renewal, or rebirth."

He gazed up, his mind calculating the arrival of the heavy hanging rain clouds. "... never without struggle, it seems."

Sensing something in the silence when the unspoken rests, she placed her small hand on Koda's mane and watched as the wolf studied the space around them, also sensing the arrival of the unseen. She looked up and watched Grandpa, watching the clouds, wondering if he sensed something too. Time passed. The moment lasted.

"It's gonna rain soon, huh, Granpa."

"Yes," he said, his eyes blinking him into a more fully conscious state. "Soon..."

The sweetness of his granddaughter's assertion had interrupted his momentary loss of self, staring at the horizon. Now he was looking down at her, but his sense of self, the man he thought himself to be, became the reflection, and along with it, came his insecurities and uncertainties. How was he going to do this thing, this ... raising of a five year and half year old child?

With a gaze beholding his granddaughter, he placed his hand on her shoulder, wondering again if all his grown-up words were making any sense, wondering too if he had any right. She's too young, he repeated to himself. I have no right. What do I know about raisin' a child? What do I know about the world?

Then he heard the whisper that would begin his transformation. The sound, like a quiet breath of the wind brushing a palm. At first, Grandpa thought he had imagined it, but the whisper had called his name ... Walter.

Walter, the voice called again. She's not

too young, Walter, the whispering said. Who better to guide her?

"Jewel?" In a sound almost too soft in the wind for a child or even a wolf to hear, he had called out the name instinctively. Still, after all these years, the anticipation of his wife's presence so natural to him, so expectant, it nearly lifted him into the air, when in an instant, the realization of her death quickly grounded him, and that she was not there, not where he could see her, and not where he could hold her anymore.

It was the disembodied voice in his mind, those words he would hear long ago on the rare occasions when he would be home long enough from a road trip, or in between trips, and find himself discussing with his own little daughter, the nature of the world, and of the universe.

Give her the words, Walter, the voice of Jewel encouraged. They are wise words.... You give them with such love.... In time, she will grow to understand their meaning.

Talk to her, Walter. Give her the words....

The beating in his heart quickened, forcing his attention back to the familiarized pain in his chest. "Dear Granddaughter," he said, as his mind began reaching into the bundle he had filled with longing and regret, "I should've been a better father to your mother while I had the chance. I should've been a better husband. All my life it seems I've always worked. I was a visitor between trips home. A part-time husband. A part-time dad. "

His physical absence from their lives had saddled him with this self-made bundle, a burden he bore even into his retirement years; now its weight and his age were not allowing him to make it up the last and final hill of his own life's journey.

"I wanted to spend more time with your mom when she was a little girl like you. I never even got to hear her first word! I wasn't there to walk her to the bus stop on her first day of school. I wasn't home to help her with homework. To see her graduate."

But his job to support the family is what they needed. What he needed to be doing. Often his work found him sleeping in his truck along roadside rest stops or in inexpensive motels that catered to truckers, away from home, in need of a cooked meal, and a hot shower. Driving big rigs all those years, he hauled deliveries to cities and small towns all over the country east of the Mississippi, across the border of Canada down to the Gulf Coast, then over to the Atlantic. Sometimes gone for days, even weeks.

"You can walk me to the bus stop, Granpa."

He looked down at the child at his side. Her wisdom returning his sense of wonder.

"You can help me with my homework. You can see me gra-jate."

A smile broke through his captive gaze, and the yearning for what should have been.

Then Koda took his place in the ritual, pressing his wolf face alongside the girl's, bowing himself in the way a wolf will do when he comforts you, his weight leaning and pressing her ever closer to Grandpa, arcing his large animal body along the back of hers, his long bushy tail brushing the back of Grandpa's leg.

Grieving is a process. It doesn't require you to be alone. Sometimes grieving together is better, than grieving alone. It feels better not being alone.

Rain Song

Close to the west the great ocean is singing.
The waves are rolling toward me,
covered with many clouds.
Even here I catch the sound.
The earth is shaking beneath me
and I hear
the deep rumbling.

Tribal Song

CHAPTER FOUR

THE RAIN BRINGS HER NAME

"Did ye know," he asked, looking at the water pooling in his hands, "this is your namesake?"

She nodded slowly, and watched the rain filling and cascading from her grandfather's hands.

"Sometimes a name comes in a dream," he began. "Sometimes it comes through observation, like watchin' how someone behaves."

"Like if someone loves horses," she said, "ands always carin' for them and ridin' a horse, then maybe her name could be She Loves Horses."

"Yes," he smiled, "somethin' just like that.... But a person's name can come in other ways too. Sometimes in a vision that is more than a dream. And sometimes it comes in a dream. And sometimes it comes because of somethin' special happenin' at the moment of birth. Somethin' that'll stay with that person her whole life. A name carries meanin'...."

"My mother named me," she said.

"Yes, she did. Ye see, your mother gave birth to you in a rain like this, Granddaughter. It was a rain that broke a terrible drought," he said. "The water was disappearin'. Fires were burnin' the Glades. Worst one started with a cigarette butt thrown from a car window. Smoke hung everywhere. Even as far up as here. Animals ... birds displaced. Deer starvin' to death, runnin' through the burnin' saw grass and Cyprus that used to be wetlands until the sugar farmers and ranchers drained the water and big energy moved in."

Her brown eyes opened wide, her jaw

dropping, she stood transfixed and disturbed in the storyteller's words.

"Panthers chokin' on the air, and cars hit them escapin' 'cross the interstate. Alligators can't find water.... Everything dyin' and thirsty. Dyin' and scorched." He repositioned himself as the pain throbbed in his knees, but still his arms extended, his hands remained together, cupped in the rain. "They said it was the worst drought and fires since they'd been keepin' records. Your mom labored from sunrise to sunrise bringin' you into this world."

The rain fell harder, the drops bigger. The sound of rain everywhere....

"We almost lost her," he continued, his voice raised above the din of the downpour, "but your mom was strong, and she was brave, and she held on, and then, the instant you took your first breath, it rained!"

He poured out the water pooled in his hand, and she watched and Koda watched. "Rained for nearly two days and because of that, saved much of the glades and the forest and of course so many of the animals. And that's how ye got your name."

"It's gonna be okay," he said. "The nature of a storm does what nature needs that storm to do. If that means makin' us afraid, then maybe that's not such a bad thing. Because it makes us brave. Maybe that's how we become smarter too. For some folks, maybe makes us more humble.

"If the nature of a storm means makin' us change too, then change can turn into a good thing, even though it can be painful while you're goin' through it."

As the hard rain softened, Grandpa stood, his back slow to straighten. And then, with Koda still pressed against her, she watched her grandfather be quiet as he looked off into a light misty drizzle, his fingers rubbing at the place over his heart.

"Humans need to know they can't control everything, Granddaughter," he said, breaking the silence, seeing into things not using his eyes. "When it comes to Nature, and sometimes when it comes to other humans. You can just know that Nature needs to be free. And we are Nature. Your name sings that connection. We need to live in agreement with nature, and not impose our will, like humans have been doin' over the earth and other people since they got the foolish notion that they can.

"Respect nature," he repeated, "and learn to find gratitude, even in a great storm, no matter the damage. For as long as we got life, we can't let our fears of losing things and sorrow over things we've lost take the place of our love for one another, for those who've passed. It's that love that keeps us movin' forward."

Slowly, he shook his head. "No, Granddaughter," he said, "like a lot of things in life, storms, and the way some people behave, are just not under our control."

A spear of lightning connecting Sky and Earth had flashed far out over the waters beyond where they could see followed after a while with a distant rumbling they could hear.

"We ought'a go in the house pretty soon," he said. But just for a moment, they stood alongside each other now in a sacred silence with the rain, she looking up her grandfather, watching beads of water trickling trails from the corners of his eyes, one pooling with a rain drop at the edge of his cheek, then falling on her arm. Koda was still wrapped around them both, and Rainy smiled.

CHAPTER FIVE

A STORM IS COMING...

More than the coming storm kept eleven year old Rainy Peek awake, more than wondering what middle school would be like tomorrow, more than even missing her mom and dad. For over six years she had lived here with Koda and Grandpa, and storms had come and gone, and some were stronger and more violent, and some dispersed before they arrived. This one, though, this one coming tonight was bringing something different. It was not a fear or dread. It was a keen awareness of suddenly everything in her life coming together. She was especially thinking about the words that people had said, the words during this particular day, as on other days, that hurt her, and it was those words that were merging with the big energy of the storm that kept tossing around in Rainy's mind as she tossed in bed.

CHAPTER SIX

BEAUTY AND THE BULLY

The school day began with an assault at the bus stop, not a physical assault, like somebody punching and kicking another human being, or hurting an animal for no good reason, but the kind of assault that uses words to hurt you personally. Words to demean and belittle you. Words shot into your brain that can never come out....

"You're only part Indian, not a real Indian," declared Terrance Walcott, standing on the highest point on the sandy shoulder of the two-lane road. He was an eighth grader, who some say should have been left behind in seventh like he was in third.

"Look at your skin," he said, and pointed with his fat finger at the sixth grade girl. "It ain't even red."

It had been three weeks since the first semester of school began, and Terrance had never spoken to Rainy, so his outburst that morning startled her in two ways. A few of the children who were there, like the ones he knew talked about him behind his back because of his being so overweight, glanced up from their texting or smart phone browsing or from themselves looking in mirrors, and over at Rainy to see what she would say, but she didn't say anything.

In the corner of her eye, she caught sight of the white plume. Before she had left the house that morning, her grandfather asked if she would like to wear it. He said that the feather came from a white heron. He had discovered it on the ground a few days earlier on his way to the mailbox.

"They're rare and sacred beings," he said. "This one must've come for you. Special Delivery."

She was mindful that wearing it would make him happy, and it was pretty. She was also aware that it drew attention to her Indian-ness.

"Soft plumes for promise," he said. "Firm stem for strength."

And so, she gave into his charm, and allowed him permission as he fastened it to a single braid that graced the side of her long sun-streaked brown hair.

Suddenly, though, she wondered if the pretty feather didn't belong there.

With her fists clenched, her lips press together, Rainy raised her dark brown eyes and looked up at Terrance. Though she appeared more than angry at the ugliness of what he had said, the betrayal felt worse, as did the embarrassment.

Her striking face, the soft shades of the pink and purple shell necklace that she always wore, the confidence in her voice the few times he heard her talk, these were all things that Terrance Walcott more or less admired in the sixth grader. He even liked the t-shirts she would wear, like the black one she had on today, tucked into her capri jeans. It pictured pastel-colored flowers shaped into a peace sign. He also especially liked another one, this shirt deep red, where a silver-painted hyena on the front, was dragging along a human skeleton.

But the t-shirts Terrance had first described to his mother as "cool Indian designs," only initiated his mother's tirade of ugly things that people can say about other people they don't even know. He never told Rainy any of this, and he never would.

All of these things, and Rainy herself, made Terrance uncomfortable being around her, but she couldn't know that. She couldn't know that his father when he visited with Terrance briefly over the summer, made fun of Rainy, and her grandfather, when Terrance had talked about them, but he did elicit a semblance of compassion, adding that some of 'em (meaning Indians) got a raw deal, but his mother?

She would just shake her head that even the idea of Indians in this small beach community was, in this day and age, surprising, as if Indians weren't supposed to exist anymore, except on reservations or "making money off casinos."

Even his stepfather had something to say between beers about Indians. His stepfather worked on oil rigs out in the Gulf of Mexico, mostly off the Louisiana coast. A lot of the time he was gone, traveling, and living on the platform. He said he didn't mind being at sea for weeks because he made good money. When he was home, it could be for several days.

He had told Terrance once, as he handed the boy a crushed can of Bud, he didn't think that they (meaning Indians) were allowed off the reservations.

"Indians never did nothin' with this country when they had it," he said, Terrance handing him another beer. "That's why we gave them reservations." He popped it open and began drinking it as he lay back in his electric, black leather recliner, remote in his lap, watching a befuddled looking man on the 62 inch big screen TV news station in HD, ranting over something to do with the government.

"So, you see," his step father continued, raising his head up, talking over the news program that had switched to a commercial where an image of a lovely butterfly had something to do with a drug that helped people sleep. "It's like this, little man," Terrance's step father said. "Americans took over land the Indians were living on in order to procure our natural resources for this country, like oil, coal, uranium, gold, farmland and so forth. It's what Darwin called, survival of the fittest." He let his head fall back and took another slug, his eyes glazed over with the return of the well-dressed, nicely combed blonde haired woman that now appeared on the television news.

"Land would go to waste, otherwise," he said, pressing the volume control of the remote, making the TV voice louder.

His stepfather not being home very often, turned out to be a good thing for Terrance, because his stepfather got drunk a lot and went on mean-spirited rants like the man on TV, and occasionally he went after Terrance.

"Besides," he said, pulling back the flip top and exploding another tall one, swallowing as much as he could with giant gulps. "Ain't no real Indians left. They're dead. Cowboys got 'em."

He laughed, poking his finger at Terrance's stomach while still clutching the can. Then his mood changed. "All you got these days is mixed bloods with coloreds and whites and immigrants. You can't even tell what they are anymore. I once seen a Negro woman... anyways, I thought she was a Negro, with that straight jet black Indian hair, and thought, How odd is that? Then I'd see an Indian on the Little Bayou fishing one day off the pier, and I know he was an Indian because he had that weird thing going on, like he understood something about fishin' nobody else did, and he had that long dark hair too, only it was turning white, with one braid between his shoulders. He was wearing sandals and looked more like an old hippie, but I knew he was an Indian....

"I'm tellin you, Little Man, they're all mixed bloods is all. It's nature's way. If you wanna see a real Indian, you gotta try and catch an episode of a Lone Ranger rerun. Now Tonto... he was the real deal. Not that Johnny Depp crap.... Too bad," his step father added, his face showing some kind of emotional loss that Terrance had not seen often in him.

It had something to do with those reruns, remembering a segment of his own childhood, when it was early morning and he felt safe watching T.V. His own father just home from the platform would be sleeping one off, his mother probably not there. "Tonto's dead too," he said suddenly and sneered at Terrance. "As are the rest of the real ones.

"And why the hell would you care about Indians, Chubby? You're not sweet on that little half breed squaw I heard you talkin' to your mom about?"

Terrance smirked and shook his head vehemently. "No," he said.

His stepfather reached into his pocket and held a wad of bills. Slipping a ten out, he gave it to Terrance. "Now here. Go by some war paint or somethin'. Get yourself some burgers." He snickered. "I hear squaws like their burgers like they like their men.

Terrance stared at the money. Couldn't make sense of his stepfather's gibbering. "Thanks," he said, wide-eyed with possibilities.

"But bring me another tall one before you head out and do something stupid."

Terrance nodded that he would and

left clutching the ten dollars, already imagining what he might get, but forgetting to bring back the beer....

Rainy couldn't know any of this. It's hard to consider how some people are, how they raise their kids, how they think, especially if you can't even imagine it yourself.

She did know that she had never called Terrance Walcott "Tundra" or "Wal-Mart" or "T-Rex," like some of the eighth grade kids did, and even the seventh graders. Once, outside behind the gym, he sat on a kid so long for calling him Tyrannosaurus, the kid almost stopped breathing. He got three days detention for that. Another time, he had socked a kid in the nose in the bathroom, and the kid's nose wouldn't stop bleeding. That got him a week suspension.

It was widely known that you didn't mess with T-Rex, because, sooner or later, it would be your misfortune. If he would catch you at the moment, which wasn't often, Terrance Walcott would punch you with his big fists until you cried or was bleeding or both. Sooner or later, though, to any kid's misfortune, no matter how long ago it happened, you would wind up getting cornered at school, like behind the gym, or in the bathroom, or at your locker. He would get you in the school bus. He would get you for something he heard you had said about him or a certain cross look he may have thought you shot his way, and you would get hurt.

He learned a new punch on the Saturday afternoon when he returned after not bringing his stepfather the beer, and he had seen a girl's bracelet Terrance had bought with his ten dollars, dangling from his jeans' pocket. Terrance never saw it coming....

He had learned "the gut punch," as the

other kids would name it. The gut punch got delivered as a direct blow to the solar plexus with a hard fist and would render anyone in bad shape, winded and sucking air, but quiet, and leaving no evidence of blood behind.

However, at that moment, when Rainy was looking up at him at the bus stop, it was Terrance that got struck. First, at the way her pretty face transformed from a look of anger, then pure horror and betrayal, to embarrassment, and then to anger. Then at a surprising gust of wind bursting out of nowhere that hit his face and flipped his Cleveland Indian baseball cap onto his shoulder. His father had given the cap to him on a visit last summer, seeing how his son was interested in Indians, and Terrance wore it every day since, though he didn't care about baseball, and didn't live with his father in Cleveland. He did manage to grab it before it got blown away, but he had placed it back crooked on his head.

Now it no longer shadowed his face.

WHAT HAVE I DONE!

What have I done
that it feels I have torn the world apart?
And the wind wailed,
You have broken
a heart.

TRIBAL SONG

CHAPTER SEVEN

THE REAL INDIANS ARE ALL DEAD

The sudden gust at the bus stop had diverted the other children's attention away from Terrance and Rainy, to the quick mess it had made of some of their clothes, and hair styles, and maybe blowing some sand on their hand-held technologies, but Rainy stayed focused on Terrance, the burst of wind framing her face with her long hair, the twirling white plume secured to the sun-streaked braid.

With his baseball cap on sideways, she didn't have to look directly at the ugly face it showed above the visor, the big nosed, red faced mascot on the front of it named Chief Wahoo, but she could see most all of Terrance's face now, and how his plump cheeks pushed up against the slits of his pale blue eyes, and pressed down against his mouth, making it, and his lips, seem small and out of proportion with the rest of him.

Undergoing Rainy's unexpected analysis, he caught a glimpse of himself mirrored in the pools of her dark eyes, which now caused Terrance to feel a semblance of uneasiness. It made him nervous at what this pretty little sixth grader had seen; and, for an instant, as he straightened his baseball cap, he got unexpectedly perplexed at the same time about the timing of that burst of wind. He wondered if it weren't some weird Indian thing that his step father had talked about and he'd seen in movies, that had to do with nature and spirits, and that spooked him.

He didn't like that feeling because it partnered with a kind of fear with which he was not familiar. It was not something he could see.

It would never be something he could know. It was nothing he could punch, or beat up. Still, Terrance had learned a ways back how to deal with unfamiliar feelings of any kind, and with a hard shove, he pushed this one back down with a disgruntled sneer, while shoving his hand down his pocket, concealing forever the necklace and silver charm he was continually carrying to school.

Yet, as is most often the case with Terrance Walcott or anybody who oppresses his feelings, nothing gets held down for long, and sooner or later that energy is going somewhere.

When the school bus pulled up, he blocked Rainy at the entrance, and before he was about to take a big breath and make the climb up the steps, lugging his backpack, he turned, and, pale blue slits glaring at Rainy, said, "My stepdad told me that the real Indians are all dead!"

Rainy's face took on a look of shock. How could you say that? she wanted to say, but he was already getting to the top step, seizing hold of the bus railing with a huff. She wanted to grab onto that backpack he was dragging behind him and yank him down, but she probably wasn't strong enough, and besides, he could fall on her. So, instead, she just averted her eyes away from the sight of this overweight bully struggling to reach the top where he had to hold onto the railing some more, before landing in the nearest seat to the front where one of the kids had rolled a soft boiled egg.

Everyone in the bus laughed when Terrance Walcott plopped down, and though he knew that they were laughing at him, Terrance appeared somewhat satisfied over the attention, particularly when Rainy walked passed him, but he didn't feel the squish, so he did not know what they were laughing at. He just kind of showed a half-hearted smirk, and when the bus door squeaked and squealed shut, and the bus started down the road, blowing out dark dirty clouds of exhaust behind it, Terrance had a sudden craving for a pack of Twinkies, which he always carried extra in his backpack.

When you want to teach children to think,

you begin by treating them seriously when

they are little, giving them responsibilities,

talking to them candidly,

providing privacy and solitude for them,

and making them readers

and thinkers of significant thoughts

from the beginning.

That's if you want to teach them to think.

BERTRAND RUSSELL
(NOBEL PRIZE FOR LITERATURE)

CHAPTER EIGHT

HIDING HISTORY

All through the human experience on this planet, at least, the little that we know of it, philosophers, writers, and scholars of history have observed that a people who do not learn their history will be forever doomed to repeat it. The key word here is doomed.

When Rainy had first started out in school, she liked reading, and she especially like reading about history, but she soon discovered that her people's history, the one her grandfather told and read to her, was very different than the one that she was reading in her textbook, which hardly mentioned American Indians, or Native Americans, at all.

"Why don't they teach what happened to our people in school, Granpa?" Rainy would ask. "Why don't they teach about the contributions of our people?"

Her grandfather understood that there was power in knowledge, that knowing things helped you think through difficult situations, and gave you a strong sense of empowerment, but he was also aware that it would not be easy for Rainy, seeing how she was so young, knowing the things he did about history.

A lot needed to be considered.

He could still recall his anger as a young man reading for the first time the detailed accounts of the Indigenous side of America's history. He remembered the eyewitness testimonies of the Pilgrims' setting fire to an entire Pequot village, and all the human beings living there, in the name of God. He read about President Andrew Jackson's forced death march of the Cherokee that American historians called the Trail of Tears.

He read about The Homestead Act that granted American citizens the right to take Indigenous people's land and country all across the Great Plains. He read further, about America's great Western expansion, which the United States government gave the name, Manifest Destiny. In this nineteenth century document, the Americans granted themselves all the land that didn't belong to the United States between the Atlantic and Pacific oceans.

Grandpa's feelings as a young man boiled over into tearful rage sometimes after reading of slaughtered buffalo killed for sport or shot for the money their hides would bring; some even killed for amusement by bored train passengers, their bodies left to rot on the disappearing prairies by the thousands; and the US Army reports of massacring Indian people where they were living peaceably at places like Sand Creek and Wounded Knee.

He read about the hangings in Mankato, Minnesota, of thirty-eight Santee men, old and young, ordered by the Great Emancipator, Abraham Lincoln, and how it was proclaimed, America's Greatest Mass Execution. He read about the gifts of small pox infected blankets taken from dying soldiers and given to Indian people as a tactic called germ warfare, and the mayhem and terror the US government and its military had inflicted on Indigenous people everywhere because none of these things were ever read nor discussed while he was in school, and they weren't discussed now.

Looking back, he could see that his young man's anger, and the anger of many others who were reading the same books, not only centered on the betrayal and brutality of the history that is all the Americas, but that he was made to believe so much differently.

Rainy, though, she was only in her first year of middle school. She was still a kid, and Grandpa felt that with few exceptions most school boards and administrators and teachers dealing with issues of education did not want her, or any of the kids, to know the Indigenous side of American history, or really anything that was Indigenous to this land. Not their art. Not their music. Not their literature. Not their accomplishments. Because it all contradicted with the history taught in school, and it was not a history of good. How could they justify the brutality they inflicted on an intelligent and culturally strong people? The less American students were taught about Indians, the better for them. They would not be holding any discussions about using an entire race of people as mascots and stereotypes. Not unless some brave teachers were willing to risk their jobs....

And so, Grandpa remained quiet for a moment while he thought some more on his granddaughter's question about the teaching of history. He even went outside with his pouch of tobacco, and with Koda at his side, stepped off the porch to make a prayer offering, sprinkling the dried flakes of tobacco leaves over the ground where he had once found an eagle feather, and on that special spot, that's where he would talk to the Great Mystery, knowing for certain that he had to choose and select words most carefully

He said, looking up to the Sky, "Great Mystery, pity me, a grandfather in need of guidance.... Thank you for my life and the life of my granddaughter. Thank you for the joy she has brought me, and thank you for the challenges she provides me. But, I need help, Great Mystery.... I need to find the courage and the wisdom that is you within me to know what's right for my granddaughter, and for Mother Earth."

After some time had passed, he came back inside and sat at the kitchen table where Rainy was already sitting and doing her homework. He held a box of matches and a big conch shell in his hands. Inside the big conch he had put some leaves of sage and cut sweet grass and pieces of cedar. Then he struck a wooden match on the side of the matchbox with the fingers of his one hand as he held the conch with the other, igniting the small pile, blowing his breath softly into the shell and fanning it carefully with the eagle feather, cleansing their space for the words about history that were about to enter it.

He blew again just enough breath to extinguish the flame and used the feather to make the smoke that smelled ever so sweet and sacred, swirl and float and coil and dissipate like you would imagine spirits unconstrained from all limitations.

Then he placed the shell on the table. It was an ancient ritual and a new ritual they shared together for the first time.

"Your mom used to read to you about our people even while she was pregnant. She did that, so you might know these things. She hoped that the stories she told you while you were still in her womb might feed your own growin' spirit, and that your spirit would know even before you were born. Then, she imagined when you were older, your mind would need to know one day, and you'd ask the questions about your people that your spirit beckoned, like the one you asked me now.

"That's why I will answer you, Rainy. I feel your mom and dad would want me to...."

He took a slow deliberate breath and closed his eyes. Releasing the breath, he opened his eyes again, and looked through the sacred smoke at his granddaughter.

"You see, Rainy, education doesn't provide kids in school the history of what happened to American Indians because it would not be a good history. How could you say, 'We are a great nation,' and pay homage to your flag while singin' the Star Spangled Banner with your hand over your heart, or sing songs like, America the Beautiful or God Bless America, when you know for a fact that this nation, for whatever the reasons, has contaminated or destroyed so much of the waters and lands of the very country you'd be singin' about? And is still doin' it today. How could ye feel singin' about the Pilgrims' pride and God's blessins on America when you know about the genocide committed against your native ancestors who once lived here? It would not be easy for most people. So, the way I understand it, they choose to not know the real history and facts about these things, and somehow, they believe their ignorance protects them. Somehow, from what they are taught and not taught, it makes what they're singin' feel good in their minds about themselves."

Rainy looked up at him through the white smoke. "What's genocide, Granpa?"

He took in another slow, but deeper breath. Then he let it go into the sweet and sacred smoke drifting above the table.

"Genocide means the death of all the fathers and mothers of one tribe or one nation or one people," he said. "It means the death of all the grandmas and grandpas, aunts and uncles, brothers and sisters, cousins, friends, all the children, and even the babies, all wiped out by people believin' that they had a right to take what was not theirs by whatever means they could. Genocide is not almost total annihilation, it is annihilation."

As the smoke thickened, its fragrance even more potent, he paused, allowing that sweet scent to disperse any anger or bitterness that could conjure. He needed to remain calm, quieting the beating drum that was his heart.

Then his eyes shifted to the front door, gazing momentarily through the screen into the yard, seeing with his mind's eye all the way to the shore, and beyond, where turquoise water sparkled in the light of the Sun, and dolphins breached and mantas swam, and life was going on as it had for a billion years. And then he saw further out, the drilling platforms disrupting the beauty and the balance....

"They'll do anything for oil, or coal, or gas, and just about anything else that makes money. That's their true history, always takin' more than they need. Not thinkin' of the mess they'll be leavin' for the children of the world, and their children's children ... only the bottom line."

His voice was low and somber, his heart, the beat a medicine drum in a healing ceremony.

"Of course," he said, "the energy of those dead tribes and nations didn't just vanish into nothin'. That energy was all put back into the collective energy of nature, and sooner or later Nature will reclaim what belonged to Nature, regardless of the history they tell."

Sweeping through the screen door, like the wings of a ghost water bird, a breeze caused the white remaining smoke from the shell to drift up.

He turned to his granddaughter, sitting near him at the table. "Do you understand, Rainy? Can ye see why our people's side of history is not included in school when it comes to the history of America?"

Pressing her lips together, she thought. Then she nodded. "I do, Granpa," she said. "Because it would not be a good history, and it would make them feel bad about themselves."

"No, it would not be a good history. But, history's a living thing, and each generation creates its own, or recreates the one they inherited. It's somethin' we should learn from, even if it's not good, it's somethin' to not go on repeatin'.

"But, instead, the only time the history of American Indians is given any attention in school is where we might be convenient and useful, like how Sacajawea lead Lewis and Clark across the West, or how Indians attacked innocent pioneer and settler families, hinderin' their way to the American dream of prosperity.

"It was a dream, all right, that became our people's nightmare...."

Leaning forward on the table, he touched the shell, and felt its smoothness. "The irony of it all seems crazy, because when a school needs a mascot with some kind of symbol of honor and courage, a fierce warrior mascot, or the name of a tribe they stole from, or wiped out, does the trick.

"They always say, The past is the past; we need to move forward, and why that is true ... that you can't change what's happened; we have a responsibility to learn what happened, to learn where we've been, and how we got where we are, so before we make that step forward into wherever it is we're going, we know how to act

48 when we get there."

Grandpa said that even Indian people played a part in some of the bad that was done, and still are to some extent. "The way I see it, Rainy, everyone can make mistakes, but only fools repeat them.... If a country, or a people, doesn't learn their history, or learn from their own mistakes, and even from the mistakes of others, they'd become a country, and a people, made up of a lot of fools."

She reached alongside her chair with her toes to find Koda who had laid next to her.

Grandpa leaned forward, elbows on the table, folded hands supporting his chin. "It's gonna be hard for ye, Rainy, knowin' the things you do, or for that matter just by bein' Indian because, even if ye never said anythin', your heritage accuses. You can't help bein' a catalyst for their collective guilt, a reminder of what they've done to become the country they are, 'the greatest country on earth,' which they readily claim to be, or of their failure.

"But, in spite of all this, it'd be good for ye to learn both sides of history, and to just try to understand how things got to be the way they are, and how people got to be the way they are. Understandin' might take some of the sting out of their behavior....

"Then the more ye understand, the better chance you'll have of helpin' to make the world a better place and that maybe you and others like ye can keep us from being doomed."

Truth does not change according to our ability

to stomach it.

FLANNERY O'CONNOR

CHAPTER NINE

DESCENDANTS OF COLONISTS...

A rare heated discussion was taking the chill out of the air-conditioned teacher's lounge one morning during the teachers' planning period. This one pertaining to the political debate of new immigration laws, "My family history goes back to the arrival of the Dutch colonists and New Amsterdam."

"They were still immigrants, Colonel," one of the younger social studies teachers responded.

"They were colonists!" Mr. Kline snapped, sitting up in his chair. "They'd become the foundation of this country."

"But there are diverse perspectives of that."

"Facts are facts, Mr. Leming is it? There's a world of difference between immigrants and colonists."

The treatment of the Indigenous people who were living here at the time the Dutch landed would give you nightmares. So, though proud of their ancestral claim to North America, Mr. Kline's family had to long ago dissociate themselves from that particular barbaric aspect of early American history, burying the evidence in the New York City archives. Now, their descendent, Mr. Kline, was a history teacher, presenting the sanitary, even heroic, version of the New Amsterdam settlement, unaware himself, in part by his own choosing, of the horror that lay hidden in those libraries.

This was Kline's thirty-fifth year of teaching at Osceola Middle. Though most everyone referred to him as the Colonel, he was a long retired veteran of the war in Viet Nam, who had also served some time as an Army reservist. Over these past ten years, he had lost his wife, and then his son, burying them both at the edge of town in St Vincent's Presbyterian cemetery where he had stood at their gravesite ceremonies, stoic as an officer ready to inspect his squad.

The school board, as well as the administrators and faculty and a lot of the parents valued his military service, and seemed, for whatever reason, guilty in his presence, so Mr. Kline, aka the Colonel, was above the status quo of teachers. To some extent, many of them felt at least partially responsible for his suffering as they regarded it as the price he paid for their freedom and his love for America.

He was six feet tall once, and lean, back in the day. Over the years he had shrunk an inch or two, and he was overweight, and nearly bald except for thin outcroppings of white hair above his ears. He was obese in his stomach, and now dealing with the onslaught of type 2 diabetes.

Prepared to leave the teacher's lounge for his next class, he rose from the old chair where he had been sitting and drinking coffee, and tossed the Styrofoam cup into the garbage. With his grade book and text under his arm, he walked to the door. For a moment he paused there, standing with his hand on the knob.

Then he turned to the small group of teachers and staff at the table, and those sitting in the older cushioned chairs, reading books or snacking, or also preparing to leave for classes, all more or less, participants in the new immigration laws discussion, and said, "If I were you, I'd be careful of this idea going around to change the curriculum. They want to assign supplemental reading requirements in our subject areas to include diverse perspectives. What they're trying to do is get us to teach negative history about our country. What good can possibly come of that kind of pedagogy? Especially in these times."

CHAPTER TEN

SAVAGES

When Rainy Peek entered Mr. Kline's classroom on this particular morning, neither of them was wanting to deal with the other. For one, she was not coming from the better place that her grandfather had mentioned where learning both sides of history helped you understand more about human behavior. And, after dealing with the issue of immigration in the teachers' lounge, the Colonel was not about to support any such notion as diverse perspectives.

Rainy Peek was, for Mr. Kline, a student he needed on his rolls if he was to achieve the teaching award he coveted, but her very presence in class disturbed his sense of balance. That meant his control. He had the authority in class, which he mistook as power.

He had only mentioned days ago of the "eloquence of mankind's greatest social achievement," the Declaration of Independence, but as he continued to read from the textbook that it "is at once the nation's most cherished symbol of liberty and Jefferson's most enduring monument," he again felt uncomfortable because of her presence in the room.

By reading further on the night before, and then researching the Declaration and the Constitution on the computer, and finding in her grandfather's library several books that referenced the influences of the Iroquois on the founding democratic principles of the newly formed United States, Rainy had already discovered Jefferson's reference in the document Mr. Kline had read was the "most cherished symbol of American liberty," that the Indigenous people she regarded as her ancestors were, according to the Declaration of Independence, "...merciless Indian savages". However, on that day, she remained silent with her newfound knowledge, but, as her grandfather had explained, even in her silent presence, dwelled accusations .... Her mere existence made him uncomfortable, and yet quite contrary, she remained his only hope for the award.

On this particular morning, though, she would break that silence.

As she slid into her desk chair on this already difficult day, her adrenalin was still coursing through her blood since that encounter at the bus stop with Terrance Walcott, so when Mr. Kline had the students turn the textbook pages to one that pictured Benjamin Franklin flying a kite in a storm, Rainy just thought, How crazy is that! She figured that he must not have an understanding of power.

Still, she remembered what her grandfather had said about trying always to understand, so she made an effort to at least sympathize with a grown man flying a kite during a storm, when her teacher, the Colonel, proclaimed that Benjamin Franklin helped discover electricity by doing that. And that "discovery" had tugged at her sense of ambivalent curiosity.

Maybe Grandpa was right....

So, she read along as Mr. Kline read aloud the part where Benjamin Franklin was called "...one of the founding fathers of the United States of America." The word father had also been used with Jefferson, but it still had the influence as a word to strike a tender chord in her, so she felt that maybe she might like to learn more about this other father, Benjamin Franklin.

Mr. Kline had lowered the book he had been reading, and addressed the class real serious, and said, "Benjamin Franklin loved this country as all the founding fathers. These were the men who set the very foundation of Western civilization here in America, and allowed for our way of life to advance."

Rainy began exploring another perspective. The night before, she had again *Googled* the <u>Declaration of Independence</u>, even the US Constitution.

When the Colonel saw her hand go up, Damn it! he wanted to say. His lips tightened, his neck tensed, and in a concealed glance behind his thick glasses, he looked up at the clock....

Some students were looking at him, then turning and glancing up at the clock too, which was behind them. Some were looking at Rainy. Others weren't paying attention to anything but the cell phones concealed under their desks. A few of the students, seeing that only about three minutes remained, were desperately quiet as they prepared to be the first to leave at the bell.

With the coveted teaching award, which could liberate him from the classes of ordinary kids, and that fall teacher's workshop in active learning, which included student/teacher interaction and would be a part of his overall score on his end of the year evaluation, each looming over his head, in a reluctant gesture, the Colonel flicked his hand, as a person might do to brush someone off, rather than invite a response. It was a gesture he'd make upon the rare occasions when a student actually *wanted* permission to speak.

"We've only got about a minute ... Miss Peek... is it?"

She forced a courteous smile, swallowed,

and sat up, her hands folded in her lap. "How could they go about loving a country, Mr. Kline, when they destroyed it at the same time?"

"What are you referring to?"

"The founding fathers.... You say they loved America, but I think what they loved was the freedom they gave themselves to take whatever they wanted. By their behavior, and by what I've seen in my life, people don't love the *land*, America. They love the *idea*."

"Miss Peek, they forged a country that would become the greatest industrial nation in the world, and the most powerful, and they accomplished this based on the rights of men to be free. Wouldn't you say that's impressive enough idea for the love of one's country?"

"But you can love somethin' without respecting it.... That's how you can love something to death."

He stared at her, and didn't speak. His mind rambled and struck out.... *You thought military school was best for him, so what if he was... different? He was your son! You still can't even use the word.... You can't! But he was your son! You loved him.... You just wanted him to make the right... choices .... You wanted the best for him because you loved him. You wanted him to like girls! You didn't stick the needle in! He did. You didn't even know....*

"Mr. Kline?"

He looked blankly at her. "What is it?" he said, weary and disconnected.

"I think the founding fathers gave themselves the right to take whatever it was they wanted. Because they gave themselves that freedom. And that's what America was for them. So, when you're talking about how much they loved their country, you're not really talking about the land."

"You're telling me ... what I'm talking about?" He squeezed his eyes shut, and took a deep breath. Then opened them and exhaled. All of a sudden, the two hundred ninety-eight page textbook he was still holding felt heavy, and yet only three pages were dedicated to the war in which he had fought and sacrificed his own soul.

Actually, less than three pages.

"Land serves a purpose, Miss Peek. Otherwise, it's wasted, and that's what the founding fathers had realized. All this land, not being fully utilized, nor cultivated to its potential, especially for an advanced civilization, inspired the early Americans. They rebelled against Great Britain for imposing taxes on them. The fought against the French. The Spanish. This land is our country, the American colonists proclaimed. We settled America. And they fought to establish a free country with land and rights for all of us...."

Have you read the Declaration of Independence lately? she wanted to say.

But she didn't.

"Problem, Miss Peek?"

She shook her, No.

His frustration at more than this, more than her arrogance to challenge and unwillingness to submit to his authority and the authority of the text, more than his life, released in a suppressed sigh of fatigue. He closed the book and, with the class in stone silence, walked back to his desk. When the bell rang, the energy inside him imploded: thoughts about the "incident" in Viet Nam seeped through his skin as sweat. The flash of his father's photo in uniform caused him to tremble, and the vacant emotions for a mother, and a wife, who distanced themselves with medication from everything, including him, left an emptiness in his thinking.

The flower arrangement; he couldn't see the true colors on the casket of his dead son! Now this know-it-all girl that he needed in his class; and those young liberal colleagues supporting revisionists' history; his wanting at any costs that teaching award which could validate his own existence and possibly liberate him from these classes of ordinary students; and the notion of his foreseeable retirement.... A war waged in his weary and uneasy state of mind. He could hardly hear the bell, and himself say, "Dismissed," nor was he even certain he had said it. What he did hear was the unrestrained scuffling of the students escaping through the door...a muffled memory echo of young soldiers' boots as the troops relieved of combat duty broke rank and raced across the tarmac at Fort Bragg....

He sat heavy in his chair, pretending to examine his attendance sheet. When Rainy Peek passed him, she only glimpsed his eyes feigning to ignore her through the thick glasses, as if she didn't matter. Like the ghost of the young peasant girl who passed him as he remained standing on the air strip with nothing between himself and the caskets adorned with American flags being unloaded from the air transport.

CHAPTER ELEVEN

THE AFTERMATH

"So," Grandpa said, taking the dinner plates down from the cupboard. "How did your meeting with Dr. Lawson go? It isn't every day you're invited to see the principal."

"It went okay. And thanks for picking me up after school, and not grillin' me on the way home."

They decided on a big salad for dinner. They made it pretty much from scratch, including the first tomatoes their Home Depot plant had given to them, and the herbs they picked up at the grocery store.

"Of course," he said, setting the table as Rainy sliced the tomatoes at the counter, holding one to her nose, inhaling the flavor before she tasted a sample.

"Well, I didn't mean anything bad about what happened in social studies today. I think that maybe I should've not said anything. I just wanted.... I should've known. Maybe I did. But sometimes...."

"I know. You've just gotta learn to pick your battles. You picked this one."

"I guess I did...."

"I told ye, knowledge is power, Rainy. It's sound crazy, but you gotta be careful with it. Use it for the greater good. Too many zealots out there, seeing knowledge as a threat to what they believe. They can get downright nasty about it."

"Is Mr. Kline a zealot?"

"No. I wouldn't think so. He's just always been what he was taught to be. He's lived and thought the way he has for so long, the idea of changin' is not somethin' he chooses to

60 deal with."

He tossed the tomatoes that she'd cut, and some lettuce and some spinach together. Sprinkled some dressing while she set the bowls on the plates and silverware and glasses on the table.

"But change is a part of life.... You told me when I was little kid ...change can turn into a good thing, even though it can be painful while you're goin' through it."

He raised his eyebrows. "Yes, I do recall saying that...."

Huh, she felt herself say and sat at the table, her legs over the side of the chair.

Grandpa reached into the refrigerator, taking out a raw chicken quarter for Koda.

"And so, Miss Rains," he said standing over the sink, hold the chicken quarter with a paper towel, "how did your meeting with the principal go?"

"She told me that Mr. Kline is a veteran and deserves our respect because he fought for our country. She said he has a lot of passion for teaching history, and that maybe I should stick to what he teaches and what the textbook says, and continue to excel on my tests. That would make him happy, she said, and make me a good student."

Grandpa held the chicken quarter in a paper towel, briefly in his hand. He had his eyes focused on it and was quiet. Then he said, "Thank you."

She understood that you always expressed your gratitude to that which sustains us, even Koda's marrow bones for chewing deserved gratitude. Grandpa had said that Koda needed the marrow bones for his teeth, and the gnawing helped him relax, gave him a sense of pleasure and contentment.

He put the chicken, bones and all, in Koda's bowl, which he promptly carried onto the porch. A minute or so later, you could hear his wolf teeth and jaw breaking the bones and chewing.

"She also said that if he complains about my behavior again, that you'd be called in for a conference, and seeing that I didn't have a father or mother, and how I was living with my grandfather, it could mean the child welfare services might have to 'intervene' (her word), though she said she wouldn't want that...."

Terror tactics. Threaten to take the children. At first, his heart pounded real hard, like it could jump right out of his chest, and he took a deep breath to settle himself, exhaling slow. Another deep breath. Exhaling. He felt himself become light headed.

As if he sensed something wrong, something upsetting the balance, Koda returned, drank some water, and sat next to the old man, leaning against his legs, and Grandpa's hand reached for Koda's head where he liked Grandpa to scratch in his ears, and it felt good to Grandpa too.

"At least she didn't give ye detention...."

They chuckled, like he'd made a joke, and then they ate, and they were quiet.

I want to know what dark matter

and dark energy are comprised of.

They remain a mystery,

a complete mystery.

No one is any closer to solving the problem

than when these two things were discovered.

-NEIL DEGRASSE TYSON

CHAPTER TWELVE

STAR TALKING: FINDING THE BALANCE

The ritual of "star talk" began around second grade and lasted for years.

Tonight, a night in the fourth grade of Rainy's education, they star talked about the recent discoveries of dark energy, and dark matter. Koda lay at their feet, working on a bone.

Grandpa held his mug in both hands, a form of meditation for him before he would begin speaking. Another aspect of the ritual.

"Some scientists and astronomers are sayin' now, that there's much more dark energy, and dark matter in the universe than anything else, even light, but that they don't know what the dark energy or dark matter is.

"Of course," Grandpa said, as the crickets chirped around them, "being in fourth grade you probably ought to show caution when it comes to scientists with their so-called theories." At that moment the cicadas sent a wave of their electric whirring over everything.

"Maybe you can help me now with this latest dark energy theory I was readin' about," he said, lifting his mug, adjusting his flip flops in the sand and lifting his legs fully onto the chair. "It has got me intrigued."

"Dark energy makes me think of people that give me a bad feeling," she said, "and certain places where I don't want to go.... I mean, when I see people who give me that feeling, I just want to get away from them."

With her fingers of one hand holding the handle, she placed her mug back on the arm of the chair, and leaned her head back as far as she could. "I don't mean now, sitting in the dark under the stars here with you and Koda. I love this kind of dark night, but without those pin points of light out there," she said, "and without you and Koda alongside me, I'd feel uneasy, like a few nights ago," she said. "I was taking out the recyclin', and I got this weird feeling, and when I looked up, I saw a shadow standing in the driveway. Just stood there looking at me, but it had no eyes, or nothin'. Just a shadow.

Koda stared at it too, and growled real low, and bumped my leg. I bent down to pet him, but he was real stiff, and his hackles were up. Then when I looked again, the shadow was gone."

"Huh," Grandpa said, rubbing his chin. The incident disturbed him. Can't never be too complacent, his mind was thinking .... Don't let your guard down. You've got to protect her....

"Shadow people," he said. "Stay away from them, Rainy."

He thought about the word, foreshadowing, a future energy, a form of dark energy that can cross the veil that separates dimensions and appears as some form of shadow in the present, and can be seen, or even felt and not seen. He was sure this was not what the scientists or astronomers were talking about, but he felt the connection.

Closing one eye, she made a fist and pressed it against her cheek and focused with her opened eye, using her forefinger and pointing up at the sky, like a telescope aimed at individual stars. Sometimes, she said, "when I hear the bad things some kids say about other kids, I start thinking about the bad things that people do, and the bad that has happened in my life. And that if I choose not to get away from them, I will have to do battle with their dark energy."

She dropped her finger telescope, and was quiet for a moment, and then she said something that startled even her. "I'll never really have my mom and dad again."

It was the first time she had ever spoken those words. But then, the idea of dark energy seemed to draw her in....

Laying back in the comfort of the Adirondack chair, her faced raised to the night, the dark energy was taking hold of her mind, like the gravity of a distant black hole, attracting her light, like the radiance of stars pulled in by its force, into the mysterious blackness of itself....

>>·<< >>·<< >>·<<

It was the first day of second grade....

Grandpa had walked with her to the bus stop. One of the older kids who was new at school and, no doubt, trying to impress Terrance Walcott and the other older kids, sat up in his seat, and said real loud without thinking, and laughing out the window, 'How!' and another boy sitting alongside him put his hand over his mouth and gave a whoop when the school bus was driving away, and they laughed.

T-Rex just smirked, his eyes following her grandfather. With his face turned towards the rear of the bus, he could see through the grimy narrow windows, the older man take a deep breath before he headed back across the street. Passing the mailbox, Terrance caught a sliver of a glimpse of the wolf greeting the old man. Shifting his attention to the Indian girl sitting in the aisle seat several up from him, he could only glimpse her too.

She sat with her folder and her rainbow colored lunch pouch in her lap, along with a worn book that had belonged to her mother, Marguerite Henry's Misty of Chincoteague, about wild horses that lived on a barrier island. The vision of her dark brown eyes drifted to the trees and her ears listening to the sounds of birds and thinking she might've heard a tree frog singing, through a cloud of exhaust and noise from the engine of the school bus.

No one could see her surprise when the toes of her red sneakers were finally able to touch the floor.

>>•<< >>•<< >>•<<

Koda shifted again, pushing beside her chair, causing her to steady her mug. A sign his bone-time was done.

"To me," Rainy said, scratching his mane with one hand as he settled, and lifting the handle of the mug with the other, "a lot more bad happens in the world than good." The sweetness of the tea did not suppress the bitterness in the words. The peculiar imbalance causing her emotions to teeter on the edge of calm. "It's like the bad is so much bigger. Is that the dark energy and dark matter the scientists are talkin' about?"

Grandpa pressed his head back against the chair. "Huh," he said, the question had evoked more reflection. He repeated the sound, and he drank his tea, and thought some more.

"I think you can look at dark energy and dark matter as metaphors like that," he replied, with some apprehension. "Not all dark is bad, though. The fertile earth is dark. The universe when we look up at the sky and stars, is dark. A place of mystery. One of the sacred colors in the circle of life is black. So not always is dark, bad. But the kind of dark energy you're talkin' about can be a metaphor for disharmony. Negative feelings. Low resonance.... Evil.

"It won't be defined that way in your science text, but it's in your Harry Potter books. Hardly a good story without them. But that's my point. The bad, as you say, or the dark in the scientists' theory, only seems that big to them, as it does to us. So, if there's no balance of light and dark, good and bad, and other things we can't even imagine or put words to, everything would be total chaos, Koyaanisqatsi," he said, using a word he'd never spoken with her. "It means out of balance, but the word's intended for civilized humans who are livin' now on Earth.... For we can't know the universe."

"Ko'-yaan- iss'-skots-zee," she repeated.

"Yes. It's like livin' in a home where nobody's centered. Everyone's out of balance. The house where they lived would be Koyaanisqatsi...."

She put her head back against the chair. "Then the people themselves would be Ko'-yaan-iss'-skots-zee."

At that moment, their eyes shot wide opened as a bright meteor fell across the sky, leaving a long and quickly disappearing trail of light behind, and they could hear one another catch their breath.

"Thank you, Ah-nuh!" Grandpa said in a whisper.

"Who is Ah-nuh, Granpa? Is that a Mayan word?"

He shook his head. "No.... Someday I will tell ye about Ah-nuh."

Her lips tightened. Her eyes looked off to the side. She was disappointed. Ah-nuh, she repeated in her mind. Something to do with the meteor. Something to do with gratitude.... Her disappointment didn't linger.... She would just have to wait. Sometimes you have to be patient.

"Ko'-yaan- iss'-skots-zee," she said again in that moment of illumination, and to herself, she thought of the word, the name, Ah-nuh.

Grandpa glanced at the flakes of tea leaves in the mug, searching the patterns that formed symbols, and then suddenly asked, "What'd ye feel when ye look up at the stars?"

"Huh," she said. "Like a tiny spec. Smaller than a speck. Smaller than even what's inside an atom... Especially my brain. Sometimes I wonder about how the light I'm seein' from them stars left way before I was born, and even you, Granpa, and even before the Earth was born. Then I think that the light that's leaving them right now while we're speaking won't get here until long after you and me and Koda are gone. Maybe even the whole world. Maybe the light from some of them stars left so long ago that the star has died and what I'm seeing is a ghost."

"A ghost star," he said. "I never thought about it like that. In all my years... a ghost star. Maybe more ghost stars than we can imagine....

"Sometimes it's good to feel small, Rains. Then what we're goin' through can't be such a big deal."

He sat up in his chair, holding his mug on the arm rest. Then he chuckled and lifted a half used pencil from his shirt pocket.

"Here," he said. "You take the pencil, Rainy."

She did.

"Now, put an imaginary dot on the Earth."

She reached over the chair. "Okay. Dot on."

"Now imagine again that the dot you just made is our Sun, and all of North America, including Canada and Mexico, is the Milky Way."

She looked down at the dot, and then look up, her eyes shifting from side to side, up and down, her mind recalling the drive with Grandpa from South Dakota when she was only five. How much earth there was! Prairie. Hills. Mountains. Rivers. Lakes. And there is this dot. Her mind expanding until it almost hurt. She was quiet.

"They say there's more stars in the Milky Way than grains of sand on all the beaches of the world. Billions of stars. Billions of galaxies. We're just like microscopic human cells on this earth. But," he said, emphasizing the but, "we are here. And no matter how small...we do exist. We are a part of it all. How special is that!"

She shifted in her body, staring back up at the sky.

His eyebrows raised, and like it just happened yesterday, he turned suddenly, thinking he had heard the sound of a bee, but it was night .... "Do you hear that buzzin' sound?"

She looked at him. "No."

Maybe his hearing was going. He had read that ringing in your ears, or a buzzing, or a whistling could mean you were losing your hearing. He heard it again. "I swear, I just heard a buzzing. Like a bee..."

Her hands were nervously drawing closer to her body, and without her thinking, she had brushed the handle of the mug just enough she almost knocked it off the chair.

"Geez," she said, annoyed at herself, yet wary of any sound or sight that resembled a bee.

"Must've been something' else...."

"Granpa," she asked, "would being angry, or afraid, make you and me dark energy?"

One of his flip flops fell under the edge of

the chair.... He had walked into the house once, holding onto a flip flop he had broken after an encounter with an angry bee....

His young wife was putting the groceries on the counter. She had warned him to leave the bee alone, that he wasn't threatening anyone, and there she was shaking her head. Her long black hair hanging to her waist, she hardly believed she had just witnessed an almost knock-down-drag-out all the way up the drive way between her husband and a honey bee because he took an unprovoked swat at that bee. But Grandpa knew that she was smiling too, for he could see her reflection in the window above the sink, looking at his reflection looking at her....

Holding the mug in his lap, his toes hanging onto the one flip flop that remained on his foot, he found himself staring down at the what was left of the darkening tea and seeing himself again in a reflection – only much older – and he was seeing in a split cluster of tea leaves clinging to the side of the mug, the symbol for a broken heart.

"Even the little bee can be angry, Rainy, and afraid," he said, coming back from a waking dream. "Though we may associate those feelings with darkness, he's certainly not dark energy or dark matter. His existence is our life! Without bees, we'd be outta food in no time. So ye see, dark and light exists in all of us because there's dark and light energy in the whole universe. How could we know joy if we didn't know sorrow? Or courage if we didn't know fear?"

"Fact is," he said, "it's not like we don't have those feelings or emotions we think of as dark inside us, or ever experience them, because we all do. We're human beings and a part of the universe; it's that we don't let them get the best of us.

"Maybe the more we remain in the light, the more we become the light," and his voice trailed off.

"Maybe," Grandpa said, after a while, "what I'm takin' outta this latest scientific theory of dark energy and matter is pretty simple. As I see it, just by me and you and Koda's presence in this world, we are the livin' proof that there's always a balance in the Great Mystery, even if it's not so visible to us on this Earth, or in the known universe of science."

He turned to look at Rainy who was sliding down a bit further on her chair, and struggling to keep her half opened eyes on the stars.

"It's simple," he said, as much to himself as to his granddaughter, and again, the echo of his father's words giving him comfort and a sense of connection.... "Our job's decidin' what part of the balance we wanna be on.... Light, or dark?"

With her eyes almost shut, she nodded that she agreed. "I feel that Balance now," she said in a sleepy voice, "right here in the front yard," her hand dropped over the arm of the chair, her fingers somewhat wriggling through Koda's mane. "Right here, 'tween my fingers ...'tween you ... me ... everything. I feel it.... It feels like light, even in the dark."

With his back resting against the wooden chair, Grandpa glanced down into his empty mug, where a few of those straggling tea leaves that escaped the straining, had re-formed, attaching to the sides and laying on the bottom. He studied them for a moment. It was something his Uncle Roger, his father's only brother, had learned in Ireland. Some called it magic. Some said witchery. His Uncle Roger said it was ancient. Before he died, he had taught some of it to Grandpa. Tea reading....

He turned slightly, so he could see his granddaughter, and he whispered to her, You will learn the science. You will make a difference.

She was still nodding that it all actually did make sense to her, this metaphor of light and dark energy, though not sure whether in her dreamy present state of mind that she or Grandpa would ever know the mystery of dark energy and dark matter that the scientists were talking about. Maybe there are just some things that can't be understood through the technical, but more through the mystical of metaphor.

Her eyes were closed, and she was yawning. Koda was standing over her.

The Song of the Stars

We are the stars which sing,
We sing with our light;
We are the birds of fire,
We fly over the sky.
Our light is our voice;
We make a road for spirits,
For the spirits to pass over....

This is the Song of the Stars.

Tribal Song

CHAPTER THIRTEEN

DARK ENERGY AND THE ENERGY OF LIGHT

Yawning when it's late at night and you're about to go to bed is one thing, but yawning in the Colonel's class was another. She looked up to see if Mr. Kline had noticed. He didn't like yawning. He said that it indicated your brain was too tired to learn anything. He said that you shouldn't stay up so late gossiping on Facebook, or "tweeting" or watching "antics" on YouTube or playing with your IPhone, or on any other of your electronic gadgets, so you're too tired for school the next day.

"It's all time you're wasting rather than studying and doing your homework," he said. "That's how you become lazy and unemployed."

She took a deep breath, and forced her eyes to open wider, almost as wide as they had when she was six years old and digging for a shell she'd seen partially buried in the sand in Grandpa's backyard. It seemed like all of a sudden right there in the yard she had come Face-time, eye to eye, with a giant king snake; only she didn't have to force her eyes opened then. She held her breath as the snake shot under the palmettos after Koda almost caught him. Even with wounded hind legs.

With her eyes opened wider now, she pushed herself up from slouching in her desk, and scanned the room of her classmates. Only a few seemed to be paying even partial attention, but she did notice something else, their textbooks were closed. Hers was opened and still on the page where Benjamin Franklin had used the word savage.

Again, she found herself staring at that word, knowing there was nothing she could do to make it ever go away, and then she kind of let this feeling of darkness that the word had created to pass in front of her, like dark energy, or dark matter, passes in front of a star.

The imagined, or real, concealment allowed her mind to fall back again. This time to that first day of third grade. It really had started off as a good day, she thought, until someone shot a word arrow at her, and it struck her heart....

>>·‹‹ >>·‹‹ >>·‹‹

It was like she could actually feel herself growing up back then. Her third grade teacher, a kind woman named Mrs. Kingsley, spoke with a gentle southern voice that could send words sliding through your ears. She had said to the class that morning that she enjoyed reading stories out loud, though she wouldn't mind at all if the children read along silently with her. This took considerable pressure off a lot of the kids because most of them didn't like to read, or couldn't read very well themselves. Rainy, though, she already loved to read, especially out loud to Grandpa. She loved it when someone read to her, like he would do occasionally, or her mom used to do. So she was looking forward to her next day of third grade and the next one after that.

Mrs. Kingsley had also told Rainy during recess that Rainy's beaded hair piece was "exquisite". Rainy explained that it was her mom's barrette, and that her mom had made it on a loom. She even asked if Mrs. Kingsley would like to touch it because Rainy knew you could tell more about it if you could feel it. So, Mrs. Kingsley said that she would love to, and proceeded to run her fingertips over the tiny colorful beads, intrigued how beaded flowers that look like real flowers could be made from geometric patterns. Of course, she was delighted the whole time she was looking at Rainy's barrette, and all the while she did, she used words, like, "incredible," "fascinating," and "so striking".

"Your mother was quite an artist," she said.

That brought a soft smile to a little girl's face. "If you look real close," she said, pointing to a beaded green leaf, "you can see a red bead in there."

Mrs. Kingsley bent forward and looked real close. She had trouble finding it, and so she lifted her glasses up that she wore on a thin silver chain around her neck, and looked through them at the barrette.

"I do see the red bead!" She removed her glasses, but kept her eyes fixed on that red bead. "Is there a reason for the red bead, Rainy?"

"My mom called it a spirit bead. She said that humans, especially women, had the gift of creating, if we choose to use it. But to never think of ourselves so perfect as to create something perfect. She said it was the way to show humility."

Suddenly more aware of a most special child, Mrs. Kingsley raised up, and with her head slightly tilted, she seemed to say with her whole face, "What a wonderful lesson...."

Rainy looked down, smiled again, and then glanced back up at her teacher.

Well, sometimes a person can be having a really good day when something happens to ruin it....

If you're an adult, it could be that you barely got out of the house on-time, and your car won't start, or you get stuck in traffic, and your boss won't like you being late for work. For a kid, it's like getting a low grade on a test, or the teacher reprimanding you for not paying attention in the last class of the afternoon, getting detention because someone pushed you in the lunch line and you get caught when you go to retaliate, or mostly, whether you're a grown up or a kid, it's when somebody says something to you, or about you, that crushes to death any good feelings you might be having that day, and wrecking the rest of it, and even causing you to be cautious of ever letting yourself have good feelings anymore at all.

Then there's something called humiliation. It's the dark side of humility. And just may be the worst experience a living being can have....

Rainy was searching through her new locker, deciding what she needed to take home with her, and getting ready to leave school for the day. It had been a good day. So far....

The third grade lockers were lined up against the wall on one side of the hallway, the older kids' lockers were on the other side. The afternoon sun was sending shafts of light through the door windows, so it was bright where the third grade lockers were, where Rainy was standing.

Two older girls, fifth graders, were huddled together across the hall in the shadow of the hallway, secretly checking their cell phones (it was against the rules to use them in the hallway between classes), and talking at their lockers. One of the girls shot that one word arrow ...savage, loud enough that Rainy could hear it, even before she felt it strike her heart, and the other girl laughed.

Now, in order to be defined as a genuine savage, the dictionary states that you would, most certainly, have the main characteristics of someone who is wild, barbarous, and cruel.

Of course, Rainy Peek was none of those things, but that didn't prevent the impact of that word striking her right in the chest. Like all kids will learn, sometimes words can make a person feel real good, and sometimes just one word can hit you harder than almost anything.

It hurts, and it makes you mad. Sometimes you don't even have to know the dictionary meaning of a word to feel its force, for the kind of sound vibration and energy that's used to speak it can knock the wind right out of you, like a punch from T-Rex, and you feel that you can't breathe.

Always, those kinds of words leave you feeling bad or mad, or both. Rainy would try to understand one day, how a person would have to truly see the world or how that person would have to truly look at other people in order to have made up such words in the first place. Grandpa disliked the name Redskins for a professional football team in the nation's capital. He said that the people who used the word today were really degrading themselves in front of the whole world.

He said that there were no such derogatory sounds in the languages of animals or birds so far as he had determined.

"I mean," he'd say, "what sounds in nature were ever conjured just to degrade something or someone?"

When Rainy squinted from the sunlight into the shadow where the fifth grade girls were standing, to identify the one who had said "savage," the girls smiled at her, but they weren't friendly smiles. They were look down on you kind of smiles. Or maybe better described as put on smiles, not unlike the ones on the faces of clowns. One of the girls had glanced down at the floor, almost like she was embarrassed, or even ashamed. The other, the one who actually said the word, the one who was actually jealous of Rainy, and threatened by the physical beauty at which she had just flung her word, grabbed her girlfriend's arm, turning her away. They shut their lockers, and hurried down the hall, the girl who had looked down, following her friend, who was whispering to her something about how they (the savages) lived with wild animals. Probably had lice, and become sluts real young. Rainy kept watching them as they faded into the dark side where they were walking.

That's when Mrs. Kingsley stepped through the open door of her classroom, and asked Rainy if everything was all right.

Clutching her backpack, she looked up and nodded that it was, but she wasn't.

"Wait here a moment," Mrs. Kingsley said, placing her hand on Rainy's shoulder. "I'll be right back." She turned and headed into her classroom, and then, like she said, she came right back. Only this time she was holding two huge homemade oatmeal cookies and offering them to Rainy.

Which she accepted. "One is for your grandfather," Mrs. Kingsley said, in her sugary Southern tone, "but I am so sorry I haven't any for your wolf."

Rainy was thinking that it was okay because she and Grandpa would share theirs with Koda even though Koda should not really be eating people food like that, but her grandfather had said that since Koda was getting on in years and his wounds were bothering him more, that it would be okay to share with him since it could help make Koda feel better and show him how grateful they were for him. Especially since he would be getting half of each which would mean he'd be getting a whole one....

"We'll share with him."

Mrs. Kingsley smiled. "I understand," she said, "we all need to feel appreciated."

Then she thanked Rainy again for allowing her to look at the barrette, and how lovely it looked in her hair, and how it was one of the most wonderful things she'd ever seen, and that she was also looking forward to seeing her tomorrow.

"I hope you're always my teacher."

Mrs. Kingsley smiled again, but this time her smile morphed into looking a little sad. "I'm retiring, Rainy," she said. "This is my last year teaching. I've been at it a longtime. And I've got an elderly mother who needs my care ...."

Rainy looked down at the cookies she was holding.

Though she'd put them in her backpack, she was still thinking about them, and the word savage, in the somewhat unusual, moderate mayhem on the bus ride home that day. If you could've put your ear next to her and tried to hear her breathing, you probably barely could. She was really quiet.

CHAPTER FOURTEEN

WHEN ENERGIES INTERACT

When she met Grandpa that afternoon at the bus stop and they walked home together, her silence ended.

Grandpa had asked if he could carry her backpack, but she said, "No. It's okay, Granpa. It's not heavy."

She didn't want him carrying it because he was old to her, and she knew he had problems with his back. Though she would never say that to him.

"Huh," he said, recognizing the weight of a burden that can't be seen with the naked eyes. "I guess, it just appears heavy."

With one hand she reached back and pulled the zipper of her back pack's pocket. "Maybe it appears so because of these," she said, and smiled.

Grandpa's eyes smiled too, then his whole entire face as she handed him a large cookie.

They started walking, she telling him about her day while they ate their cookies, but making certain to break off a piece of each to share with Koda when they got home.

"It pretty near seems, Miss Rainy Peek," he said, chewing his half of the cookie, "that your experience proved out to be, more or less, a lesson given to you by the power of words.... Like most powers, it's got two sides."

Then he thought some more while he savored his last portion of the cookie, and just before they reached the house where Koda was standing to greet them on the porch, he dipped into his pocket and pulled out the other half that he had saved.

Koda, of course, having smelled the cookies long before they actually made it to the front of the house, came down the steps in total control, not like dogs will often do even just hearing the word, cookie, or crazy like some people might do for something they want. He sniffed Rainy first, assessing her emotions. Then he took his half carefully from Grandpa's hand, so as not to accidently hurt Grandpa, because Koda had huge teeth, and a lot of them, and a jaw that could crush a man's hand like breaking a cracker.... Then Grandpa watched as Rainy had given her half to Koda as well and observing how Koda used his tongue, and not his teeth at all, taking it from her, and even chewed his half of Rainy's cookie more like a delicacy. Which the last piece most often is.

When Grandpa noticed Koda's bushy tail slightly wagging, it caused him to smile, for they had made Koda happy, and as Grandpa stood there for a moment shaking his head while looking at Koda, causing Rainy to be happy, he got to see another morsel of a wolf's incredible relationship with the pack, and he and Koda and Rainy were the pack. A pack is family of those who love one another, respect one another, and contribute to the welfare of one another.

Then Grandpa rubbed his chin, thinking more about Rainy's situation at school that day with those older girls using the word savage so Rainy could hear it.

As he made it up to the top of the porch, he opened the screen door, but before he headed inside, he stopped and turned. Standing in the doorway, his gaze fell on his granddaughter who was sitting on the bottom step, scratching Koda's chest as he lay on the ground.

Suddenly, Koda's head jerked up, and in

that one terribly fast motion, he had just snapped at a honey bee, buzzing near Rainy's face. Like the bee just disappeared, he had taken off that fast, no doubt still feeling the power of that snap, and probably thinking he was lucky to be still flying at all. Of course, Grandpa also knew that if the bee had stung Koda in the mouth, it would've been a painful situation for everyone, especially for the bee and for Koda. Grandpa figured that Koda must've known what he was doing. I'd done the same thing once, he thought, shaking his head.

They settled into the moment. Rainy scratching Koda, hugging and kissing him. Her backpack on the step.

"Rainy," Grandpa said, "please tell Mrs. Kingsley I was grateful for the cookie, and that it was real good," and he thanked Rainy too.

Then he said, "You mentioned Mrs. Kingsley had an elderly mother to take care of, and that she'd been teachin' a really long time, so I can relate to how hard it can be caring for someone you love who needs ye. I can understand that point in someone's life when they need to retire...."

He didn't like that word, retire. It always took on the meaning that something was ending, that nothing was beginning. But always, living in the Circle of life, he understood, more-so now, than he did back then, when somethin' ends, something new begins....

Then he said that Rainy was fortunate that she got to have Mrs. Kingsley for a teacher and not to let her disappointment about her retirement take anything away from that, but instead appreciate their time together even more. He asked how that barrette might look one day in Mrs. Kingsley's hair.

Rainy's smile telling him, even as her fingers ran along the rough surface of the wood where she was sitting on the porch steps. "We really do have to paint these steps."

"Huh," Grandpa said, looking down at them and thinking that she was right. Old chipped grey was not exactly a pleasant sight when you walked towards the house.

Koda lifted his head off the ground; his eyes focused on Grandpa, and then like a cat's tail will twitch when the cat is fixed on something, Koda's tail rose and then lay back down. It was his way of showing he approved of Rainy's suggestion, and Grandpa's sentiment as well, and then, and in the way that a wolf can do with simple gestures and using mind projections, he thanked Grandpa for his half of the cookie too, and for caring for him and giving him a purpose and a place to live out his life. Then he sniffed the air and laid his head back on the ground, his tongue hanging out passed his big toothed smile, and as Rainy scratched his white chest, he would close his eyes, and let the energy of the pack embrace him.

CHAPTER FIFTEEN

MEDITATION

Days later, during third grade recess, Rainy actually wanted to play kick ball. It was something she didn't do often, but today she felt different, and she had that feeling of growing again. Her legs were certainly doing just that and getting stronger, and she wanted to test them. However, she was wearing her barrette. She asked permission from one of the supervising teachers if she could put it in her desk back in the classroom as she was concerned something would happen to it....

She discovered the hallway empty, as the younger grades were in recess, and the older ones still eating lunch. This left an unexpected silence that filled the building.

When she got to the door of her classroom, it was opened just enough for her fingers to get through and pull it open slightly before she stopped.

The lights were off. The blinds had been shut. The room in a shadow of itself.

Mrs. Kingsley was at her desk, her feet off the floor, sitting crossed-legged in her chair. She sat in this position with her back perfectly straight, her hands resting on her thighs, palms up, fingertips touching. Her eyes were closed, but her lips were moving with words Rainy could not hear, and there was a peacefulness about her that Rainy could not disturb. She imagined Mrs. Kingsley had lifted off the chair, just enough to appear like she was floating....

Rainy blinked, and looked wide-eyed, expecting Mrs. Kingsley to have raised even higher, but she was still in the chair, and not floating in the air.

Slow and silent, she closed the door as she had found it, and just as slow and silent, she walked away without making a sound.

On the field outside, one of the kids said, he'd "never seen a girl kick so hard."

CHAPTER SIXTEEN

NON-LINEAR TIME

Now it is true that if you could open an ancient Mayan book which was called a codex some would more or less open like an accordion as if unfolding. Often it would have glyphs, which are like picture words and symbols, and these glyphs, whether they go up and down, or even across a page, tell stories moving within circles and cycles of natural time. The truth is, in telling the story of a person's life, such a writer, or artist, would have to include how that person's life relates to the movement of the stars, and the other planets, and even the cycles of the Moon and Earth. For everything is connected. Their work would even encompass the rain and the clouds that bring the rain.

Often, a writer begins a story at the beginning of the journey, Point A, and everything moves in an orderly fashion to Point B, the middle, and to Point C, the ending. The experiences that happen along the way, the plot, move along in sequential order, told in a straight line.

But, natural time, and cycles, don't run in a straight line, like you're born here at this point, and then, straight line, you die here at this point. Think of it more like a circle. Think of life as a passage of cycles, like seasons. Phases of the moon, or Moon cycles. Think of life as one stage transitioning into the next. That's how a Mayan book recorded the passage of natural time. Sometimes, in the telling of a story, it takes a few steps back into the past, to see where you came from, then a page could turn and spin and spiral your mind, and the stuff that happens in-between all that; then you may even circle back, and then forwards again. You see, Time, as the ancients understood it, belongs to the Mystery.... We can only know for certain that things often happen in cycles, and move in cycles and circles....

Those who dream by day are cognizant of many things that escape those who dream only at night.

EDGAR ALLEN POE

CHAPTER SEVENTEEN

DAYDREAMING

Rainy found herself circling in time like that, but then, of course, coming back and still occupying a seat in Mr. Kline's social science classroom. The Colonel had been going through his sixth grade lessons of Benjamin Franklin and the other founding fathers, and giving his homework assignment, but hardly anything at all was filtering through her third grade recollections of Mrs. Kingsley, and of those older girls who became shadows walking into a metaphor of dark energy, becoming themselves a metaphor of dark matter. No, neither the Colonel's words nor the words he was reading from the textbook could break through to Rainy, that is, until the Colonel called her name.

"Miss Peek!" he said in a voice that sounded like he was addressing a soldier, or maybe a POW. He leaned forward glaring at her. "Are you on the same page as the rest of us?"

Startled, she knew that, of course, she wasn't. Then, embarrassed, she shook her head.

Now Mr. Kline was very well aware that Rainy had never received anything less than an A in his history tests, and that his own evaluation at the end of the year depended, to a large extent, on the grades his students had earned.

In that regard, Rainy was a prize. The price he paid, though, had caused him personal conflict. These were the history lessons Mr. Kline believed to be important in the development of a young student's mind, and so, because of Rainy's presence in his class, he felt the need to make the extra effort to drive home the fact the United States of America was, and still is, the greatest country in the world

"Miss Peek, do you know how I know that you are not on the same page?"

She didn't want to say the actual words.

"We closed our books ten minutes ago, Miss Peek. You are supposed to be taking notes on our discussion of the founding fathers."

She glanced up, but her eyes did not make direct contact with his.

"Do you have a problem with that, Miss Peek?"

"No," she said, squirming in her seat, shaking her head to emphasize the fact that she did not have a problem. Feeling the stares of everybody in the classroom, she closed her textbook real quiet, pushed it aside, and opened her notebook, turning to a blank page.

The Colonel's blue googly eyes magnified through his glasses.

"No, Sir, indeed," he said, standing upright, like a big bellied soldier at attention, holding a textbook instead of a gun, the dark frames hiding his bushy grey eyebrows, the shiny bald head reflecting the light from the ceiling. His thin lips tightened, so that it appeared he didn't have any, and his head nodded agreeably. In his mind, he had reestablished his dominance, his idea of balance, so to speak, not just in the classroom, but with Rainy, and with the very idea of male dominance and superiority as his concrete cracking foundation. He was right. What he taught was truth. He was reestablishing order in his world. A world where men, like him, held control. Now he felt free to resume his lecture on the founding fathers, emphasizing the Declaration of Independence, and the words, all men are created equal, and to teach her once and for all, just who was responsible for the greatest influences of American democracy and origin.

And so, he had gone on to read from the text and elaborate about the ancient Greeks and democracy, about the Roman Senate, and even about the Magna Carta, but he never mentioned how the Constitution of the Iroquois Indians was the U.S. Constitution's main model, the same Indians (the Ho-dau-no-sau-nee) whose symbol of the eagle the Americans borrowed as their national symbol, had also shared their knowledge of democracy. The Colonel never mentioned that. He never mentioned that in the minds of the Ho-dau-no-sau-nee, equality included women.

He never mentioned how Benjamin Franklin said, it would be a strange thing if Six Nations of ignorant savages should be capable of forming a scheme for such a union and be able to execute it in such a manner that is has subsisted through the ages and appears indissoluble; and yet that a like union should be impracticable for ten or a dozen English colonies....

So, Rainy started to shut Mr. Kline out again. He was speaking, but his voice just became like the sounds of background noise. A continual droning that you might hear when they first begin drilling underwater. Shutting him out was all she felt she could do in the moment. It was intentional. What Grandpa had said about having to learn both sides of history wasn't cutting it for her this time, and that blank page in her notebook just beckoned....

Then she thought that maybe she shouldn't. Mr. Kline would probably see her, pencil in hand, head down, concentrating on what she was doing, and he would suspect that she wasn't taking notes, or even paying attention, and he was always saying, "You are not in elementary school. You're in middle school. You need to act your age. A few more years ...you'll be having to make your own way in this world."

So, instead of drawing, and being the possible recipient of that, she chose to retaliate for his dismissal of the Native part of history in a way that she knew would shake the Colonel to the core, but she didn't think her actions through.... She didn't consider the possible ramifications of what she was about to do.

Youth often acts impulsively.

And so, she picked her battle, and raised her hand .... And all hell broke loose.

The Water Monster Unktehila, Queries the Witch,
Ina Bdu Ha Sni...

You say, Ina Bdu Ha Sni,
They do not have hearts.
Do you mean, They are heartless?
But certainly, they must have some kind or
unkind of beating in their chest,
Forcing their memories to flow
somewhere.
How else, you say, could they steal two
continents
And still feel they don't belong anywhere?
You say, They are susto.
Do you mean, Without souls?
How can anyone be soulless?
What kind of creatures are they?
How did they come to exist?
You say, Never speak of this
Or they will crack the Sky!
But then, how do you know so much?
You say, Because I am the witch
Who made them.
But why? Unktehila asked.
... Because I can, I am Ina Bdu Ha Sni, the
Motherless.

CHAPTER EIGHTEEN

TOO YOUNG FOR THE TRUTH

Grandpa hadn't been called to the Principal's Office since he refused to cut his shoulder length wavy black hair back in 1958, after he had just started high school. That was more lifetimes ago than even Grandpa wanted to think about. Now he walked in with his hair still long, only pulled into a thin white braid that hung down the center of his back. He was wearing a yellow shirt, black pants, a shell necklace Rainy had made for him, and a silver bracelet on his wrist that his wife Jewel had given him not long after they got married, but that too, it seemed, was lifetimes ago.

"Good morning, Mr. Peek," the tall woman with short blonde hair, wearing navy blue pants and jacket, and a white blouse said behind her large desk. "I'm Dr. Margaret Lawson," she said, standing and extending a firm hand shake with Grandpa.

Grandpa nodded. "Good morning," he replied, shaking her hand.

A man was seated in one of the chairs in front of the principal's desk.

"This is our guidance counselor, Mr. Mills," the principal said.

Mr. Mills gestured with a small smile and a slight hand wave.

Dr. Lawson asked if Grandpa would like to sit, so he did, straight up, not leaning against the back of the chair. With his hands resting on the chair's arms, he was assessing the two people in the office, but had become suddenly very much aware of the beating of his own heart. It was pounding in his chest, and slightly out of rhythm, which would occasionally happen when he grew anxious, so he was trying to make it settle down with slow deliberate breathing and with the force of own his will.

"Mr. Peek," the principal began, "we enjoy having your granddaughter here. She seems like a good natured child, though quite introverted at times, and she provides some diversity for our student body."

"I don't understand, Dr. Lawson. Why am I here? Has anything happened to Rainy?"

"Oh, no! Nothing happened to her. We're very protective of our students here at Osceola Middle. It's just that we have a problem with something she had said in class the other day. That is, her social studies class with Colonel ... I mean, Mr. Kline."

Grandpa glanced at the gentleman next to him, the guidance counselor.

The principal leaned forward, her arms on the desk, supporting her. "Mr. Kline complained that Rainy asked him about genocide the other day in class. Two of the children went home and asked their parents about it because Mr. Kline claims that it was not part of the discussion. He made certain to tell me that it made him very uncomfortable. He even felt forced to dismiss the class a few minutes early to avoid a response. Something he has never done."

"I understand," Grandpa said.

"Well, you can imagine. I had one boy's parents calling me here at the office, and a school board member at my home, wanting to know why they were discussing genocide in a sixth grade class. I told them what had happened, and that it was not discussed. Now in eighth grade we do teach a unit on the Holocaust for our Honors students. They can even read books about it."

"You're referring to the Jewish Holocaust?" Grandpa said.

"Why, yes, of course." Dr. Margaret Lawson seemed puzzled. She had never considered other holocausts. Had there been other holocausts? After all, the capital H designated this as the only one, so in her mind, and in the minds of most people, any others were relegated to some lesser status of annihilation, and significance.

So, Dr. Margaret Lawson, the school's principal for the past ten years, paused, regrouped her intentions, and erased complications created from Grandpa's question. "We even let our eighth grade honors read that famous book," she continued, instantly angry at herself because she couldn't remember the title. Regretful she had even mentioned it. Then, like an unclear thought of scrabble letters floating into her head, she was trying to form them ... "I can't recall its title."

At that point, she glared at Mr. Mills who looked surprised and shrugged and shook his head.

"It was written by a Jew," she asserted, desperate to reclaim her academic station.

"I believe he actually escaped the Holocaust," added Mr. Mills.

"I feel you might be thinkin' of the book, Night, by Elie Wisel," Grandpa said, looking at the principal. "He survived Auschwitz...." He glanced at the counselor.

"My father was among the first soldiers to liberate the people in Dachau, Dr. Lawson... Mr. Mills." Then his eyes narrowed, and his gaze scanned the area of her desk just in front of him, his focus flicking from corner to corner, like he was seeking out that place somewhere in the turbulence where you can find calm, like a storm tracker pilot flying into the eye of a hurricane. It was in that unsettling and eerie calm where Grandpa could often find composure and understanding.

Then he said, "I told Rainy about genocide, Dr. Lawson. It came up in a conversation she'd wanted about why the history of her people was not taught in school. I explained to her what genocide is, and how it was part of the history of what happened to her people. But I didn't tell her all of it. I didn't tell her how some historians claim the Nazis established their concentration camps after studying the U.S. policy imposed on American Indians."

Dr. Lawson's face flushed red, like she could've blended in with the stripes on the miniature flag near the phone on her desk, and she cleared her throat. "Yes, Mr. Peek, but Rainy is not a full Indian, only part, am I correct? You did legally change her last name?" She sorted through some related papers on her desk: memos, school records, and letters.

"Yes, the idea was to make it easier for her in school."

"Of course, Mr. Peek. We realize she has no parents." She lifted one page from the shuffle. "A question of negligence apparently came up when she was in fourth grade.... I understand there was an incident."

He stared at her. "Yes, there was an incident, but I never heard of a complaint against me."

"Well, it was probably something over that age old discussion of whether grandparents were capable of raising small children, and you being a single grandparent...well, the question had come up."

"Not with my knowledge."

She glanced through other papers. "And though I'm not personally familiar with the Indian movement of the 60's and 70's like you are, especially as your having been arrested back then...." The principal lowered her eyes to the paper she placed atop the others, and followed her finger as she scanned it, reading excerpts aloud. "I understand your arrest had to do with... interfering on a federal Indian reservation with a mining facility the elected tribal officials had legally authorized."

"The charges were dropped," Grandpa said, the bewilderment at what she knew about his past apparent on his face.

"I understand," Dr. Lawson said, with a failed tone of empathy in her words. "Everyone has a point of view, but the record of that arrest could threaten custody of your granddaughter, though we would never recommend that, nor have we."

Grandpa's eyes narrowed again, but he was not calm, not on the inside. His chest constricted as if the agitation had become an anaconda coiling around him. Then he took a deep, slow breath. His chest expanded, and with a controlled nearly, silent exhale, the anaconda mercifully released him.

"You may not be aware, Mr. Peek, but we do try and provide our students with a well-rounded view of history. They learn about countries and cultures all over the world. We even had a TV set up in some of the classrooms last year, so they could watch the announcement of the Royal baby's birth in London. Our advanced eighth graders watched Mandela's funeral.

"Unfortunately, it would be impossible to provide everyone's version of history, and that must include yours." She seemed to suddenly switch to higher gear, higher ground. "I mean, most of our students know that a hundred miles away, we have the Seminole casino and Hard Rock Café. I must confess, I've been there myself. Won some money at blackjack. I even got to bring my kids to the craft store and zoo. Quite an extravagant place they've got there."

Then she downshifted, reaching the top of her higher ground. "Now I understand what you're trying to do with your granddaughter. Some Indian tribes had gone through struggles in the past, but we have to protect our children here at Osceola Middle and not burden them with too much, Mr. Peek. These are fragile times. These are fragile kids. This country is going through a lot right now, and neither you, nor would we, want any trouble from social services for you, or your granddaughter, because of some irate parent or school board member."

Grandpa nodded slowly, his eyes peering into the eye of the storm, but in his peripheral vision, a hurricane was raging. He was thinking about his youthful days in school. How he learned that you either went along with them, or you dropped out. He knew what dropping out had cost him. The pain in his back that he was feeling now and the uneven heartbeat caused by a job he took because he didn't have a better education.... He felt like just dropping his head in his hands and breaking down, crying, even screaming; We failed! I failed. It was all for nothin'!

He was thinking that after all these years, they haven't changed. After all the protests he went through when he was a young man, trying to bring justice to the lives of Indian people, trying to stop America's ecocide, trying to create change without dying, the people he saw beaten, the ones murdered, the ones who had killed themselves, the ones he helped bury, the ones who were jailed.

All trying to make the world a better place the only way they knew how, trying to make them change, and we failed.... Casinos? Zoos? Now he was thinking how many of the Indian people had instead, changed, buying into a profit-at-all-costs way of life, accepting a history that is not theirs, praying in their native languages to a God that is not the Great Mystery, succumbing to the missionaries and to religions that are not theirs, just so they could get along, condoning the idea that the earth is nothing but a resource, that greed is good, that taking more than you need is what it's all about.

Pledging allegiance to a flag that your ancestors were holding up with a white flag in clear sight and were gunned down just the same. Wearing the uniforms of the very military that invaded your land and killed your own people. We have changed and they have not.... Grandpa blinked back into the eye of the storm, where the uneasy calm had once again appeared, and he glanced up and looked at the principal. "I'm teaching my granddaughter the truth, Dr. Lawson," he said.

"Yes, but keep it in your own home. It's your version of the truth, and our sixth graders are too young."

"For the truth? Tell me, Dr. Lawson, can omission of truth not be a form of lying? If they're not too young for lies, then why are they too young for truth?"

The principal stood and smiled forcibly, and the counselor, following her lead, did the same.

Grandpa stood.

"I think you understand, Mr. Peek. It's so

much easier this way."

"Yes," Grandpa said. "I imagine so."

...come to nature, feel its power,

let it help you, one needs time

and patience for that.

Time to think,

to figure it all out.

You have so little time for contemplations,

it's always rush, rush, rush with you.

It lessens a person's life,

all that grind,

that hurrying and scurrying

about....

- LAME DEER

CHAPTER NINETEEN

FROM THE ART OF PAINTING ON A SUNDAY MORNING:

Rainy had begun pressing the last of the painter's tape against the edge of the step. "I'm not sure about middle school next year."

Grandpa sat on the side of the Adirondack chair, holding an old brush in one hand, and a new can of paint in his lap. "Why's that?"

"The kids seem really mean sometimes.... Almost crazy."

Grandpa said she was probably right. "It's understandable, though," he said, picking some of the old gray off the brush handle. "Tough age for kids. A lot of them unloved. Some of 'em already tryin' to hang onto their souls.... sometimes just the struggle makes them crazy." He put his paint can on the ground. "But," he said, "you'll find kids who aren't crazy, one or two maybe, like when you met Mrs. Kingsley...."

"But she wasn't a kid."

He agreed, but saying she's just more proof that not all people are crazy, and not all teachers are just doing what they do to maintain the status quo.

He put the old brush in his lap and looked at her, sitting on the step, cutting tape with her teeth. "Now, ye gonna tell me what happened on the bus?"

"How did you know?"

"Just logic. That's pretty much the only time you share space with the middle school."

"Oh," she said, looking at the blue roll of tape in her hands that keeps the lines between the colors. "This seventh grader...Tamika Williams...

she stands up at her seat with her cell phone and turns around and asks me if I go to church.

"I felt real uncomfortable, but I said, No. Then she says every Sunday her mother takes her and her brother and sister to church. And then she asks me if I had a religion, and I said I was Indigenous.

"Then she starts her fingers moving on her phone screen, so I figured she's looking up Indigenous, but can't spell it. She said she didn't know what that all meant, which I didn't think she would, and then this big kid yells from the back of the bus for her to sit down or he'd use her little brother's dick for bait when he went fishing. She said something nasty back at him, which doesn't need repeating, and then the bus driver pulled over and told everybody to sit down and shut up or he would start taking names...."

Grandpa was shaking his head. "Well, maybe that's the first time Tamika ever heard that word, Indigenous. She's probably just curious. Doesn't know etiquette. Still, by the time ye get to middle school a kid should know better. There're lines you don't cross, and asking personal questions of somebody ye hardly know at all about church, and religion, that's personal. Boundaries should be respected."

She had a long piece of the blue tape stuck on her fingers. "Sometimes you need lines," she said, cutting the tape with her teeth. "You need boundaries...."

"As I see it," Grandpa said, "a synagogue, mosque, shrine, temple, church, call it what ye will, they're all places people go to pray. They call 'em houses of worship, or places of worship.... I look around, and know this is where we go to pray. And none of those places or houses of worship anywhere could not be more pleasing

106 on a Sunday mornin' than what I'm seein' all around us right now....And nothin' could be more sacred. This is our church, iff'n someone asks. Nature. The Sky and Earth."

With the tape halfway hanging from the last step, she paused, took a breath, and did look around.

It is beautiful, she thought, the different kinds of bird songs and sounds of the morning greeting the day. The new spring green glistening everywhere. The pink lilies ready to bloom at the end of the driveway. Koda perusing the perimeter of the yard, pawing at something in the sand....A place of worship anywhere couldn't be more... beautiful.

When the blood in your veins returns to the Sea,
and the Earth in your bones returns to the ground,
perhaps then you will remember
that this land does not belong to you.
It is you who belongs to this land.

INDIGENOUS THOUGHT

CHAPTER TWENTY

VOICES OF THE ANCESTORS

Occasionally, when Mr. Kline got the notion, he left his desk to read out loud to the class. Rainy figured that he did so as not to fall asleep to his own voice.

Paying closer attention to the Colonel's movements, she was not necessarily focusing so much on what he was reading, or saying, but rather more on him, standing alongside his big metal desk in a white shirt that appeared like it could've been made of some kind of cardboard, his dark grey suit jacket seemingly too warm for wearing, and always, his miniature American flag pinned to the lapel. His blue eyes to match his tie, stared down through his black- framed glasses into the textbook he was holding like he was about to read scripture from a Bible. He started to walk around while he was reading. She thought it a good thing, his moving like he did, so his blood could circulate better. Grandpa had said to Rainy once, though he was pleased she was doing such extensive research for her science homework, and on her writing projects, that he felt she was spending too much time in a chair sitting in front of the computer.

"It's important to get up and walk around," he said. "Look outside at the sunlight's reflection on the oak leaves. Move around. Go outside. Hug Koda. Give him a kiss, let him kiss ye back. Keeps the blood flowin'."

He said that the water that carries blood in our bodies can stagnate, and like a stagnant pool, or really anything that stagnates, it could become unhealthy, and even old buildings can, like Osceola Middle School, become unhealthy.

It was nearing the end of its time.

>>•<< >>•<< >>•<<

Since the school was opened in 1961, a renovation was required in 1974 to keep it up to code, which meant its tall old windows needed to be replaced for more energy efficient smaller ones, or have them bricked up altogether, but the education budget without warning got cut, so a few of the old fashioned windows had still remained in some of the classrooms. Then, a 1985 renovation to replace the rest of the windows came to an abrupt halt when asbestos was discovered nearly everywhere, requiring the budget this time to be redirected at the removal of all the asbestos from under the floor tiles and in the walls. However, the new school, still under construction, and far away from the location of the old school (so it could bus in more students from other communities), wouldn't be opening for another year, and there would be no worry about windows in that place, for it was designed totally without them.

Grandpa said it looked like a factory.

But for now, education in this small, quickly growing beach community of America's children, needed to be carried out in an old building with windows, and oh yes, a few trailers for classrooms in a parking lot they paved over a "vacant field". And though most of the middle school teachers opted for rooms where the big windows had been replaced or dried wall closed, Mr. Kline said that he preferred a classroom with them.

"There's a history in the classroom where I teach," he had declared, during a discussion one day in the faculty lounge.

They didn't know that he was dealing

with the onslaught of Type 2 diabetes, which was gradually taking away colors from his eyes. He could help determine to what degree this was occurring by looking at the leaves of the oaks outside his classroom windows because slowly they were turning ashen green. The red stripes of the flag in his classroom, were turning grey, on their way to becoming black.

"I've taught generations of students in my room...," he said, "some of them sat in those same desks. Looking through those very widows at a world they knew nothing about. In my classroom, my students learned the courage and conviction it took to make this country great. And some of them who sat in that room grew up and sacrificed their lives defending our way of life. Gave their arms and legs," he said. "One girl I taught became a mother of two sons killed in Iraq. At least four generations and four wars should mean something...."

A few of the teachers counted on their fingers; others, in their heads. Just how many wars had this country fought since the school opened? And was this all really about windows in a classroom?

>>•<< >>•<< >>•<<

For now, though, as he had for past generations, with his trusty textbook in hand, Mr. Kline was in his comfort zone headed towards the old classroom windows with his eyes focused on each page he read. Always, like a ritual of the hour, he would stop and lean against the window sill for a rest while he continued to read. That way he would not run into something, and he could also look up to make sure everyone was following along and not daydreaming out a window, and he could check the color of those leaves to see if he could still see green.

As he resumed his reading on the forming of the *Constitution* and the *Articles of Confederation,* he realized a few of his students were, in fact, daydreaming out the windows and not paying attention.

He reached for the cord, and shut the blinds, calling out an order for Sean Stevens, whose desk was at the front of the room, near the light switches and the flag, to turn on all the overhead florescent lights. Then he ambled towards the door, still part of the reading ritual, where he would inevitably step into the American flag, which hung on a stick down from the wall, right alongside of the door, and it would brush ever slightly over the skin at the top of his head.

He concealed his throat movement as his swallowed hard when he saw Rainy Peek's hand raised. Hers was the only one, and when he acknowledged her, which wasn't often, she asked him why there were so many American flags in and around the building.

"What do you mean...so many?"

"There's one in every classroom," she said. "One in the lunchroom, one in the gym, one in the auditorium, one in the library, one in the school office, one in the principal's office ... on her desk too, one in the vice-principal's office, one in the guidance counselor's office, and the big one on the pole in front of the school...." She said some of the cars that dropped kids off had American flag bumper stickers or plastic ones attached to their car antennas. Some of the houses on the beach had flagpoles with American flags. She even noted that Mr. Kline wore one on his jacket.

The Colonel's heart started thumping like a bass drum in a marching band. The pale pink of his face grew flushed, her *genocide* inquiry months ago still stalking along the surface of his mind. The question, the word, the memory prowling further into a 20 year old second lieutenant's attached forever haunting images of the fathers, mothers, and children, and the grandfathers and grandmothers, all herded and huddled into a ditch at the edge of a village called My Lai. *I didn't kill them.... I was obeying orders. You're not going to put this on me!*

Not this time, Little Girl. I don't care how high your grades are.... But he did care. He needed those scores.

Clutching the textbook, he stood in front of his desk, taking a position of authority in the center of the room. "Displaying our flag is a sign of patriotism, Miss Peek. It shows the world that we love America. We follow American values. People in these parts are proud of that.... It is *Miss Peek.* Am I correct?"

She nodded, her eyes glancing up from her desk at his human form. Her imagining him among the walking dead, the soulless. The ones that can somehow retain their human forms, though the dark energy which sustains them continues to rob them of the spirit being that was once human about them. The questioning of her name, a tactic he had already used.

The confused looks, and detached expressions on the faces of his students, were not the encouraging signs of support that years ago his affirmations and authority would have commanded, and so his reaction refocused on her. "After all," he continued, "it is our country, Miss Peek." But somehow saying the words didn't make it true, not to her.... "Displaying the American flag shows our pride. Don't you think?"

Her eyes darting from side to side to avoid direct contact with his, allowing for no sign of aggression on her part, and so she nodded again, slightly, reserving her affirmation to what her own heart was saying about the meaning of our country.

"America is our country, Miss Peek. It belongs to us, the American people. That includes me and you." Maybe if he says it enough times.... How could this be questioned? It mustn't be. "And everywhere we go the flag reminds us of this, and it reminds us of the sacrifices men have made to keep us free...." Now leaning against his desk, tiny beads of sweat forming on the sides of his head reflecting the ceiling lights, he held the textbook with both hands, raising it to his chest. "In the very desk you're seated in, a young man once sat. That young man grew up, went to high school, and less than a year after graduating, lost his legs in Afghanistan. The American flag symbolizes such sacrifice. It stands for our way of life, which makes us the greatest country in the world.... So it's pride, Miss Peek. Pride in the flag and the freedom it represents."

She wanted to say, Isn't pride one of your seven deadly sins? And what about greed? But she didn't. Nobody said anything. But now she could feel the curious glances and partial stares from some of the students aimed in her direction. She caught sight of Sean Stevens' concern over the Colonel's next move.

Don't get us extra homework. Don't make us have to stay after the bell rings. The room was silent. Everyone on edge in anticipation of additional assignments. Mr. Kline's face had turned quite red, but the pale pink hue was, for the moment, returning. The heat in his head receding, as his heart slowed and softened its pounding. He saw his fingers quivering while he lowered the book, though, and he wondered if it was the type 2 diabetes causing this. Or maybe an onset of Parkinson's that his doctor had warned could appear. Or maybe it was simply her.

His breathing, which had grown somewhat labored, was becoming more normal, but his eyes, which had turned a colder blue, remained fixated on the student, the smart and arrogant little Indian girl, who would enable him to win the teaching award; Don't push me! the eyes were saying through the thick lenses of dark framed glasses, again making them appear too large for his head. I can make life miserable for you and your grandfather.... But still, he needed her in that class. He needed that award. It was a contradiction. Everything was becoming a contradiction.

He took shallow breaths, releasing them as tactfully as he could. He fought to not show any physical sign that she had affected him. "Did I answer your question, Miss Peek?"

More silence while the unspoken then resided in her own gesture of another head nod and glance.

But how did this land become your country, Mr. Kline? Her lips remained closed.

She just needed to permit her knowledge of history to empower her self-confidence, but her wisdom not to allow it to be used against her.

So, another uneasy quiet hung in the room. She imagined her voice, the one inside her head, the silent voice, the one behind the glance, becoming the ancestors' voice. The orator. The voice of all those who have none in the affairs of men....

He had lifted himself from the edge of his desk, and walked around it, to his chair, where he stood....

She looked up with her eyes as her head

remained partially down....

This is not your country, Mr. Kline. It was never yours. For the Earth does not belong to any of us; we belong to the Earth.... Our people were the first human beings of America, and we were the only human beings for thousands and thousands of years. You could have come here and shared the land with us, Mr. Kline. You could've been humble. You could've adapted to our way of life and not imposed your will upon our people and upon the land. This can never be your country, Mr. Kline, because your heart has never adapted. It is not indigenous. You've never felt you belong here, and that's what makes you so uncomfortable.

She sat still in a room of silence. Quiet, empowered without speaking, her mind making words in the calm confidence she had found in her knowledge and in her connection to the ancestors of beings while her fingers folded the corner tip of the open page of her textbook.

She was fighting without fighting.

Then the bell rang.

"Dismissed," he said as always in half command, half irritation, his students pouring from the room through the door, their faces still so young, unlike the faces on the soldiers his new assignment as a Colonel in 1973, had required he welcome home, as they regrouped outside the plane, standing at programmed attention with those "thousand mile stares," preparing to break across the air strip back to a world in America they would never know in the same way again. And always the ghosts following them....

He shook his head, and paused once behind his desk, his body heavy with self-righteous anger, guilt gnawing like a rat on the bone of his skull. In a controlled fall as if in slow motion, he sat in his chair. Reaching for a red pen, that his increasing problems with color blindness had changed to black, he attempted to scribble something down on a notepad by his textbook while it remained clear in his head, a "written report," as the principal, Dr. Lawson, had suggested. "It has to be dated. Be sure and put the date."

What's the date? He did not know.

Right now, concentrate, "document" her behavior: confrontational attitude... What's with the pen? Why do I have a leaky pen? In... quiry... dis...rup...tive... he wrote. Shows lack of re...spect for flag... unwil...ling...ness... to ... Damn this pen!

It was leaking, turning into splotches of red that his color blind eyes saw only as black, which smeared the incursive rant, like spilled oil or toxic waste. It even got on his fingers, this thick black ink, so he tossed the broken pen down into the empty garbage can at the side of his desk, and in fatigue and exasperation slouched back against his chair, wiping his fingers with tissue paper, but the ink stained his skin red, but black, and he kept wiping, but it would not come off. I *didn't shoot them! My son died because he was a homosexual.... There, I've said! He kept wiping.... I did what I was told. That's what a soldier does. I served my country. I loved my son!*

He turned his flushed face to the windows, as a glimpse of the gleaming sunlight outside, and the movements of the leaves, would have helped him recover, helped divert his disorder. But the blinds were shut. Only a small shadow floated between him and the windows.

Red inked smeared words on his

notepad, now staining his fingers like blood if you could see it, but was black to him.

...When I read about butterflies,

I realized that they are a metaphor

for the totality of the universe.

How is any of this possible?

How did any of this happen?

From the formation of a galaxy

to the wings of a monarch!

No one truly knows the answers.

It is all such a great mystery.

THE LAST THING RAY BRADBURY
WROTE BEFORE HIS DEATH

CHAPTER TWENTY-ONE

STAR-TALKING: THE WORDS THAT GIVE MEANING...

"Did you ever wonder, Rainy, that if ye couldn't put your thoughts into words, you wouldn't know what ye was thinkin'?"

Grandpa rested his dolphin mug on the wide arm of the Adirondack chair. Rainy was sitting in her chair, Koda pulling up and laying alongside her. She sipped from a special white porcelain cup with a tiny handle, and a white porcelain saucer. When she graduated fourth grade last year, he had given them to her. Grandpa's Uncle Roger had brought them back from Ireland. It was an heirloom on the Irish side of the family, and she liked it a lot. It made her feel older, and elegant.

She had asked Grandpa if she could use it tonight.

He was looking down the dark winding driveway, and she was stirring her tea with a small silver spoon he had reserved for such an occasion. Reaching into his shirt pocket, he removed two shiny abalone earrings, and he laid them on his lap. Then he began telling the story. It was a story he said had influenced his whole entire life....

"It's been said, *we are made of stories.*" He sipped some tea from his dolphin mug and placed it on the wide arm of the chair. "I'd backed the rig up to the docks around dark," he began. "An Arctic front packin' strong winds and snow was bearin' down, and I was lucky I'd made my delivery. As I was standin' in the cold, this Indian man stepped up to me. I swear he could've been hundred years old. Shoulder length white hair. Odd clothes. Bundled up.... But what struck me most, he was wearin' abalone earrings. These....

"Of course, this all happened years ago when I was young, so time might've made my recollectin' a little hazy in places...embellished in others. It's the nature of storytellin'. The core of the story, however, never changes. It's the truth of its meanin'.

"Had to be my first job driving a rig. I do remember that.... And I was feelin' angry back then cause I got cheated out of my education. I got this job that was a dead-end. What knowledge, what wisdom can I learn drivin' a rig?

"And I remember the ol' man sayin' the weather would be real bad for travelin' and I'd have to stay in the truck until the storm passed, which could be all night. He said that he liked the idea of having another Indian for company, and invited me to stay at his place."

As Grandpa sat back in his chair, she watched his eyes close like he was going to sleep, but she knew he was awake, just needing the darkness to travel, for some things he could see clearer with his eyes closed, and other things not so clear, more like looking through the haze, like what was forming up by the mailbox near the road..... Shortly after he and the old Indian man had arrived at the apartment, Grandpa said that he was sitting at the kitchen table in a room that appeared empty.

"I noticed you lookin' at my earrings," the old man said to me.

"of course", I apologized and said I was just surprised to see such exquisite shells in the middle of the continent. Where there was no ocean.

He smiled, and said, "Yes, I imagine it is."

Sitting at the square table with two chairs, Grandpa looked beyond the kitchen, where the area was unlit. He guessed it must've been where the old man slept because there was a single bed in the shadow against one of the walls. He also noticed a partially opened door. Saw only darkness in there, so thick, he recalled, it could've had substance.

"Probably just a closet. But then my imagination was getting' stirred up...."

But, before his mind could go any further, the old man had made his new young friend a peanut butter and strawberry jam sandwich, which he had presented on a small blue plate, and brought him a glass of water, and the glass was blue. Grandpa was surprised and grateful, and that it felt good being in a warm place and out of the truck.

He said he was about ready to lift his sandwich for a bite, when the old man asked, "You got tobacco, Nephew?"

Grandpa nodded, and placed the sandwich back down. Then he dug into his pants pocket and pulled out a small deerskin pouch. Untying it, he reached in with his fingers and removed a pinch of dried leaves, showing them to the old man. He explained that he carried it for medicine and for prayers while he was traveling. The old man closed his eyes, briefly acknowledging the gift, and then told him to put the tobacco in the center of the table. Grandpa did so.

As he began eating, the old man sat down across from him, and out of the blue asked, "What do you believe about the universe,

Nephew? What is the universe to you?"

The profoundness of the old man's question somewhat startled him, but it also resonated. He liked his intellect challenged, having missed out on a formal education.

His eyes narrowed. He gulped some water. He rubbed his chin. And even though the question itself had surprised him, he couldn't help but feel a kinship with the old man. It was the second time he had referred to Grandpa as Nephew.

The old man, eyes looking down, his arms resting on the table, patiently waited for Grandpa's response.

It didn't take long before Grandpa's frustration set in because he couldn't find the right words to answer the inquiry about the universe. "I know what it is I believe about the universe.... I just can't put it into words."

Rainy didn't think there was hardly anything at all that her grandfather couldn't put into words. She scratched Koda's mane, and listened, and with her imagination, she watched while her grandfather's story turned another page ....

He lifted his mug, drank some warm tea.

"Back then, Rainy," he said, "I may've been in my twenties, but I was still a kid in a lot of ways. I didn't know a whole lot about anything....

"'It's not about what you believe, Nephew; it's more what you feel. And what your mind thinks. If you can't put your feelings, or your thoughts, into words,' the old man said, 'then maybe you don't know what they are...'."

Grandpa leaned back from the table. Of course I know what my thoughts are. He lifted his glass nearly straight up, rinsing down the peanut butter and strawberry jam, and swallowing the last drops of water.

"It's okay, Nephew," the old man said, and smiled, removing Grandpa's glass and plate from the table. "Did you enjoy your sandwich?"

"Yes, Uncle, thank you." But even as he said this, he contemplated the question, trying to find the best words he could to describe what he believed about the universe, or more what he felt and thought about the universe. Brushing his fingers on his shirt, he looked fairly confident at the old man across the circle that had somehow formed at a small square table....

"Uncle, this is what I feel.... This is what I think.... Everything's somehow connected to somethin' unimaginable."

Then, the young man that was Grandpa had paused, wrung his hands. "This universe, and for all I know, all the universes, are all too mysterious for me to know in ways I can't put in words.... I mean, how can I describe what I feel is a Totality that always was, an unimaginable Oneness that is now, and will forever be? It's like tryin' to know what infinity is. It's just somethin' I as a human being cannot comprehend, somethin' I don't have words for...."

"You mean... Wah-kon-tah," the old man said.

"Wah-kon-tah...." Grandpa repeated. "What does that mean?"

"It is the source of wonder," the old man answered. "It is the Totality that you speak of. The Oneness of all things that ever were, are, and will forever be. It is the name in my tribal language for the undefinable, the Great Holy Mystery.... I know all names for the Undefinable: Gitchie Manido, he said in Ojibway.... Maheo, he said in Cheyenne.... Awonawilona.... Ichebiniatha.... Huaca.... Manitou, he said in

Wampanoag.... Hunab Ku' in Mayan.... Then he said in Onondaga, Sakoiatisan, ... Wakon'da, he said in Ponca.... And then more and more... Ke'-vish-a-tak-vish .... Whee-me-me-ow-ah.... Naimuena...."

The old man went on and on, reciting name after name after name after name after name, like they were musical notes, and as he did, they began to form strings, or threads, and these strings stretched into space and beyond, weaving into one endless spreading cloth of time all things together that ever were, and are, and will forever be....

His presence and the incantation of names had to some extent altered Grandpa's reality, drawing him into another perception of time and space.

The old man knew them all, the tribal names of what no human being can comprehend. By the hundreds, he knew the name; by the thousands. He spoke of the concept in Druid, he called it out in Gaelic.... He spoke of it in Lallans, the ancient language of the Scotts. Io, he said in Maori. Even in the dialects of the Aborigines. The Mandingo. He said it in Swahili. In Rapu Nui from Easter Island. Yonke, he said in Zulu.... Brahma, he said in Hindu. The Tao, he said in the words of Lao-tzu.

Grandpa paused, and turned to look at his granddaughter. She too was experiencing a time bend. Everything was moving faster, and yet she could imagine it all with such clarity, the words, the colorful threads spreading out over time and space. She could hear it all in the same way. She could feel them. How can this be?

"I know, Rainy," he said. "Imagine how I felt that night.... But then, it began to make sense to me. I understood what I believed, or more what I felt and thought, about the universe, about this world, about me…. It was somethin'. I imagined all our ancestors felt and thought as well. Only for me it was an epiphany because I finally had the words."

Rainy turned to him with a look of pure longing. "Granpa?"

"Yes."

"What's the Dakota name for the Great Holy Mystery?"

"Wakan-Tanka."

Her mind in that instance seemed like it was swirling with the threads around the stars. "Wakan-Tanka," she whispered.

It all began to make sense to her too. It all really was a Great Mystery, something unimaginable that she was a part of. Something incomprehensible. Something more sacred than anyone could ever know. And, it was the center of her being. The spinning slowed, and she drank some more tea. It tasted different, though; stronger, more precise in flavor than she had tasted it before.

"What happened then, Granpa? Did the old man say anything else?"

"Didn't need to," he said, shrugging his shoulders in matter of fact sort of way. "But he was gone when I woke up…."

"What'd ye mean? Did he say, I'll see ye later, or something… anything?"

Grandpa shook his head slow. "Nope," he said. "I mean, he was gone…." He lifted the earrings that remained in his lap the whole time. "I found these in my jacket pocket when I was standing outside the truck the next morning."

He brushed away a mosquito, dropped his other flip flop, and crossed his legs at the ankles. "I remember that I'd went back to my cab at the loadin' docks, and I recall climbing up and reachin' under the seat for my thermos, as I was hopin' to grab some coffee somewhere. That's when I got surprised... someone was callin' for me, and when I opened my door, one of the younger men, I'm guessin' around my age, that worked there, was now standin' in the parking lot in about four inches of snow holdin' a big container of his own, asking me if I wanted some.... I climbed down, and stood there in the cold holdin' my thermos while he poured the coffee, and then he looked me over...."

"Geez, man," he said, kind'a pitifully.... putting the lid back on the coffee. "Rough night?"

He had glimpsed a quick reflection of himself in the side view mirror before he opened the door and had made the dangerous descent from the cab into the snowy parking lot. Standing still, he combed his fingers through his hair, and tucked the front of his shirt in, noticing in his subconscious, a small dark-red stain on the front. He realized that he must've looked like he personally had gotten tossed around in that storm.

"No," he said to the young dock worker. "It wasn't a rough night at all. Fact is, I slept pretty good. The ol' Indian guy that works with ye on the docks, he let me stay at his place."

The young man about the same age as Grandpa, raised an eyebrow. "Ain't no old Indian works here."

"Yeah, he lives about two blocks away... old apartment."

"You mean that ol' buildin' round the corner?"

Grandpa nodded.

"That place's been condemned for goin' on a year. Sometimes the cops pick up homeless hangin' out in there, addicts and such, but no electricity, no water...."

Grandpa's face took on the expression like you do when you hear something you don't understand. "That's when I reached my free hand into my jacket pocket to get warm, when I discovered the earrings."

Now, an old man himself, he rested his head back on the Adirondack chair, and stopped talking. The story had reached its climax.

A veil of wispy clouds covered the stars. He could still see them, the stars, but the veil had made him once again aware that a separation between worlds does exist, between universes, even separations in our minds, and sometimes they must be so thin that a spirit, or even a forgotten memory, could, for whatever reason, pass through at some moment, and then go back again.

Rainy turned towards her grandfather. "He was some kind of spirit."

Grandpa nodded. He was remembering the fire and his mother standing weakly the night before she died, alongside its blaze, stoking the flame with her art. He was remembering... sacrifice. He was remembering the Ah-nuh.

"Some things can't be explained," he said. "I mean, the old man knew all those names, in all the languages."

"You think you might've dreamed it?"

"Sure. I mean, it's possible. Then what a dream it was! Maybe I never did leave the truck that night.... I've thought about the possibilities over the years, and what I'm left with is this gift," and he held up the earrings, "and the words that would forever give meaning to my life...."

He sighed.

"Until I met that ol' man, I never

appreciated how important puttin' thoughts into words really was, or even to say the words, Great Mystery...."

She pressed her head back too, the mind-spin, slowing.... "Wakan Tanka," she whispered with her breath, as though the speed she'd been mind-traveling forced her to hold it in the whole time. The fingers of her one hand buried in Koda's mane.

"Let me see your cup," Grandpa said.

He held it and looked into it. When his head lifted, his eyes turned to her, alternating back into the cup, describing as best he could what he saw looking through the veil of time, stimulated by tea leaves that had remained in various positions.

"Fire.... water.... And, there... at the bottom, near the edge...a leaf...you...emerging...."

He focused where one leaf remained near a tiny cluster of leaves that had clung to the side. "You're sittin'... alone.... And there... The leaves form a crescent.... Towards the top on the cup, near the rim, tea flecks shaped a cloud....

"Thunder," he said, and smiled, "and rain...."

Weeping, I, the singer, weave my song of

flowers of sadness;

I call to memory the youths...gone to

the land of the dead; once noble and powerful

here on Earth,

The youths were dried up like feathers,

were split into fragments like an emerald....

AZTEC POEM

CHAPTER TWENTY-TWO

CIRCLES AND SPIRALS AND MAYAN GLYPHS

"It's all Florida history," Mr. Kline said. He was standing behind his desk, looking out the windows on a sunny day where drifting puffs of small cumulous clouds passed in front of the sun, casting shadows and light....

Later in the semester, he was reviewing past lessons on the Spanish exploration of Florida. Facing the board, he picked up a black marker, and in script wrote three names: Hernan De Soto, Ponce De Leon, and Narvaez.

"That is script writing," he said, stepping away from the board, his back still to the class, "....in case any of you had forgotten."

Most of them had not learned script writing.

Placing the marker on his desk, he turned. "I call them, the big three."

He reached for his textbook, picked it up, and flipped the pages right to the place he had marked. Then, with textbook in hands, he began the reading ritual, heading for the window side of the room. That's when Rainy began a ritual of her own called unintentional daydreaming. It's the kind of daydreaming that just happens when you're not even aware it's happening. So, here's Mr. Kline with his textbook opened, scanning a searching eye over the classroom of thirty-five students, like he was spying rows of newly enlisted recruits, but instead of shouting orders, he was telling his students in a firm, and controlled voice, to keep their eyes opened and glued (his word) to their textbooks. Then, half sitting on the window sill, he told them that on this day in 1513, Ponce De Leon and his soldiers first landed in the New World in this place they named La Florida, the book said, because ... It was around Easter and there were so many flowers. He told them there was a celebration and a reenactment of the landing in one of the nearby beach communities.

"We've got extraordinary history right where we live," he said.

A kid named Darian Parker raised his hand. Of course, the Colonel didn't like it when his students raised their hands, especially if they were asking unrelated question. Still, he was a teacher, and as such, obligated by the school board, to provide what had been decreed as "active learning". The idea was supposed to provide students the opportunity for questions and discussion that teachers would decide were relevant. So, Darian Parker asked why the students at Osceola Middle didn't get a holiday.

"Because, Mr. Parker," the Colonel responded, in his usual exasperated and condescending tone, "the landing didn't happen here. It happened near here, and some schools do take students on a field trip to the landing reenactment site, but only as a learning experience." He emphasized, learning experience.

Stephen Spencer Jr. raised his hand. Rainy knew all their names, and observable behaviors.

She was aware that Spencer Jr. often pretended to show special interest in subjects he perceived were important to Mr. Kline, despite the fact he did poorly on a lot of the tests, and insulted him behind his back, when the Colonel couldn't hear.

His older sister, a cheerleader for the

basketball team, the Warhawks, attended a few classes with Sadie Willis. Her name was Sharon. Sharon Spencer. Their parents, Sonja and Stephen Sr., were local realtors. The mother was a member of the PTA. The father was elected to the school board. Though they were rarely seen on the beach itself, they lived in a new beach house. Not a cottage type beach house either. This one had four floors and a deck on top. Like her parents, Sharon Spencer looked down on most everybody, except those that could be useful to her. Once at lunch with Rainy, Sadie noted that ...the whole entire family has the initials, SS.

"My granpa said, there are no such things as coincidences."

"You got that right."

Stephen Spencer Jr. sat in the front row by the door, choosing a desk close to the flag. His fair brown hair was short and spiked, and he often wore anything that had the Florida State mascot on it. Today it was a t-shirt with Go Noles printed at the bottom of the mascot's ugly head. Mr. Kline dropped his book to his lap and released another exasperated sigh.

"Yes, Mr. Spencer?"

"De Soto Middle got half a day so they could go to the reenactment, and the parade. My cousin goes there, and I..."

"Mr. Spencer, what's your point?" Mr. Kline knew enough to be careful with this exchange because of the positions of power of the father and mother. Politics, of course.

"Well, Sir, Mr. Kline, he's not goin'."

"What do you mean, He's not going? And why should I care?"

"He told me he'll be home playing Grand Theft Auto."

The students laughed. Even Rainy

smiled. Everyone knew it was an R rated video, except Mr. Kline. He didn't even know there were such things as rated game videos, and had only heard of Grand Theft Auto once, when teachers were discussing the game's "blatant exploitation of theft and violence," and "how horrible women were portrayed." The discussion had taken place over lunch in the teacher's room.

"So, let me get this straight, Mr. Spencer, you interrupted class to tell me your cousin is skipping out on the commemoration of a great moment in the history of the New World, to go home and watch a video game that promotes theft and violence?"

The Colonel didn't see the irony. But Rainy did.

Mr. Kline stood up, his silhouette against the window darkened by a passing cloud. Looking up from the textbook, he shook his head, his mind wandering. *Maybe I'll retire at the end of this year. .... I've been teaching for decades.... Win that award...move up to administration. Not have to deal with these little shits. Maybe, he imagined, a vice principal position at an A rated school, move up to principal, get out of teaching altogether... or if you're still stuck here, at least get assigned the new honors classes .... You've got seniority.* His mind assuring him, things will get better, he looked again at Stephen Spencer Jr. "Well, I regret to inform your, Mr. Spencer, we'll have a full day here at Osceola.

"And, no parade. You'll have to do your video thievery after school, and why not, unless you have a desire to complete all the questions at the end of this chapter." The Colonel understood that assigning Stephen Spencer extra homework for asking questions in class might bring the query of his petulant parents. The Colonel had raised his eyebrows over the dark rim of his glasses, sliding down his nose, and said without using any words, No more interruptions! Now repositioning the text book in front of him, he readjusted his glasses, and sat once again at the edge of the window sill, and resumed reading, the words in monotonous-monotone, telling how Narvaez, De Leon and another explorer, De Soto, had to fight off pestilence, insects, snakes, alligators, and, yes, hostile Indians (probably the same type of merciless savages mentioned in the Declaration of Independence), never mentioning (because it would not be a good history) how those brave Conquistadors and their Spanish soldiers had introduced horrible diseases to the tribes in Florida, and how they had terrorized and killed everything in their path on their way to discover the Fountain of Youth, or to get rich on gold, which they never could find either one.

And, as a result of their frustration, (again omitted from the text because it would not be a good history), the Spaniards cut a bloody trail up through Florida of near total destruction, the surviving indigenous human beings left behind wrought with disease, sorrow, more death, and, of course, the Catholic missionaries (some of them becoming "martyrs" according to the textbook) as "they were killed seeking to make converts of the heathens". It appeared that just as the Conquistadors believed God gave them the right of discovery, the missionaries believed God wanted Indian converts, even under pain of their Indian death. Not far from the southern coast of Florida, on the island of Cuba, a Taino leader named Hatuey lead a guerrilla war against the Conquistadors (not in the history text, of course). It has been documented that Hatuey, the Taino cacique (leader), had been betrayed and captured.

At a Spanish camp, Hatuey was tied to a stake where he was burned alive. Just before lighting the fire, however, it was documented (and everyone knows how important documentation is) that a Catholic priest offered him salvation. Holding the cross the priest was wearing up to Hatuey's face, he gave the Indigenous leader a final opportunity to accept Jesus as his personal savior. It was recorded that Hatuey answered, saying, He wanted nothing to do with a God that allows such ruthless violence and brutality....

De Las Casas, a Catholic bishop, also documented the fate of a local Taíno village after Hatuey's death. Over two thousand Taino people, who had received the Spaniards as guests, gave them food, and gave them drink, were immediately, after the cacique's death, wiped out. "They set upon the Indians," the bishop wrote, "slashing, disemboweling and slaughtering them until their blood ran like a river."

Of the few survivors, they were sent to the mines. Bishop De Las Casas described how the Spaniards "required of them tasks utterly beyond their strength, bending them to the earth with crushing burdens, harnessing them to loads which they could not drag, and with fiendish sport and mockery, hacking off their hands and feet, and mutilating their bodies in ways which will not bear description."

Hatuey, nor what was done to the indigenous people, are mentioned in the social studies textbook. There is a popular Cuban beer, though, named *Hatuey*.

These accounts affirm what the philosophers and scholars of history understood, especially with gruesome scenes today depicted on TV and YouTube. ...People who do not learn their history are forever doomed to repeat it. In this situation, it has to do with human history as a collective, especially when religious extremists are involved and those fat cats wanting to get rich from stealing resources play a cooperative role....

But Rainy knew all this. She had read about the early history of the Americas' exploration from the books Grandpa had kept on his bookshelves. He told her that she would read disturbing things, even see troubling paintings, photographs, and drawings in those books, about humanity, and inhumanity, but if she felt she was old enough to learn the history, he would not stop her, and if she had any questions, or needed to talk about anything she had read, he would be there for her.

Before Mr. Kline's class on The Big Three, she also researched on the computer, the De Soto Pageant, celebrating the Spanish landing (or invasion, as Grandpa would call it) with a reenactment and parade. Shadows of clouds outside floated across her mind just as they had over whatever lesson the Colonel was teaching that day.

So, unintentional daydreaming beckoned her without her even knowing. About the only time Mr. Kline had managed to engage her attention was his reading about the hostile Calusa Indians who attacked Ponce De Leon, shooting him in the thigh (Grandpa said that he actually got shot in the butt, but that wouldn't sound too honorable, so they changed it to say he got shot in the thigh) with a poison arrow, which had ultimately, according to the textbook, managed months later to kill the brave explorer.

Well, the swift moving morning clouds had now passed, leaving the Sun to shower his light and heat on everything. The classroom even grew brighter, though the blinds did the work of shielding out any direct light with the exception of this particular spot on this particular morning when a shaft of a sun ray filtered through Mr. Kline's classroom window at just the perfect angle, creating a golden glow that had fallen like a radiant shawl over Rainy Peek, and though her eyes had remained fixed on the textbook page, her mind's eye strayed from the printed words, the warmth from the light shawl momentarily rekindling an unintentional daydream.

Call it a reaction of his military training, if you want, but just at that moment the Colonel glanced over his glasses, and capturing a glimpse of peacefulness in the golden light on Rainy Peek's face, he discerned almost at once that she was not listening. This was important test material.

And so, the Colonel shut the blinds, saying it was getting too hot, and that it was too bright, that the glare was making it hard for them to read, but Rainy never flinched. She kept her eyes glued (as ordered) on the book, but did not let go of that serene feeling and warmth inside her left in the brief light of the radiant shawl. Instead, she just allowed the darkness to drift in front of her, like dark matter passing before a star.

>>•<< >>•<< >>•<<

Without closing her eyes, she felt like she was floating away from her body, floating into another time, a thousand and more miles away, floating like the snowflakes across a gray morning long ago that turned everything they touched to white.... As they fell, she could see her breath, and her mother's breath, squatting alongside her. Fitted in her new snow boots, and a snow suite bundle, she stood embraced in her mother's' arms, and close to her mother's body, feeling warm and secure, like every child ought always to feel in someone's arms.

"My, Rains, you're gettin' so big! I'm not sure I can pick you up anymore.... You're growing too fast! Too soon for me." Then she grabbed hold of one of her daughter's legs. "And these are gettin' so long!" Then she kissed her rosy cheek. "Just think, Rainy, you're exactly five and a half years old on this day and at this exact time in the morning. Except there's a time change of an hour. And, of course, it's snowing... not raining."

They stood in front of the door of their small reservation house, in big jackets with hoods, while watching Rainy's dad, boots sunk in new powder, ankle deep on top of a white pile of hard accumulated snow plowed up days earlier, a portable CD player right alongside him on top of the mound, and holding a frozen broom in his gloved hands, like it was a guitar. He even used an electrical cord he got from their bedroom closet for a guitar strap.

"Well, Ladies, Music Lovers, Fans of All Ages," he called to them. "I'm just dress rehearsing for your concert today, which I will personally perform for you, my loyal fans, during my sunset show in the snow." Then he looked at his daughter. "Geez, Rains, if you were born on a morning like this, your mom might've called you Snowy.... Then I'd be callin' you Snows!" He smiled the kind of smile you make when everything in your life feels right. Cold gust blowing warm feelings. Snow falling in his blue eyes. The Sun rising unseen in a Cirrus sky.

"What'd you think, Ladies?"

"Frank," her mom called out. "You might fall and hurt your leg—again."

It had been a month since he and a couple of his diabetic Dakota patients were moving heavy equipment into the clinic. He had twisted a knee and strained a ligament just as they were maneuvering an X-ray machine into place. He only limped for a week while using a cane, but with another, unusual Artic front descending in late autumn, the sharp pains had remained long after, and often struck hardest at night.

"Oh, Maggie, I'm dedicating this song to you, and to our precious daughter," and he winked. Snow that had accumulated on his eye lashes fell, partially melted down his reddened cheeks. "And, to my dad too."

Maggie loved him. Deeply. It was like she could feel his hands sometimes holding her heart, protecting her and loving her.... Rainy loved him with the light of a thousand suns, but something made her feel like sometimes she missed him even when he was present. He worked long hours and spent a lot of time driving from the clinic to the hospital in Fargo. When he was home, he'd answer calls from patients, no matter the time of day or night.

"Besides," he said, "Rod Stewart never fell during a performance."

"Frank, you don't know that!"

He didn't know that the rock star of the 70's had never fallen during one of his concerts. He was just a boy then sitting in the front leather seat, driving in the car with his father, a doctor himself, behind the wheel of a white Volvo, and whenever his dad would hear the song, Maggie Mae, on the radio, he would say, in a Swedish accent, "Frank, crank it up. Let's get some use oudda deez fine Bowers and Wilkens speakers."

At the moment, Rainy's dad, Maggie's husband, standing on top of this five foot snow pile, had declared himself, "Ice Man Rock," and leaned over real careful, pressing the play button on the CD player.

As the guitar from the speakers resonated, he began strumming their kitchen broom. The fingers of his snowy black gloves sliding up and down the imaginary bridge of the imaginary guitar, like he had rehearsed this song and this moment his whole life. He didn't look much like the serious and handsome endocrinologist student that Maggie, on a student scholarship herself in education, had dated. He didn't look like the doctor who graduated at the head of his class at Harvard Medical School, with his blonde shoulder cropped hair now sticking out like elongated crystals of frozen sunlight. He looked like Ice Man Rock, or in Dakota, more appropriately said, Ice Rock Man.

The cold wind was picking up, and it began snowing sideways. He kept singing the memorized lyrics to Maggie Mae, and working that old broom stick guitar until the ground unexplainably shook, not a violent knock-you-down shake, more subtle, almost imperceptible, but the drift he was standing on followed the laws of nature and gave way, and he dropped, along with the CD player, quite suddenly like there was nothing but air under him, burying him in snow up to his chest.

"Frank!" Maggie cried out, as much from his fall as from the shaking ground.

He had to crawl on his belly, and sort of roll and slide down the remainder of the drift, his face wet and colored like a bad sunburn.

"I'm good," he said. "What was that?"

"I don't know. That's the second one this week, though."

Still, as a victorious warrior emerges from

a horse fall with his weapon in hand, he held the broom-stick guitar over his head, protecting it as if it had belonged to Rod Stewart himself, and wearing a startled smile frozen in his daughter's memory of the last morning they would ever spend together.

As Maggie and he were trying to determine what happened, the sight of him covered in snow, still holding the broom-stick guitar, had caused the child that was their daughter to laugh so hard her tears might have gotten frozen too. They all laughed to tears, freezing in trails down their cheeks.

Maybe that's what *frozen in time* means because the image was still there, even as she sat, staring into a textbook in the Colonel's sixth grade social studies class, a frozen image remaining in her mind, of the three of them together for the last time, and they were happy.

》•《 》•《 》•《

A few days later, back in the Colonel's classroom, after she had finished her multiple choice test on *The Big Three*, and the rest of the Conquistadors and their "explorations," so-to-speak, of Florida, Rainy was sitting at her desk when her imagination gradually began to open once more across another page of the codex, focusing on a single faded glyph up in the crinkled corner of her mind, found again in that place of unintentional daydreaming....

》•《 》•《 》•《

Next thing, her mother was leaning over Rainy's crib, gazing down at her, but Rainy was a baby, an infant, and her mom's face was smiling and adoring as so many mothers' faces are when beholding their babies, and her long black hair was feather-brushing across Rainy's little wriggling fingers....

>>•<< >>•<< >>•<<

On that particular unintentional daydreaming session, while the other kids were still working on the test, and the classroom was quiet, she had taken a half sheet of the scrap paper, which Mr. Kline allowed them to keep on their desks. With her eyes focused on the paper, she traced the image of her hand, then began drawing circles with designs in them and spirals, each looking like the ones her Dakota ancestors painted on their lodges, or on their bodies, and then retracing her mind's image of other drawings she was seeing, these of mysterious beings etched on rocks and cliffs many thousands of years old. She even sketched from memory one part of a Mayan glyph she had seen in one of her grandfather's books about the Mayan people.

It was an image of Kulkulcan.

>>•<< >>•<< >>•<<

At the beginning of the semester, Mr. Kline had noticed her drawings after a True or False test, this one, on the Old World. She had finished checking the boxes before anyone else after reading the single sentence questions. Disturbed what she was doing, the Colonel had stepped in front of her desk and leaned over so close to her face she could smell his creamed coffee-stale breath.

"Miss Peek, is it?" He knew her name. Even then when she was a new student at the beginning of the semester. It would become part of his procedural acknowledgment. Her reputation for high grades, however, preceded her, and that was what he cared about most. Her strong sense of self and identity had been exhibited more than a few times in previous classes where she attended elementary school. That idea of self-assertion, especially from an Indian, and a girl, disturbed him, but he was willing to risk the discomfort of his male ego for the teaching award she'd help him win at the end of the semester. He knew that just by acting uncertain of who she was, he could make her feel less significant to him. Not empower her. Keep her off balance. His intention did not go unnoticed. His smelly breath, his violation of her space, and his obtrusive cold blue magnified orbs staring from behind the thick glass lenses in black frames, enabled her to already assess the kind of man he was, just as Koda would have done, as wolves (and a lot of dogs) will do with all men they can see, men they can smell, or hear, or sense in any number of ways, the ones not hiding behind a rock or a tree a football field away, downwind against their pale faces, concealing their human scent and malice, their dead eye taking dead aim through a telescopic scope....

Without moving her head, she looked up. "Yes, Sir," she said, glancing up at his blue gumball eyes.

"You should have better things to do than doodling, Miss Peek," he said in a low hard voice, his mouth inches from her ear, and pointing to an image on the paper. "What is that?"

"He's a spider. He is Iktomi, the Trickster."

"And that? My Lord, is that... a snake?"

"It's Kulkulcan, the Feathered Serpent."

The Colonel huffed, and stood, like this one was beyond anything he could fix, and then he shook his head, clearing it for the prize, quickly realizing that this one was still his ticket.

"No matter what you call it, Miss Peek, it is doodling" – if not downright improper and heathen, he was thinking but didn't say. Another mandatory fall workshop for teachers on cultural sensitivity had helped him out a little. He didn't want to say something that could be construed as culturally insensitive and jeopardize his eligibility for that teaching award, the grand prize he could not win without her.

As he didn't want to push it too far because she was, after all, the student who had already scored the highest grades, he backed off. He knew not to mess too much with a good thing, and Rainy Peek could be a really good thing for him. She was the kind of student he could always count on to set the curve for the entire sixth grade class when it came to tests. And she was his.

>>·<< >>·<< >>·<<

Since the Colonel would not let them read books for pleasure, or study from others, while a test was in progress, she didn't have anything better to do, especially if daydreaming wasn't working for her. She continued making her drawings on scrap paper, even after an Old World true or false test, at the beginning of the semester, and even after a longer multiple choice test on the Conquistadors weeks later, because the Colonel had not really ordered her to stop. At least if she was doodling, he figured, she appeared to be problem solving, which meant that she would not be a bother to the other students, nor give any impressions of them being any less intelligent, though they all knew.... And while she sketched one more image of a long haired pregnant woman, the students still trying to figure out answers, or even making desperate guesses as they went, she imagined how lucky some children are because they get to love their mothers through a good part of their growing up years, and how lucky mothers can be if they get to love even one child throughout their own lives. She wondered about a mother who did not love her child in that way.

How can that be? What kind of thing has to happen?

On that particular morning a few weeks ago in Mr. Kline's class, somewhere in the blood, Rainy had tapped into the Great Mystery within herself, and somewhere deep inside of her, she understood the feelings in the symbols she drew. She understood their importance. She understood without even knowing, that the *circle* is the ending of one cycle and the beginning of another. It is perpetual and complete. The *spiral*, something evolving, or emerging, like a human learning and becoming the *being* in the *human*. She grew closer to the mysterious pictographs pictured in her grandfather's books, etched in stone, the gods and star people of the heavens, the ancient memories and ancestors and the sky mechanics of the universe. And the Mayan serpent glyph of Kulkulcan on his own cyclical journey traveling the earth and beyond.

Then, like a ghost whisper inside your mind, when you hear someone clearly call your name, but there isn't anybody there, Rainy at her desk staring at those designs, suddenly imagined her mom's voice. *Rainy....*

She heard it.

Rainy....

It fluttered as delicate and faint as moth wings brushing her ear, but then the Colonel's voice broke in like a soldier busting open your

146 bedroom door.

"Test time is *over*," he pronounced. "Put your pencils down. I'll be collecting your papers."

He moved through the rows of desks, gruffly picking up tests, glancing at a few with a serious but somewhat approving expression, and shaking his head at most of the others with scorn. When he stood over Rainy Peek's desk, holding her test, skimming her answers, he barely was able to restrain his vain approval squinting over his glasses. Maintaining a face without emotion, he half nodded favorably as he gazed down at her, confident about *himself*.

The unit test he was holding showed without doubt that *he* really had done *his* job. The only person to doubt the standard history of the discovery of the New World had answered all his questions perfectly.

Her glorious excellence in the multiple choice test on the Conquistadors had proved it. No more fear of challenges to *society's* truth. No more discomfort for him at having to discuss her perception of what had really occurred in the Americas with the arrival of Columbus and the Conquistadors.

The Colonel had, indeed, succeeded in teaching Rainy Peek one of the first lessons of the standardized and status quo history of how things were and how things got to be the way they are in this world, and in this great country. Her indoctrination, if not assimilation, was proving successful.

But then, in the delight of his assumed victory and brief illusory moment at receiving the end of the year teaching award she was going to win for him, he noticed the scrap paper on her desk, the marks made into circles and spirals and strange forms, and the glyph of what he only knew was an evil snake, *the devil himself,* and everything would suddenly go blank for Mr. Kline.

You see, back in the day of Indian Boarding Schools, when native children were forcibly taken long distances away from their families and homes to be *reeducated,* there was a saying, or more like a motto. It was even engraved in a plaque on the door of a school's entrance. The teachers lived by it; *Kill the Indian; save the man.*

Now Mr. Kline's sense of self-importance, culminating at the end of the school year with his award presentation, the check he would receive for his students' success, the recognition by the faculty that mostly didn't like him but secretly needed him to help perpetuate the illusion of their country's greater honor and meaning of sacrifice, would disappear. Even the desire for becoming a principal, or teaching the new honors classes, had been in this instant reduced in their worth.

He had failed. *He had failed in his Viet Nam mission. He had failed with his son! He had failed with this student.* His mind was reeling.

In that one minute, as he stood over Rainy Peek's desk, staring down at the images of circles and spirals and unknown creatures and a menacing serpent god, who *really was* a true American cultural hero, he needed to steady himself, to catch his breath. His head was light and dizzy. He could lose his balance. He could lose control of his human form and actually fall. For the balance had all of a sudden and unexpectedly shifted back.

It didn't belong to him.

Like the air, like the water, like the land, it could never belong to him.

Love Comes in Many Forms...
The touch of a hand on your shoulder, a kiss
from someone you love...
A dog's lick on your cheeks.
Loves comes in many forms, the colors of shells
that make up a necklace, the colors of beads
that decorate your hair, colors of feathers
of courting birds, colors on the wings of
butterflies touching flowers
Colors of the sky
at dawn.
The colors of peoples and animals and the
colors of banana leaves and mango leaves and
the cool shade of palms and turquoise shades
of the water.
Love comes as a song as a poem, as a gesture
of friendship,
Human or not.
Love comes with generosity and kindness
and in the faces of the ones you've always
known,
and sometimes in the ones you just met,
The ones you never forget who take you in and
hold you in their hearts.
The ones who know your spirit.

CHAPTER TWENTY-THREE

HOLDING ON AND LETTING GO

It always seemed to her that she worked hard to hold onto different images of her parents' faces, fearing that they could fade away. She tried not to let her mind forget the sound of their laughter and their voices, afraid they could disappear forever. If you've ever lost someone you loved like that, you understand. Sometimes just the smell of a certain kind of perfume or a cologne could make them feel so close. Hearing a certain song. Being in a certain place. But, if you haven't yet had that empty feeling that loss can leave with you, at least you know that when you do, you won't be alone.

Her mom's cell phone was not recovered, and her father's crushed between frozen rock and metal. The pictures they saved were gone. Since no one in the family even owned a camera, Grandpa had just a few photographs. They were pictures of how Rainy wanted to remember them, but they were pictures, always the same ones, still and silent in that one moment, and looking at them would always touch her heart, and the fact that she could actually hold them in her hands gave her something tangible, but it wasn't the same as seeing her parents and hearing them in her mind, so she kept calling on those memories. Sometimes in the boredom of class. Sometimes in the madness of the school bus. Sometimes lying in her bed hoping she would go to sleep and dream she was with them again.

Today, though, as Terrance T-Rex Walmart Walcott and Ben the Father of our Country Franklin had competed for the Bully of the Year Award, and Mr. Kline, not making the situation any better for any kind of daydreaming to work but quickly becoming a strong contender for the sorry award himself, Rainy was having too much trouble escaping what the bully seventh grader, should be eighth grader, had said to her that morning, and trying to understand the mindset of the bully founding father that had called her ancestors savages, and how she could never call him, nor ever think of calling him, EVER, the father of her country. It also made her think about her and Grandpa and Koda, not even having a country.

What does it mean to not have a country when you're living on the back of a Turtle shell your ancestors for tens of thousands of years called Mother? It was the first time she had grown concerned at the core of her being, that the United States of America, as it was conceived some merely 200 plus years ago, and as it exists even now, could never fully include them.

Her mother's own tribe, bickering over how much Dakota blood a person would have to be, to be an enrolled member of their tribe to benefit from casino money offered no country of belonging. No nation. Her grandfather of mixed ancestry as well as she, was not a Mayan living in Mexico. He was not a Scott or Celtic.

Even with the exception of a few places in North America, Koda had no place for his country where they would not try and kill him. And so, if this can be all true, did this mean for certain that Rainy, Grandpa, and Koda really didn't have a country, and would never have a country? The core of her being was shaken....

In her mind's eye, Mr. Kline had become a blurry form that resembled the Michelin Man sporting a blue suit jacket in front of the classroom, and his textbook versions of

American history a mumbo-jumbo of words that at the moment made no sense at all, but she could see and hear past them, and then, into that wormhole of moments, into that tunnel of time, she began to ... fall and spin, and spin and fall... fall...fall.

>>·<< >>·<< >>·<<

Without ever closing her brown eyes that morning while Mr. Kline went on about the courage and fortitude of the American colonists, she just gazed down at her desk at a painted page in the imaginary codex of her life, contemplating the ones she loved most in the world....

Grandpa's white spider web hair tucked behind his ears, the evidence of acquired trials and wisdom, his newly ordered grey sweat shirt, hanging past his waist with the words painted in red across his chest: Indigenous; his baggy safari shorts and his tan and lean muscular legs; and Koda, a hundred and twenty pounds of wolf, the scars on his back legs physical reminders of the cowardice and cruelty of men, now standing and pressing alongside of Grandpa in a wolf hug, the fingers of Grandpa's free hand feeling into Koda's thick mane; his other hand, holding the silver dolphin mug of decaf, raising it to wave to her as she walked towards the bus stop at the end of the driveway...

CHAPTER TWENTY-FOUR

PERSONAL QUESTIONS/PERSONAL BOUNDARIES

Some days were just like this.

Days when Rainy seemed to draw curious people to her just by being who she was. These curious people were a lot like those dark clouds you see moving fast across the sky sometimes when a tropical storm or hurricane is forming somewhere nearby, the way they are purposely drawn to that energy and to wherever the center of the storm would be. Something about the quiet power of calmness in Rainy's center that seemed to attract them, even adults; maybe it allowed them to feel that they were a part of something much bigger, or maybe it was something they had forgotten that they wanted to be closer to, or that it was something they had lost, but somehow Rainy drew them to her.

There were those few, though, like Mrs. Kingsley back in third grade, whose own peaceful nature and sense of calm had by the laws of attraction, connected them to each other. There are always those few you can find on life's journey like Mrs. Kingsley, who are kind, wanting to lend their own good energy to yours, not just sap it, disrespect it, or take yours away.

But, of course, as things appear to be the way they are these days, there are still the others....

"Do you live in a teepee?" they would ask.

"How come your hair's not black? How come you got blonde highlights?"

"Are you called a squaw?"

"How   come   you   don't   live   on

a reservation?"

"What tribe are you?"

"Do you go to church?"

And, of course, the big one, the one some just couldn't resist asking for whatever reason.... "Do you believe in God?

Now and then, they would say things, or ask questions they were curious about that hurt without even meaning to. Some people feel they have the right to go up to perfect strangers and ask a personal question. Without even knowing you, they might say, "Do you mind if I ask you a personal question?" Then they proceed to ask you before you can even respond, or they act terribly offended if you say, no. And yet, they're the ones that are doing the offending, and they give that right to themselves, and don't consider that what they're asking might be shared with them should they get to know you as a friend, first, and maybe then as friends, it would be your choice, for you to share something personal.

Maybe, Grandpa would say, it's that gotta-have-it-now, or me-first mentality that allows such people to cross lines of social etiquette, which he explained were manners, or maybe it was using too much technology and getting used to instant feedback looking too much at computer screens and smart phone screens, and screens of all kinds, and not looking at, or having interaction with, another real-live-standing-in-front-of-you human being. Then he said that sometimes having a culture, or even a religion, taught folks about etiquette and help ed keep people respectful and mindful of crossing personal boundaries.

A third grade teacher, Mrs. Karen Christiansen, wearing a handsome gold cross necklace once proclaimed to Rainy, "You're a pretty little girl. I'm curious, are you part Indian?"

Since Rainy had never thought of herself that way, and her grandfather had never talked about her like that, she somewhat understood at least the Indian part of the question, so she slowly nodded, agreeing more or less that she was.

However, the question lingered in her brain, and she carried those words, part Indian, around with her for the rest of that school day. As her and Grandpa walked down the driveway from the mailbox, she asked Grandpa if she was part Indian.

At first, he just stopped walking, as if something had made him. Then he pursed his lips and released his breath in exasperation, shaking his head in disgust, for he didn't want to think in this day and age that a grownup person, especially a teacher, could still be asking a child such a question.

"Which part of your body did that teacher expect you to point to that is Indian?" he said, and began walking again.

She raised her eyes, and shrugged, and hurried to keep up with his longer strides.

When they got back to the house, Koda sniffed Rainy all over, moving her back with his nose, turning her around, assessing the kind of interactions she had that day, assessing her emotions, and her kisses which she gave to him all over his face.

Grandpa smiled and shook his head again.

He had taken a braid of sweet grass from a drawer in his desk, along with a shell about the size of your hand, and asking that she sit at the kitchen table with him, he lit the end of the braid and placed it in the shell, the fragrant incense swirling around the table, and then he sat down with that serious look in his eyes like he had something to say about the idea of being part Indian....

>>·<< >>·<< >>·<<

"Rainy, where ye sit right now, point to the part of you that's Indian, and the part that's not."

She looked at herself. Looked at her arms, her hands, her legs. Her toes scratching Koda's back. She was wearing a red t-shirt with a peace sign in black on the front, plain black shorts, and bare feet with a shell bracelet around one of her ankles. She touched her necklace of coquina shells. Then looked up at her grandfather. She looked down at herself again.

"I can't do that."

"That's because Indians don't come in parts," he said right off and direct. "Back in the day, that's not how our people saw one another."

She was still looking down at her body.

"Ye see, Rainy, my dad was proud of his Scott-Irish and Indian ancestry on his father's side, and his German ancestry on his mother's, but my dad considered himself an Indian. On the other hand, his brother Roger didn't really see himself that way. He chose to blend in, almost invisible like.... He hated confrontations, and if you're an Indian livin' in this country, you're bound to be havin' confrontations.... Uncle Roger never really said how he saw himself. But, don't get me wrong, Uncle Roger was a good man, and he knew things...."

Rainy peeled a mango. They had found the mangos on the ground a few days ago. They found them early, before anything else could eat them. Now they were ripe and juicy. Grandpa handed her another plate for the peels and another paper towel. Then he sat down and sipped his black coffee.

"What'd you mean?"

"My dad felt different than Uncle Roger. He liked wearin' Indian things when he could. When he was allowed. He didn't care if it was a string of Navajo silver and turquoise around his neck, a Dakota beaded wrist band, or a Seminole jacket. It's not like he went around carrying a sign that read, I'M AN INDIAN, especially when being Indian could bring serious trouble down on you; it's just that's how he always saw himself, even though he had blue eyes, light brown hair, and fair skin, ... an Indian warrior of Celtic ancestry, he used to say.

"Your great Uncle Roger kept it more inside. But he had a way of seeing' things too... like a power that was old, he could tell what you were feeling, and even see into the future where you might be headin'."

He watched her delight on the luscious mango pieces. He continued to sip his coffee.

"Now while it's true," he said, "that federal and tribal governments divide us up by blood quantum, settin' us apart, declaring someone is an Indian or not on account of how much Indian blood that person has, or others judge our Indian-ness by the way they think we ought to look, we don't need to be ashamed of our non-native ancestry to feel proud that we're Indian, or that we don't have enough blood to be an Indian.

"Take your dad," he said, and just the mention of the word dad caused her to hold the piece in her fingers, and look up at Grandpa. "His ancestors were not from this land, but his people were a tribe once. As I suspect all peoples were. It's only in the process of their becomin' civilized, that they lost touch with that Indigenous tribal part of themselves. Their wisdom was lost too. For it was, by and by, that technology became more important to civilized people than their relationship with Nature. That, and makin' money. And their religions made it all possible....

"You'd better eat that piece, Rainy, before it slips outta your hand and onto your lap."

"What about my dad?" she asked, sliding a chunk of mango in her mouth.

"Your father," he said, taking a drink of coffee, "he still felt that tribal connection. He still had not lost touch with his Indigenous spiritual being. Which was probably why he fell so in love with your mother, and she in love with him."

Then he sighed, a slight sound of air leaving with his breath that he didn't mean to make, something that loss and remembered grief can cause you to do sometimes when you're not even aware of how much you still miss those you loved....

With a mouthful of mango, and juice dripping down the corners of her mouth, and her fingers, she looked up at her grandfather again. She could feel his sudden reminder of great loss and understood, and she could see her own feelings at some future time, like her great Uncle Roger.

"Your dad was a good man," Grandpa said, "and you should be proud to have his blood in you as well your mom's. He wanted you to be raised as an Indian because the way our ancestors saw the world has not been totally lost. He wanted ye to live your life in the Indian way, to be a human being...as did your mom."

Across the front yard, a warm humid gust ignited the electric high-pitched droning of cicadas. It swept through the house with the spirits of all things beautiful. It lifted the checkered table cloth, touched the faces of the two human beings seated next to one another, and whisked away the words and burning incense before heading out the opened window over the kitchen sink, stirring the leaves and Spanish moss of the old oaks in the back of the house as it went, while the vibrant whirring of the cicadas ascended and faded into the air, their prayer/song for rain now in the wind.

Koda had laid quietly on the floor near Rainy and lifted his head as the wind and cicada sounds passed, listening and sniffing for the messages they carried.

Then everything quieted. A pause in the world. Everything still. Quiet and still, in this moment in the center of calm.

With his elbows on the table, Grandpa folded both his hands and rested them against his forehead. "It's not about being ashamed of the blood of other cultures and races that make you who you are," he said, looking up and over his hands at his granddaughter. "It's about seein' your whole self, in your case, as a human being. Blood runs the heart; the heart knows what it is…. You can see yourself as Indian…as Native… as Mayan… as Dakota…. As Indigenous. Nobody defines you, but you."

He poured some more coffee. "Or, maybe you choose otherwise," he declared, placing his hands around his mug. "Maybe you don't see yourself that way. And, if you do now, maybe one day you won't."

She wiped her mouth with the paper towel and gazed at him. He took a sip from his mug. She was trying to comprehend in her eight, going on nine, year old brain what to her seemed incomprehensible.

"It's your life," he said, looking at her. "It's your heart. Just know that however ye see yourself, Rainy, I'll always love ye because whoever you are, or choose to be, I know you'll be a good person.... A human being ...."

He stopped talking, and turned his eyes to the front yard beyond the screen door. Resting his head in his hand, elbow on the table, the silence allowed for the ideas and feelings to settle, giving Rainy pause to feel her own heart beating beneath her chest, her own pulse moving through the center of herself, and Koda's mane in her toes as he lay at her feet, all three beings in the center of all things.

"Granpa?" she asked softly.

He turned his eyes to her, brow raised, one side of his face supported still with his opened hand. "Yes?" he said, his own curiosity prompting his response to the unexpected.

"Granpa?" she repeated.

"Yes, Rainy," he repeated.

"Do you believe in God?"

"Huh," he said, pausing after the sound you make when hear something that surprises you. His brow dropped this time as his expression turned from surprise, to one of deep consideration to a profound question. "Well," he said, raising his head, his fingers stroking his chin, "the way I look at it, Rainy ..., if some people believe in God ... then God exists for them...." He paused again. "He's a part of the Great Mystery."

She nodded. "Makes sense."

He smiled and nodded too.

Then, she slid off her chair, cleaned her place on the table, and, calling for Koda's companionship, headed out the door, a whole person, a whole human being, and Grandpa eased back in the chair, arms on the table, watched and wondered.

"We are related through our Mother, the Earth;

whether we share blood is irrelevant

because we share a connection to the Earth,

and her many creatures, deeper

than others.

We are connected by the Moon

and the Stardust we are made from."

- SHIMMERING HORSE WOMAN IN MOONLIGHT

CHAPTER TWENTY-FIVE

OPENING A CAN OF WORMS

On this particular sixth grade afternoon, after Terrance Walcott and Mr. Kline had already clouded her morning up with their shadow take on things, when Rainy thought she had finally managed to find her peace in her preferred seat at a small lunch table where she could eat alone, a girl in the seventh grade, with smooth chocolate skin sat across from her at the same table.

Green, yellow, and black bows were clipped to her shiny dreads, and copper-tinted strands threaded through them, not unlike the blonde sun-streaks in Rainy's hair. Sliding her tray onto the same table, she sat down across from her, and would go where no one, outside of Grandpa, had ever gone with Rainy Peek.

Rainy lifted her eyes without raising her head and watched without looking, how the girl with the colored bows and dreadlocks adjusted everything on her tray so that it appeared in perfect organized order: fork on one side, spoon alongside it, both on the carefully folded and positioned napkin, waxy orange juice carton in the back aligned with the tray, plate of spaghetti, centered, another napkin unfolded in her lap. It was like she was preparing a hospital surgical tray.

"My name's Sadie Willis," she said, moving the spaghetti around in her dish, observing the opened orange juice container alongside Rainy's tray. "We can choose what we drink, don't get any choice what to eat," she said. "Looks like they stole earth worms from the science lab."

Rainy glanced up. A slight smile curved

162 the blush lips of her trying-to-be stoic face.

Sadie ate some, then tapped her lips lightly with a napkin. "I know your name's Rainy Peek, and I know we didn't know each other until now, but I was thinking of you today," she said, opening the juice carton and taking a sip. "This morning, in my seventh grade social studies class with Mr. Kline, he was talkin' somethin' about how we had bought Alaska from Russia when a kid named T-Rex, who's really an eighth grader but repeatin' seventh grade social studies, said he saw on TV that in Alaska you can make money shooting wolves from planes. He said he could get rich in Alaska shooting wolves."

Rainy's eyes fixed down on her plate. For an instant everything left her mind but one thought; ending Terrance Walcott's existence on this planet right then and there with her mind, so he would not maliciously hurt another life form. And maybe, she did. She wanted his meanness out of this world. Off the planet! Gone for good!

The girl sitting across from her could feel the intensity of Rainy's thoughts. "One of the kids asked Mr. Kline why they shot wolves," she continued, putting the orange juice back on the tray, making certain it was in the same position she had first placed it. "I mean, I never heard of such a thing. If it wasn't for the stupid question.... Well, the Colonel explained they shot wolves because wolves are wild animals and killed antelope and other game that sportsman hunted, and sportsmen are good for Alaska's economy. He said it might not be a bad idea for T-Rex to move to Alaska. He said the big money's in oil, though, and Alaska has a lot of it, but that maybe while T-Rex was waitin' to get rich on oil, he could shoot wolves from planes.

"Some kids laughed," Sadie added. "But I

didn't. It made me mad."

Now Rainy's heart had dropped, just like if you were to let go of something and it just falls. Catching it the moment before it landed heavy in her stomach, she brought it back to her chest where it resumed its pounding, but then she just kind of froze there at the small table, staring down at her plate, her rosy cheeks flushed, still with that one horror of thought filling all the space in her brain, trying hard not to imagine Terrance Walcott hanging high out of a plane taking aim with a 7 mm Magnum, the wolves below on the ground falling and collapsing from running into exhaustion in the deep snow, bloodied and dead for no good reason by his gun....

"Some kids say you live with an old man and a wolf because you don't have parents."

"That's my granpa," Rainy said. "Koda's a rescue."

Sadie paused, allowing the mind of the girl sitting across from her a chance to recover and maybe add something to what was appearing to be a mostly one way conversation.

"I think wolves are glorious," she said, "and I think grandparents are awesome. I live with my grandmother mostly," she said. "She's my mother's mom, and it hurts her a lot to see her daughter so messed up, like she don't understand what happened.... But I think she does.... Anyhow, my mom stays with us sometimes. We just never know when...."

Rainy stirred the tomato sauced worms, dangling them from her fork, lifting them towards her lips, and nodded that she had heard what Sadie had said.

Sadie finished swallowing her worms.

"I kinda wound up takin' care of my grandma," she said, patting the corners of her mouth again with a napkin, and glancing at Rainy. "She got a stroke last summer. She still likes to read a lot, and still helps me with my homework when she can, though she doesn't have a particular liking for Mr. Kline. She says he don't teach hardly nothin' about real history."

Sadie ate another forkful, wiped her lips with the napkin–again, drank some more orange juice, and added some more thoughts about her grandmother's condition.

"My granma can't move her right arm, not her leg very well either. The right side of her face kinda droops down. She has some trouble talkin'. The rehab lady showed me what to do to keep her movin'. I'm forever tryin' to get her to read, which helps her pronounce words."

"That's real bad," Rainy said, making brief eye contact. "Sorry...."

"My parents aren't married, and my dad's gone back to Jamaica," Sadie continued. "He lost his job up in Harbor Inlet. He was a truck mechanic. I remember him when I was a little .... He'd work on ol' lawn mowers until late at night. He'd lay the parts on the ground, all in a special order, and piece by piece, like a metal jigsaw puzzle, he'd clean 'em and put 'em back together. Get 'em runnin'. He could fix jus about anythin...." She dug into her spaghetti worms and twirled them on her fork. "Except my mom. Couldn't fix her....

"Hmm," she said in a half sigh, and ate what was on her fork, then laid the fork back on the tray in the exact spot where it had been, picked up her napkin, and patted her lips. "At his job, the owners of the garage used to get my father to do things nobody else wanted to do cause he only had a green card. A lot of times he had to work late at night. But this one time, they told him that before he went home, to load his pickup with their nasty waste and go to this place somewhere where they'd mapped out, where no one was likely to see him, and dump it. He wouldn't do it.... He told 'em it was against the law, but he told me that wasn't the only reason. He said his first job 'round here was his favorite, drivin' a school bus....

"We were sittin' on Granma's couch. He's explainin' why he didn't have a job no more. 'I seen wid mi own eyes, Sadie, wat dumpin' can look like. Oh Mon,' he said, shaking his head, '... never gonna forget dat sight, Sadie. A little Indian girl cryin' over a ded frog. Kids all wretchin' in de bus. Bad, bad! De smell in dat ditch...worse than shit.... Notten but ded!'

"He leaned over and looked right at me. 'I felt Jah's eyes see into mi soul dat mornin', Sadie. I'm looken into de side view mirror. Dem eyes looken back at me. Dem eyes belonged to one of Jah's special creatures I never seen till den....No way mi gonna dump. "

Her eyes lids snapped wide open, as you might wake from a lucid daydream.

"Jah is what he calls God.... Anyway, they fired him," she said, "and he couldn't find work. Probably cause of the way he looked and how he spoke English.... Couldn't get any references. He stopped by my granma's house two or three times that year, holidays and my birthday, but cause he had no job, he was an illegal, and he got sent back to Jamaica. My mom's mostly never 'round cause she's always gettin' high on somethin' or rehabbin' somewheres. She told me, my dad only came over to see her cause he was in need. Granma says it was cause he wanted to see me."

She took another drink of the

orange juice.

Rainy nodded, agreeing, "Probably so," but she was also thinking far back in her brain, tracing a memory feeling. It began as soon as she'd noticed Sadie's dreads. A good feeling, but it also cast a shadow of sadness.... She sees this man. She knows him. A grimy red cloth covered his nose and mouth. His dark eyes, anxious, but kind, and dark cheeks above the cloth.... She sees him. His black hair pulled back in dreads, some grey along the sides and behind his ears. He doesn't speak like the others, but she understands everything he tells her that morning....

She shook her head to clear it, and blinked back to this moment she was sitting across the table from a seventh grade girl she'd just met, and they were eating lunch together at school....

"Your father sounds like a decent man." Rainy said, almost in a whisper, about Sadie's dad wanting to see her. "Your granma would know...."

The girl with long pretty dreads cast a curious gaze at the sixth grader. She had observed everything, and was thinking, *There's something about you.* Then, an unusual awareness that she didn't have words for, came over her, in a similar way it had come over Rainy, like this moment in time between the two of them was somehow remembered. Her grandma called those sensations, spirit feelings, but others, she said, called it Deja vu. Careful not to be intrusive, Sadie shifted her eyes to the spaghetti worms dangling from her fork.

"Can you go see him?" Rainy asked.

"My dad?" She shook her head. "No. He's in jail." Her shoulders sunk forward. "Got busted for growing ganja. But he could get out soon cause the government's makin' new laws. Still, he's got a record, so he can't never come back...."

Taking a deep breath, she straightened, and reached for her juice. "I knew he smoked it," she said, taking a drink, "but he told me he never did to just get high, or be silly. He believed ganja helped him, '...to gain wisdom of mi spiritual self,' he'd say. 'To be closer to Jah.... It's mi religion,' he'd tell me."

She shrugged, tapped her lips with the napkin, and twirled some more of the wormy spaghetti on her plate. At that moment she observed an eighth grader selling a small Zip-loc with two joints in it to T-Rex who was standing where the lunch trays were stacked. "You got parents?" she asked, shifting the attention to her new friend, hopeful her impatience at the direct question, and her own offering up personal information, would reap more response.

Rainy kept eating, taking on the challenge of sucking one real long tomato sauced squiggly through a slight opening between her lips.

"Do you got a mom?" Sadie asked.

Rainy's fork hooked a heap more of spaghetti, and then more or less she forced it in, so she couldn't talk even if she had wanted to.

How do you sit at a lunch table eating with someone you just met and explain that your parents were killed in a car accident coming to pick you up from kindergarten, when a drunk teenager named Arlo Looking Glass ran their car off a slick road in the middle of a snowy afternoon into a steep ravine of nothing but jagged rocks and icy boulders, with an old pickup he'd stolen from his own grandfather on the day of your five and a half year old birthday?

How could you share something like that with someone you just met, having kept it in all these years? And yet, with her new best friend,

168 Sadie Willis, she would....

Afterwards, as the cafeteria ladies were going around picking up trays and straightening up the empty chairs and cleaning off the messy tables after all the other students had gone outside for a few minutes of cell phone activity, the two girls sat across from one another without talking much, and then Rainy looked up into very dark and familiar eyes....

"Everydey buck-it go a well," she said. "Wan day de battam drap out."

"It was you!" Sadie cried in a barely audible whisper. "You were the little girl."

THE STORM AND THE SPIRIT

After the confrontation that morning when Terrance Walcott's misinformation about Indians got all messed up with his feelings for Rainy, and he had to dump that mess on her at the bus stop, and Ben Franklin's immortal one word in Mr. Kline's history textbook, not to mention that at lunch she had finally said the words she'd always been afraid to say about her parents death to someone she'd just met, the nighttime seemed like it should be so welcoming. Maybe she would get to go to sleep peacefully and dream about being with her mom and dad, but outside Grandpa's small house near the beach, the sky was rumbling off shore, and flashes of light were streaking across the dark distant sky, and the wind gusts were growing stronger and more persistent. Earlier that evening the TV weatherman had said a tropical disturbance was brewing in the Gulf.

For Rainy, it was beginning to seem like that burst of wind that nearly flipped Terrance Walcott's Cleveland Indian baseball cap off his head really was just a sign of things to come....

>>•<< >>•<< >>•<<

Grandpa had said goodnight before he closed her door, but she could tell that he was experiencing a kind of tropical disturbance within himself, maybe even as powerful as the coming storm. He had heard it on the local news from the detached anchorwoman before the announcement of the storm ... Influenced by big oil, state legislators push to lift the ban restricting offshore drilling.

When the words first struck him, he closed the Mayan art book in his lap and let out a painful moan, like a person expressing sudden deep grief after learning of a loved one's death and not wanting to believe its truth. Then he clenched his fists.

"Greedy bastards," he murmured to himself. "It's never enough for them. Never enough...."

He spoke in a low primal growl, almost as low as his breath, so that Rainy could not hear above the rolling thunder of the shaking sky. He would step out onto the front porch, as she lay in bed, his heart pounding in his chest the way a heart pounds when something terrible has happened, and he would step down into the front yard and over to that special place where he had found the eagle feather, and where he had made tobacco offerings while speaking to the Great Mystery, and he would collapse to his knees as the weight of his anguish became too much for him to bear, and, embracing the need to be closer to the Earth, he bent further until one side of his face pressed against the sandy ground.

A light rain would begin to fall, his fingers clutching the sand, his tears mixing with the rain, a weeping grief-stricken child that is an old man grasping hold of the Mother that he loved with all his being, and, for the moment, feeling too small to protect her from more of what was coming, and what she had already begun to know of those who didn't know the Way to live. Drilling....

>>•<< >>•<< >>•<<

Inside her room, she too anguished over a world she could not understand. She lay uneasy in her bed with tired eyes that would not stay closed long enough for her to sleep. But always, alongside of her, within reach, her outstretched fingers kneaded through Koda's thick mane, as he curled on the throw rug by the bed, comforting her, and listening to the sky and Grandpa weeping while the wind was speaking, and feeling with all his senses for what was coming that was different that was coming on this storm.

Outside the bedroom window, tree frogs called to one another and did not seem to stop, and cicadas sang louder, and crickets chirped, constant, restless and alert. Even the blue jays, mockers, and doves nestled down in their nests as strong breezes shook the leaves of the avocado tree and whispered louder through the long winding branches of oaks, and rattled with more force the fronds of the tall palms.

A storm is coming, the whispering said; a storm is coming, the rattling said.

The gusts grew angrier, and soon their power began erasing the tell-tale whisperings, and all she could hear was the wailing of the wind. It stirred feelings inside of her, and her own silent wailing began. Great oak branches bowed and swayed, and the fronds of the palms twirled and twisted, the dead and dying ones tore away. Koda took notice of other things, the kind of things that a human could not see or hear or smell, and watched alongside Rainy, sensing with all his being that something more, something different, was coming with the storm.

The crack of thunder was drawing closer, and now the sky rained harder. Rolling on her pillow, she faced her bedroom window, thinking her own fear was right there, and she needed to know. White streaks of lightning ignited the fierce black sky and flashed across the mirrors

172

of her dark eyes. She shivered and, for just a moment, shut them, and in the blackness behind her lids she felt herself detaching, like light from the body of the sun, like the spirits of a billion cells becoming one spirit all connected to each other, but disconnecting from a physical form.

Opening her eyes, she noticed the numerous beads of water and water trails running down her bedroom window, appearing like the ever so many lakes and ponds and sun pools, and ever so many rivers and streams and tributaries, running all over and through the body of the earth, and all a part of the same water, the earth's water, her water, the water that could wash everything away. She pulled her covers up to her chin and over her necklace of purple and pink coquina shells.

Though she didn't feel threatened in a dangerous way about this storm, she felt something most unusual about it, and, like Koda, she knew; this storm that was coming was in different. This storm carried an eerie anticipation with it, an excited strangeness that made her anxious, like lots of feelings mixed with other feelings that had welled-up inside of her, feelings that formed questions for which she had no answers. What does it mean to be a real Indian? Why did my parents have to die? Why can't I have a mother? Then, finally, the question that disturbed her most, How can people be so cruel?

Koda understood his young companion's uneasiness. There were certainly times in his earlier life, when he was a free being living in the balance of innate wisdom, that insecurity had stalked him in a coward killer's form. Then, one cold and rainy autumn day in the mountains it struck. Koda understood the young girl's unrest, but even he, a million years descended from that innate wisdom, could not comprehend the kind of humans that were so insecure that they had no relationship with nature, the kind who are so insecure that they make themselves think the whole world is theirs for the taking, or the killing. Before he was born, in his mother's womb, Koda had learned to accept that which he could only know in his blood – and to be mindful of those that didn't know. How could any intelligent life form understand what's it's like to kill out of hate. Out of stupidity.

As lightning cracked the night and thunder shook the world and the wind howled and whipped about, her mind had conceded to the moment. Gradually sapped of thoughts, her body suddenly tired of feelings, her eyes wearied as if sleep was now approaching. Slowly, her lids began to close, but slowly too her restless spirit stirred inside of her, and then, like the steam rising from Grandpa's morning coffee, like the autumn mist ascending, Rainy's spirit rose from her own body.

At first, she thought how strange it was to float above herself. For a moment she lingered there in the bedroom air watching her closed eyes, her fingers peeking out from the covers and touching her necklace, Koda looking up as though he could see or sense her spirit's presence. Then, before she could gather another thought, something swept her away. It was a force that she had never known, and out the room she flew over Grandpa still knelt in the sand in the downpour, raising his wet face to sense something passing over, his blurry flooded eyes watching what he could not see as it moved quickly through the trees.

CHAPTER TWENTY-SEVEN

A SPIRIT JOURNEY

Down the path that lead to the beach, she found herself flying, not like a bird with wings, but as a spirit without a body.

Though she became afraid, the sensation of flying and being so free was greater than the fear, and she let go. She flew past the orange groves along the trail, over the dunes near the shore, and out across the churning open water. And in all the mighty movement of wind, and the torrential rain that was her namesake, and the crashing wild waves that had carried the first life to shore, Rainy Peek's spirit was strangely calm, even peaceful.

She could see everything all around her, but as a spirit without a body, all these sensations became as one, and all she could feel now was the sheer wonder in what she saw.

Even as sheets of rain fell like the oceans were just forming, and white crested waves tossed and splashed like they wanted to go everywhere, she still felt only wonder as the storm of the sky had merged with the sea, and the worlds of sleeping and awake and of dreaming and not dreaming all came together. Rainy was a part of it all.

She let her spirit swim through the pouring rain and whirl with the powerful wind, and then rising, she caused herself to all at once fall, and down she dove beneath the water's surface, down and down, where the movement of the water seemed calmer, deeper and deeper. As she approached the bottom, she slowed, and there, on the sandy ocean floor, rocking like an empty cradle, the wreck of an old Spanish galleon.

The instant she arrived the silver dolphin appeared, seemingly out of nowhere, her long silky nose caressing the girl's cheek. She didn't understand as a spirit she could feel the kiss, but she sensed it.

As the storm above was hurriedly passing, and the waves were calming, and the clouds were parting, her spirit watched the light of the waning half-moon all at once illuminating the dolphin now swimming in deliberate circles around a large cabin door. The door was clinging precariously to one hinge, and fluttering, as if a door can be impatient, in the movement of the water the dolphin created.

Now there may come a time in any of our lives when we will question real magic, but what is magic if not the world?

In the spirit of a young girl, she could see in the liquid luminous moonlight, the ship's broken masts, the dark portals where fish of different kinds swam in and out, but she remained transfixed on the silver dolphin circling, harder and faster, with great intent, and the big door now flailing in the dolphin's powerful currents.

Around and around, the dolphin spun, faster and faster, with more concentrated force in each revolution.

Finally, it separated from the cabin, the door, lifting up, and breaking free. Up it went, spinning, this great door, and up it floated towards the surface of the sea, and up the circling dolphin swam, rising as its escort into the light, and a new world of endless possibilities....

CHAPTER TWENTY-EIGHT

MORE THAN A DREAM

She sat at the edge of her bed, her bare feet flat partially on the floor and on the throw rug where Koda had slept; her senses returning, she could still feel his warmth. She rubbed her half-opened eyes and looked to see if she was wet, if there was water on the floor.

Her grandfather squatted, greeting Koda who had greeted him at the bedroom door. Rainy smiled at the way the older man knelt, rubbing the wolf's head with one hand while scratching his own with the other.

"Did you dream last night, Granddaughter?" he asked. His question was familiar. He would occasionally ask it, but this time Rainy could not really say that she had dreamed.

"It was more than a dream, Granpa."

As they helped each other with breakfast, Rainy breaking and scrambling the eggs, Grandpa pouring them in the pan, Rainy setting the table, Grandpa serving the wheat toast and honey jam, they were thinking about how to put into words what they wanted to say.

Finally, her grandfather asked, "What was the feeling you had when you woke from the dream that was more than a dream?"

With Koda at her feet, she sat at the small square kitchen table, and thought, her finger tracing circles and spirals on the red and white checkered table cloth. "I felt excited. Like something big happened... It's so hard to find the words.... It was like everything was real, but I woke up, and I wasn't wet from the storm or

from the Gulf, but I don't feel it was a dream....
It was real."

She brushed strands of her hair from
her eyes, and tucked the loose braid where the
white heron plume once decorated, behind her
ear. Her feet found Koda's mane. The thick wolf
hair felt good between her toes, and he liked the
feeling as they kneaded around his neck, but any
time they headed for his back, his nose nudged
her to stop.

While she ate, she thought some more
about her dream that was more than a dream.
Thoughts began to form words that began to
form more questions.

CHAPTER TWENTY-NINE

HATE IS NOT A GOOD THING

"Granpa, how did Koda come to live here?"

The question hadn't surprised him, but it surprised her because she didn't even realize she had been thinking about it. Maybe being old enough to go to middle school made her older and more aware of things in the past she may have missed.

"I mean, Koda's a wolf, and wolves don't usually live in houses with human beings in Florida, or in houses anywhere. Some kids say it's weird because we live with a wolf; some say it's cool. Not that I care at all what they think. I love him, Granpa. Koda saved my life. I can't imagine the world without him. I was just wonderin' how it happened that he's here.... And I know what they do to wolves in Alaska, and other places. Something happened to him.... I see the way he limps sometimes. Did he lose his parents too? Did you take him in like you did me? What happened to his legs?"

Grandpa had always thought that if you were old enough to think of a sensible question, and brave enough to ask, then you're owed an answer. "But, ye gotta know right off," he said, "the answers you're seekin' may not be necessarily ones you'd be expecting, or even wanting to hear.... For such is the nature of questions."

He'd been scrubbing the frying pan in the sink, but listening to his granddaughter's query, he shut the water, dried his hands, and turned to face her.

"Everything," he said, "and everybody has a story. There's a story about Koda comin' here, but it's also woven into other stories, about me, 'bout your family, and even about the dark and light energy of people in the world. Koda's story is our story. The wolf's story, is the Indian's story too. It's about pain and joy. Hate and love. Extermination and survival."

Turning to face the kitchen window, he closed his eyes for a moment, as it was easier for him to see back in time that way. "I was drivin' my rig through the mountains, headin' north into Chattanooga. I was feelin' kinda strange and worried in the same instant because it was my last run."

His eyes opened, and he rubbed his lower back with his hands.

"It was gettin' too much for me to sit behind the wheel of a truck anymore. Always rushin' to keep a schedule, bein' at a certain place for delivery or pick up at a certain time, and besides all that, my night vision was going. You don't wanna be drivin' a big rig at night through the mountains, or even a minivan, for that matter, when you can't see well."

Then he paused, slipping into that half dreamy place of nostalgia and reminiscence.

"Anyhow, your mom," he continued, "who was also my daughter, and your dad, who had become my son-in-law, had left with you for South Dakota. They'd be working on the reservation where your grandmother Jewel was born. That was your mom's mother, and my wife."

He reached in a kitchen drawer and pulled out an old map. He put it on the counter, opened it up, and put his finger on the small printed words, Red River Indian Reservation. "That's a piece of land that was not given to the Dakota, but land that they managed to hold onto by treaty.

He stared at the map, recounting a

few places. Places before the casinos. Before the parking lots. Before the smorgasbord of churches. The old barn behind where Jewel's grandparents' house used to be, near the river where they kissed and made love in the summer grass. The hills on the North Dakota side of the reservation where they held the naming ceremony for a nephew, the eagles circling above. The town on the reservation border where he'd been jailed for three days for suspicion of being an outside agitator.

"You never got to know your Dakota grandma. She was like the land that gave her life. Open and happy as the hills... and strong. A heart big as a Dakota sky. But," he said, "not so strong she could withstand the monster of diabetes...."

He leaned forward, facing the window. His elbows rested on the counter in a way that relieved some of the pressure from his back.

"After she'd become pregnant with your mom, she'd been diagnosed.... Your grandma fought that monster every day. Ain't no medicine can cure it, Rainy, not the kind of diabetes your grandma had, the kind a person's born with. The kind that just sits back and waits till you're vulnerable, like when she was pregnant. It's unrelentin'," he said. "We even called it the monster. "Your Grandma used to say, on her worst days, she could feel it slitherin' around in her veins; its million razor-sharp claws shreddin' her from the inside out. It used to fish hook itself behind her eyes, crawl up and down her legs in the middle of the night, its needle teeth stealin' her sleep, robbin' her of her dreamtime. It swam in her belly, makin' its foulness rise up, until she tasted it in her mouth like a filthy poison. "Your grandma fought it, though; every day, she battled it and I'd look in her eyes and see how tired all that fighting made her. Sometimes, I even think I saw that hideous damn thing looking back at me, hiding like a coward inside of her. "There's nothing you can do," it would say. "I'm here and there's nothing you can do about it." "People used to tell your grandma how beautiful she was and how she didn't look sick. She'd smile, thank them for their kind words, and all the while she knew, I knew, that monster was ripping and tearing, slashing and burning its way through her." I watched her stick needles in her fingers to test her blood more times than I can imagine. Pin prick and bleed. Pin prick and bleed. I can never forget the sound of that needle snappin' and the sight of her squeezing her fingers for the sample of blood.... Then one day she looked up at me, and said that every time she tested her blood, she was sending the energy pain of the pin into her skin with gratitude, and the energy of the life in her blood with love, to Ah-nuh. In this way, she was making her offerings for our daughter, your mother, even before she was born. He had spoken that mysterious word again, Ah-nuh. Though now, she understood something more.... "It is not a Mayan word, Grandfather." "It is the word I was given as the name they call themselves. I'm certain most tribal peoples had their own names and rituals for Ah-nuh, the great spirit of the water."

"Sacrifice of some kind is a part of the ritual in giving to Ah-nuh, isn't it?" Perhaps she had asked one question too many. She must learn patience. She understood this.

"I can only assume, Rainy, that's why your grandma as she grew older never complained about the demands on her body of diabetes. Her pretty fingers were so soft too, when ye think they'd be hard and calloused."

He looked at his hands, remembering how hers felt when he held them. How empty they felt after she was gone. Like his own hands didn't matter to him anymore. "Nothing mattered.... That's how it felt," he said. "That's when ye feel that what ye got taken from you, or what you got done to ye, seems that there ain't nothin' to be grateful for.... You know the feelin'.... She may've shown anger and frustration at times because of the monster she was fightin'. It's another kind of monster that's gonna make the Earth fight for her life too.... Only that monster won't win."

He stretched his back, pressed his lips together, and gazed down at the windowsill where he and Rainy had a big aloe plant growing in a painted pot that she had made in her fourth grade art class.

It weakened her little by little, until I swear, there was only her heart left beatin', and it took that too."

He turned. "You gotta watch out for it, Rains. He pressed his back with more pressure against the counter, the force on his muscles making the pain feel better, and that way he was facing Rainy again too. "I'm only tellin' ye this because your grandma's a part of who you are.

"I'm tellin' you because I know it's not good to hate, but sometimes such strong feelings come outta love; sometimes they come outta ignorance and fear, and sometimes outta being hurt. Either way, hate is not a good thing. Still, I swear, that monster Diabetes is the only thing I'd ever hated so long."

Grandpa's eyes shifted from Koda lying on the floor next to Rainy, to Rainy, sitting in the chair at the table bent over Koda.

"I also have hated men who shoot wolves," he said. "They are, I have ascertained, to be included among the lowest forms of soulless life on this planet." She raised up in the chair. She stared at her grandfather with a look you would see in a person's eyes who had just heard something shocking, something real hard to hear, something that could make you sick with terror and enraged with anger at the same time, colliding. Her hand running fingers through Koda's mane, had simultaneously stopped.

A man shot Koda....

CHAPTER THIRTY

EVERYTHING HAS A PURPOSE

He was still leaning with his back against the kitchen sink, the steam rising up from his mug, his eyes slowly shutting, drawing in a deep breath from the opened window above the sink; she knew he was traveling to that place in his mind where memories lived....

"I was makin' my last delivery that night," he said, "and I could see a storm bearin' down from the direction I was headed."

"Were you heading West, Granpa?"

"Yes. West."

"Was it just before dark?"

He opened his eyes again, a reverent expression across his face. He didn't see the cardinals in the back yard in the early morning sun that would have reminded him of the coming Spring Equinox. He didn't see the fleeting shadow of the hawk pass over. "Yes, it was, even darker because of the storm.... Most other times I'd have pulled over. But I kept goin'. Seems I got caught up in contemplatin' what it was gonna be like... livin' alone for the rest of my life. Without family around me, and no job. Some retirement.... I was a soon-to-be a man without any purpose."

The slant of the sunlight on the young palm at the edge of the yard caught his eye again.

Then he saw the cardinals constructing a nest in the crutch of the fronds. He smiled, "It'll be spring soon," he said.

"You know, I don't feel most people have a purpose anymore for bein' on this earth...unless of course it's to make money. The measure of a successful life.... Have a lot of money, so you can buy a lot of things. It's all 'bout the bottom line."

He was thinking, You can't buy a father. You can't buy a mother. You can't buy a soul, but did not say it.

He turned once again to see his granddaughter and Koda involved in a sort of synergy of love. Hanging over the chair, her dark brown hair with it long streaks of sunlight brushed across the white haired belly of the wolf while she scratched him as he stretched out on the kitchen floor just beneath her.

"There's a kid in my class at school; his name is Jebidiah." She was speaking upside-down. "Everybody calls him Jeby. He says his reason for livin' is to spread the word of God. He said him and his parents are goin' down to South America to bring Jesus to the Indians."

"Huh," Grandpa said. "I've heard some argue that spreadin' the word of God is the highest purpose there is." And then his voice trailed off, becoming distant and faint. "And they'll head down as a group to South America.... Hire a guide. Make their way into the jungle.... Make contact with a tribe that wants little or nothin' to do with civilized people and their wars and their religions, and they'll bring the word of God alright, they'll bring Jesus hangin' on a cross, right along with the diseases that will wipe out that tribe in a year.

"No," he said; his voice hollow. "That ain't the kind a purpose I'm talkin' about."

Rainy stopped scratching Koda. "Do I have a purpose?"

The wolf had stretched out with his front paw, and grabbed her arm.

"I mean, besides you, Koda." She smiled, but felt in some way she was like his sister, his companion, even something to him like a mother....

She looked up at her grandfather, holding his mug in one hand, the thumb of his other hooked into a belt loop.

"Of course, you've a purpose...."

He was standing near the mailbox with Koda in the shadows of the live oak branches and palms, watching her across the street. She had only been attending her new kindergarten for a couple of weeks. She was staring into a ditch as a bus driver with a red bandanna across his face, long dreads tied back behind his shoulders, was taking her small hand....

"What about my mom?" She had not stopped scratching Koda's belly. "Was I...?" Her grandfather had turned again, abruptly this time, to the window. He anticipated the question that would come.

"Was I ... Maggie's purpose?

"You were more than her purpose," he said. "You were Maggie's reason for breathin'. But your mom had another purpose. The great spirit of the water, the Ah-nuh, came to her in a dream. Your mom was about nine years old at the time"

"Can you share it with me, Granpa?"

"Yes," he said. "I feel your mom would've wanted that. So, what I recall is her describing that in the dream a mother sting ray stung her real bad and caused her to bleed, but the ray took pity on her too, and with a waving of her wings, made the pain go away, and stopped the bleeding.

"Why did the ray strike her?"

"Because the mother ray was protecting her eggs, but she was also Ah-nuh, and the Ah-nuh sustain themselves through the energies of love and gratitude and respect. They nourish from the sacrifices given to them...."

"In return for the love and for the blood sacrifice of your mother, the Ah-nuh gave to her a sense of purpose, telling her to be aware and respect the natural world around her, that your mom was not the most important being in the universe, and what your mother learned of life, like the lesson given in this sacred dream, she was to pass on one day to other children and maybe help them avoid causin' themselves and others such pain."

"So Mom became a teacher."

"And that's why everything needs a purpose, Granddaughter. So they don't go around doin' foolish and hurtful things. We're here to find a way to live in balance...to live in harmony with life...to help sustain life. That's why you and me are here ... why Koda's here too...."

CHAPTER THIRTY-ONE

PREDATORS

A couple of years ago, on a warm afternoon in early February, Grandpa had been working hard in the backyard. For the first time since Rainy had been living with him and attending school, he had been a few minutes late for the arrival of her bus. Which he had always made certain, he was not. On that warm afternoon, he never meant to be. He just got sidetracked, and then he'd realize like a bolt of lightning had struck the ground close to him, that he was late. Damn! Damn! How could I do that! He would mutter as he turned the corner of the house and crossed the front yard, heading down the winding driveway to the mail box. What the hell's wrong with you?

She was in fourth grade back then, and something was about to happen that would impact each of them for the rest of their lives: Grandpa's, Rainy's, and Koda's too.... Someone, some...thing, was about to shake their world....

Grandpa had been raking since late morning, for the oak leaves had been falling all week. Sometimes at night the leaves would make the sound of rain on the roof whenever a cold or warm wind would rush through the branches. Once in a while, they would step outside to see if it really was raining, but it wouldn't be – just the oak leaves falling in winter.

He'd lean the rake up against one of the trees, and drink glasses of water from a pitcher he had filled to stay hydrated and would rest for brief intervals. Things that his granddaughter insisted he do. Sometimes he would have to take pause, deliberately feeling his heart speed up, then suddenly feel it slowing down, and all the while trying to will it into a steadier rhythm. Which every so often with the medication, and with controlled deep breathing, he could do. Occasionally, the arrhythmia gave him the sensation of a spirit detaching from the body, but again, he would will it back. He didn't fool himself. He knew his time in this life was getting shorter, and even that hundred year old oak couldn't will her leaves back when it was their time to separate. Everything has a season. Everything in its time.

The day had grown cloudy as the morning turned into afternoon, and he hadn't noticed the sun's position, so he had temporarily lost track of the day – but it was the time of day that Rainy's bus would be pulling up to the corner across the street from their mailbox.

In the five years Rainy had been living there and attending school, he had never failed to watch her from behind the mailbox with Koda at his side, getting on the bus every morning, or see her leave the bus and cross the street every afternoon, often waiting halfway up the driveway as to make her feel more independent, but not insecure. As long as there was no physical clashes, which there wasn't, he never interfered with the issues that occurred among the kids, but just kept an eye on things. On rare occasions, he would see a parent sitting in a car doing the same.

He was leaning on the rake, feeling good about all the work he had done, when he looked over at Koda who was standing near one of the huge piles of oak leaves. For an instant it did enter his subconscious that Koda was saying something to him, but he was tired and his mouth was exceedingly dry from the work and the heart medications he had taken earlier. So instead of

Koda's alert attaining Grandpa's consciousness, Grandpa went over and sat at Grandma's little outdoor table, and poured another glass of water from the pitcher he had left there.

Relaxing in the wrought iron chair, he downed a full glass in a few gulps, and wiping his lips with the back of his hand, started thinking that maybe tomorrow he would gather the leaf piles he had made and get them ready for recycling.

Then he saw the marks of the old oak's lower branch and slipped into that place of unintentional daydreaming.... His daughter Maggie flying high on the tire swing...right behind her bedroom. My goodness, he thought; that tree must be at least a hundred years old! And right there he imagined Jewel sitting across the table, her crow black hair whipping like a horse's mane in the wind. She was reading a Stephen King novel, and looked up at him, but she did not smile. He remembered how she loved books, was always carrying one it seemed.

He didn't like horror stories, though. She'd distract him from the subject, saying that memories were stories too, and that human beings were made of stories. So, if we have no stories, in a way it would be like we were never here. Back then, even when they were young, the idea of no longer having stories as they grew old, made them both shiver.

Such a wonderful time of discourse, he was thinking, but as the image of his wife dissipated into air, he wondered, why she hadn't smiled. She would always smile in these brief interludes of memory....

With the engine still running, the strange man watched through the windshield and opened driver's window of his dinged up two door '84 white Buick. Alongside him on the torn front seat cover, a dirty rag concealing the knife and rope and tape. And as the school bus squeaked and squealed to a stop, its black guard rails screeched and lowered in the front of the bus bumper, getting stuck half way down.

It was the moment for which he had waited. A few days over the last few months of concealment and observation had provided him his chance. He never did see the grandfather, nor the wolf....

As the school bus doors snapped half opened, the four children whose stop it was, squeezed through, and jumped off; the two fifth grade girls heading up the sandy shoulder alongside the drainage ditch single file towards their houses, texting the whole time, and the two other kids separating as they crossed the street. The heavy fifth grade boy, IPhone in his hand, and carrying a backpack, angled north to the spot where a nanny/housekeeper was ready with engine running to pick him up, and walking slowly to keep the space behind him, the striking fourth grade girl with long hair was heading south towards the mailbox where the driveway lead to her home.

All of the kids had moved in the opposite direction of the man still parked in the inconspicuous old Buick on the sandy shoulder of the street running perpendicular to the one where the bus had stopped. It was the fourth grader that was his target. It was Rainy.

As his sunken and pale blue eyes fixated on her, he bit down on his dry, cracked lower lip until it bled. The metallic taste of the blood and the image of the girl made his heart race. And he began to sweat.

In another moment, the guard rails

jerked back up, the sound of air releasing, tires spinning, and the big yellow school bus was whining down the road spitting dust and black smoke.

With the car's engine idling, he slowly and quietly lifted the door handle, and pushed open the door just enough to slip his left leg out of the car, his shoe not quite touching the pavement. He sat in the driver's seat, tensed and still, anticipating the other kids to make their separations from her complete. When it seemed clear, he put the car in gear and crept along, steering in the direction Rainy was walking, his leg still sticking out from the opened door.

The man had a bony, skeletal face. His beard, thick brown and grey stubbles, and his hair, the same shades, and short. Even his tee shirt was grey, with black music notes stenciled across the front. He looked the way you would imagine how a zombie looks, his pallid eyes void of anything but what was in focus, and that was the eye-catching fourth grader walking across the street, and turning down the sand and shell driveway.

She was about a quarter of the way to the house, walking along one of the ruts, glancing up and wondering where Grandpa was, when the Buick turned the corner, its side mirror inches from the mailbox, its tires crushing some of the lilies not yet in bloom.

Hearing the tires crunching the sand and shells, she turned, and saw him. He had already stopped the car, shoved the gear shift into Park, and with the engine running, had slid out the door, walking quickly and directly for her, one hand gripping the knife.

If you've ever seen wolves run, you know how fast and powerful they can be. A wolf can pull down a 130 lbs. male antelope in a matter of seconds.

Rainy didn't see Koda, but she could only glimpse the blurry form that had rushed passed her, and she could hear the thunder of paws on ground, and feel a primal guttural growl that in her life she had never heard or felt before, and she saw immediate terror strike the face of the scrawny man who had swirled around, racing back to his car only a few yards away.

Grabbing the frame of the car door's opened window, he had dropped the knife on the ground, using the leverage to sling himself into the seat, one trembling hand shifting the gear stick to Drive, and quickly grabbing hold of the steering wheel, his foot already pressed on the accelerator pedal, while the other hand reached out the opened window to slam the door, as Koda hit.

Five finger bones and a wrist snapped under 1500 pounds of pressure per square inch. 42 teeth: 20 in the upper jaw, including six incisors, two canine, eight premolars, and four molars, and 22 teeth in the lower jaw of six incisors, two canine, eight premolars, and six molars.

The horrorstruck man yanked his arm back through the window, spinning the car around, thinking he was just going to run over the lilies, but not knowing they concealed his view of a small ditch that caused the Buick to almost stall out, his wheels whining and screaming, taking off again, mashing the pine cones, saw grass, and palmettos scattered along both sides of the driveway, skidding out nearly hitting the mailbox, his bloody hand broken and torn in the wolf's crushing grip, ripped loose from the man's arm, dangling from Koda's mouth.

Grandpa had scooped Rainy up, holding her as tight as he could, and they watched the car swerving wildly and kicking up sand and dirt as it sped down the road; Koda, a little ways up from where the car had first stopped in the driveway, dropping bloody parts of the man's hand from his teeth, snapping at his nose and sniffing the black ring in the shape of a human skull around one of the severed fingers, sniffing where the knife lay in the sand and shells....

The county sheriff stood in one of the driveway ruts where Rainy had been standing, the knife secured in a plastic Ziploc under the note pad on which he was writing, and intermittingly talking with the two of them, Grandpa's hand constricted around Rainy's.

"What kinda dog is that?" the sheriff asked, observing Koda sitting on the porch.

"He's a registered Malamute mix," Grandpa said. "You can check with Dr. Anne Hines in town. She licensed him."

The sheriff didn't say anything, just wrote some more, glancing now and then up at Koda. Most folks in the area had figured that Koda was a wolf. They had heard rumors of his rescue, and his residence. Every so often, they'd imagine a howl. But nobody complained. Neither Koda nor Grandpa had given them any reason. Nor Rainy, though child protective services had once responded to a school request, and asked to see Koda's dog license and seemed reassured of Rainy's welfare and Grandpa's sanity when they did.

"Besides," some people said, "Her grandfather's an Indian," as if that would explain the whole idea of Koda.

"Thanks for getting here so fast, Officer," Grandpa said. "It's like my cell phone was in my hand," which was still shaking. "Then I saw your car."

"Well," the sheriff said, his eyes switching from Koda back to the note pad. "We received another call a few minutes before yours." He flipped the pages back and read. "... Some kid. Rides her bus.... I don't seem to have a name... called 911 on his cell phone. Saw the guy. Described the car.

"You know, Mr. Peek," the sheriff said, "Your dog up there tore a man's hand off, and now I gotta go back up that driveway and collect what's left as evidence, not a'ginst yer dog, Sir, though he looks quite like, I 'magine," and he looked again at Koda on the porch, "one of his ancestors."

"No, Sir, nothin' a'ginst yer dog. Had me a Shepherd once. Pretty gal. Real protective." He looked one more time at Koda. "I swear he could pass for her ancestor." He glanced down at his note pad, and sighed. "But we do need evidence.... The guy was after your granddaughter. Probably stalkin' her past couple a days.... Maybe longer. He's a registered sex offender, a pedophile. A real bad hombre. He's not to be within 500 feet of a school or a school bus stop. Or live in a neighborhood where there're children. We got him at the hospital. If he lives," the officer cleared his throat, "and it's not likely he will, but iff'n he does, he won't be gettin' outta jail anytime soon, and iff'n he does ever get out, he won't have a hand, or even much of an arm for that matter...."

The sheriff clicked his pen, folded up his note pad, and pushed them inside his uniformed shirt pocket. Then he rested his hand on the holster of his gun.

"I hope things are okay with ye, Sir." He had observed Grandpa's trembling hand, still holding the cell phone. For an instant, Grandpa reminded him of his own father in the last years of life.

Then he looked down at Rainy, and clutched her grandfather's hand real firm, like a promise.

"I gotta girl your age," he said, releasing the hand shake. "Fourth grade, right?"

Rainy nodded.

"I'm sorry this happened to ye, Rainy Peek. Sorry to you too, Sir. Could've been worse, though...." He looked up for the last time at Koda still sitting on the porch, watching, every once in a while his tongue stretching out over his face.

"You gotta a great friend, there," the sheriff said, lifting his hand from the holster and patting Rainy's head. "He got a name?"

"Koda."

The officer smiled and nodded. Then he handed Grandpa a business card, said if he needed anything, to call, and as he turned and started walking back to his squad car to get the equipment he would need for collecting the evidence, he said in a low voice, not just to himself, but really meant for the whole world,

"No one ever oughtta be tryin' to hurt little kids."

⟫•⟪ ⟫•⟪ ⟫•⟪

When something horrible happens and somehow you manage to escape the worst of it, the experience alone leaves you feeling changed. That night, Grandpa and Rainy sat close together on the couch. The TV was on real low, but no one was really watching it even as the incident had made the local news. Grandpa and Rainy and Koda had walked the driveway earlier before dark, Grandpa holding the burning braid of sweet grass the whole time. Tomorrow they'd fix what they could of the lilies and offer tobacco, thanking them for their bravery.

His cell phone rang several times throughout the evening, and occasionally he would answer it, saying that Rainy was alright, and thanked the person for calling. One of the calls was a news reporter, but Grandpa sensed that no good could come from making this a story for Rainy to have to deal with, nor all the attention it would draw on Koda, and even him, and so, he simply said that he didn't want to talk about it. He just wanted to be close to his granddaughter.

The reporter told Grandpa that the sexual abuser of children had died in the ER.

From loss of blood....

CHAPTER THIRTY-TWO

KODA

Grandpa took another drink of his morning coffee, turned, and resumed his gaze through the kitchen window into the backyard. Rainy had asked him how Koda came to live here. He had only shared the whole story with Dr. Anne, the veterinarian who licensed Koda, a malamute mix, so the county where they lived wouldn't execute him for being a wolf.

"It was like your first day at middle school," he said, "when you didn't quite know what was comin' at ye. Just knew you were heading into it. That's what it was like for me....

"It was my last run. My last job. All I was thinkin' about was headin' into the first phase of the ending of my life. I was on my way up Eagle Mountain," he said, "just this side of Chattanooga. Dark clouds moving fast right over me, and then it started rainin'.... I could tell right away the blacktop was slick, so I had to downshift more than usual, puttin' a bad strain on my back. Then it started pouring, sheets of water. A lot of folks pulled into the last rest stop before you head up the mountain. Lots of truckers too. I could see right off this was not gonna be no ordinary storm, but I just kept going. I didn't fear anything anymore, except maybe being alone and having no purpose to my life."

He rolled his back again on the edge of the sink, turning along the counter, pressing his back against it, and faced the table.

"What I saw first, Rainy, were two bright golden eyes up ahead. My headlights had caught their reflection. Right off, I knew they didn't belong to no ordinary bein'. As I got closer, I wondered if maybe they weren't eyes at all. Maybe they were just a pair of orbs floating around the mountain. Then it started rainin' so hard I couldn't see much past the front end. And what was I thinking? I have to get a grip, I said to myself. I knew trucker stories about spirits they'd seen in these mountains in the form of lights, and I knew what they meant, drivin' a truck all those years, late at night, no one on the road. A man can see things.

"But, I'd never seen spirits like that, so I knew they had to be eyes. As I crept through the wind and rain up that mountain, those eyes were looking right at me. I know it might sound a little strange, but I felt as if those eyes knew me, like whoever they belonged to, was waitin' for me."

He paused, catching hold of his own breath, and turning again, caught sight out the window of some young squirrels tumbling in the yard, but making haste directly to the closet tree as everything that lived around the house was very much aware of a predator's presence. So nothing ever got too comfortable on the ground for any length of time that wasn't short lived.

"I pulled over tellin' myself that a dog might'a gotten hit, maybe knocked into the ditch that ran parallel to the road." He lifted his mug from the counter, sipped just enough to wet his lips, and placed it back down. "But I'd never seen a dog with golden eyes either. Specially like that." He paused again, turned and looked at Rainy, and then at Koda. "Thing is, I knew what it was I had seen all along...."

"What do you mean?"

"I mean, wouldn't you know, he was not a dog lying in that ditch, blood and rain mixed together, lying in his own blood pool. Nope," he said, his eyebrows raised, his head shaking slowly. "Definitely, not a dog."

Switching his perception once more, he gripped his coffee with both hands, and, facing the window, closed his eyes again, real tight, his eyes moving behind the lids, like the closed eyes of a man who is dreaming, searching for that moment when he could see it all clearly, and he found it, again, almost too clear because he saw how hurt the animal was, and the memory of it all was now hurting him. His eyes opened, he put the mug down and pushed it away, his hands gripping the edge of the sink, his head tilted back, as if he were trying to keep his feelings from pouring out....

"Someone," he said, his voice raw and raspy, his hands still grasping the counter's edge, "some two-legged that calls himself a man, had done this terrible thing. I can't imagine the kind of mind that would want to murder somethin' so magnificent. Have to be the kind without a soul."

Releasing his grip on the counter, he cleared his eyes with one hand and used the other to keep himself balanced as he leaned over the sink for support.

"I remember," he continued, his gaze out the window, blurred and intense. "I had to swallow any fear comin' up in my throat right down because I needed to act. But I had to be careful too, seein' he was wounded, and I had left my rig alongside the highway, emergency lights flashin', and now it's rainin' real hard, waves of rain, sheets of rain, and the wind's blowin' cold because I can see my breath swept away, but I don't feel the cold, even though my body's shakin', and my flannel shirt, and my pants too, are all soppin' wet. I got mud in my shoes and up my legs, and I'm slidin' over to him, and I hear the traffic on the slick blacktop whizzin' by, the trucks and cars, and the hissin' sounds of their tires, and I slide some more in the mud, and then I hit bottom but before I could even gather my wits, there I am face to face with this great wolf in the pourin' freezin' rain aware that he could take my head off in a moment if he had a mind to, and I could see the rain soakin' blood coverin' his back legs, and the bloody fury paws, and my heart just feels like its poundin' through my chest, but I try and stay calm for him as I know he needed to trust me, and so I glanced at him so he could see my eyes, so he could see inside me, the kind of man I was, and that I was not out to hurt him in any way. And then, without lookin' him directly in the eye for any length of time whatsoever, I make every effort to breathe calm, and then I say one of the few Indian words I know ...."

Rainy was staring up at Grandpa as he turned to her. "What did you say?"

"I raised my hand," he said, "only slightly," and he looked at her, holding his hand up. "Like this," he said, and placed it over his heart. "And I kept it here just long enough for him to know I bore no ill intent, and then I said ... Koda. Koda. It was a word in the language of your mother's and your grandmother's people. That night, shielded from the wind down in that ditch, the word became my breath, and just kind of hung there between us, like the spirit of the word itself had become visible, connectin' us... forever."

Then he took a deep breath, folded his arms, loosely, and pressed his back against the sink. "Words are powerful things," he said. "I know you're aware of this. No matter what language we speak. There's a vibration that goes with any word, and you can feel it.

"Isn't any word more appropriate," he

said. "Ye see, koda has a special meanin' that goes with the sound, a vibration that carries the depth of meaning with it, and I was lucky I knew such a word."

"What does it mean?"

"Friend," Grandpa said, the whites of his wet brown eyes turning a shade red, reflecting on some things he was remembering about seeing Koda that night, some he did not want to put into words, as though maybe there shouldn't be words for such a thing. "Koda means friend in the old way," he said, repeating the meaning again as though the very sound in either language was still magic to him, still sacred. "A koda will never betray you. A koda loves you. The spirit of a koda's friendship runs deeper than blood." He paused and gazed at the wolf under his granddaughter's bare feet.

"What happened then, Granpa?"

He rubbed his chin. "Well," he said, "I grabbed a blanket, and I really don't know how I did it, but somehow managed to get him into the cab. He curled on the blanket on the floor. I drove to the next exit and got off. That's when I saw... there was this sign, Animal Hospital, and an arrow.... Some might call it lucky.

"The vet on duty saw right off that he'd been shot. One in the back clear through." Grandpa pointed with his finger at Koda's rear. "The bullet had hit the left hind leg and grazed against the bone. After the X-rays, he told me the wolf would never run in the wild again, and that they'd put him down for no charge as wolves were illegal in that state anyhow."

"Being a wolf's illegal?"

"It is... bein' a wolf's against the law in most states. That's why Dr. Anne had licensed Koda, a Malamute mix. She knew it was to keep him legal. And alive. She's just never said nothin'. Otherwise, the county animal control would've put him down."

"Why? Cause he's a wolf? I mean what kinda sense is that?"

"It doesn't if you're Indigenous. Maybe because the Europeans who came here carried stories with them about wolves. Mostly horror legends, and I assume that over generations maybe that fear got implanted in their DNA, and that makes them afraid of wolves. Or maybe wolves can't be controlled or trained because they're wild, and free, and maybe that scares them, and maybe, like us, wolves remind them of what America was, and what people like them ruined, and that frightens them too.... And people will often destroy what they're afraid of.

"Still, we gotta remember, not all Americans are like that.... That's why I was so grateful for those folks where I first took Koda. The vet there told me he did a residence at Yellowstone where wolves are now allowed to live. His assistant once worked at a sanctuary for wolves. They both understood. I was lucky to find them.

"I had offered to pay them my entire last pay check, promised to send the rest, if they could just save him, and let me take him home, which was far away in another state. They said they'd do that, but I wouldn't need to send any more money, nor did they take any." He looked at Rainy. She was bent over her chair and scratching Koda with a tenderness the wolf had come to love.

"I think I know why he never wants me to scratch his back," she said.

"And why's that?"

"He's concerned I might hurt him."

"Could be," Grandpa said, rubbing his chin again, and realizing he hadn't shaved yet. "But I feel there could be another reason.... Ye see, Rainy, maybe Koda doesn't want ye to feel his wounds because he doesn't want to burden ye with the sorrow. He knows you've empathy for him. But, it's his choice to keep ye from the sorrow. Protect you from feelin' sad for him when you don't need to because it wouldn't be good for either of you.

"A wolf is like that. And some people. They can be proud like that, and they can love ye like that too."

"Granpa," she said, not lifting her eyes. "Is that why you decided to stay in the world? So you could care for Koda?"

"Huh," he said. He had forgotten telling her about his disconnection to life. "I suppose it's true. I couldn't save him and abandon him. "

"Then Koda rescued you too that night." She glanced up again, her head upside down. "I guess that makes us all rescues."

CHAPTER THIRTY-THREE

IN THE ABSENCE OF CHANGE

In the absence of change, what is left?

It was early in the morning when Grandpa stood in the doorway, a few feet from the screen door. He was looking at Rainy, leaning against the wall, arms folded, standing partly in the kitchen and partly in the hall that lead to their bedrooms. She was already thinking about what she might wear to school. Grandpa, however, had that serious look in his eyes, a way of looking at her when he wanted to share something he felt important.

"Rainy Peek," he announced, "after years of elementary school, now you're officially in middle school. In three years you'll be attendin' high school. At no time, ye never experienced an Indigenous Holiday, and it doesn't appear that'll happen any time in the near future.... "Therefore, on this sunny and very lovely spring day, I bequeath, and do hereby pronounce, and proclaim, an Indigenous holiday."

She didn't move. She just remained between the kitchen and the hallway like it was some kind of intersection, and she had gotten stuck on the corner. She rubbed her eyes, shook her head. She wasn't dreaming. With her arms folded again, she assessed the sudden situation that she appeared to somehow find herself.

Indigenous holiday? The words formed a fuzzy meaning in her awakening brain. She gazed quizzically at Grandpa. "I don't get it," she said. "What do you mean?"

"Well, there're school holidays for historic events, and Americans who are considered patriots, and others who have lead the struggle for human rights. But not one holiday for American Indians. It seems each year they're taken us more and more out of history altogether. Even Thanksgiving. Pretty soon, they'll be making Thanksgivin' the Pilgrims' idea. Which just isn't right.

"And so," he said, "let's call this day, Rainy Peek's Official Indigenous Holiday, and it's yours. Just yours."

"But we'll get in trouble at school again."

"It'll be okay. It's not like you're just takin' a day off and goin' to the mall.... We'll deal with the school if it comes to that.... Besides, it's almost summer...."

His arms reached out, his hands opened. It was as if he held the day itself in them, offering it to her, his eyes twinkling above a big grin that didn't distract from their sincerity.

"All you have to do is step through this doorway, and start lookin' for those answers that you're seekin'... the ones I can't give you. However, ye know there's no guarantee on the answers ye get; except, you can't even hope to find any if ye don't take any chances. And, sometimes, Granddaughter, you got to take that chance. You gotta trust...."

With arms folding tighter, she scoffed. "Trust?" she said.

"Granpa, my parents were killed by a drunk teenager. Not-to-mention, school. I might as well be a freak. Maybe I am. My teachers won't talk anything about Indians because it makes them uncomfortable," which was the word Dr. Lawson, the principal, had used when discussing this with her. "So, what do I trust?"

"Trust in the nature of you. Trust in this great unimaginable Mystery that you're a part of. Trust in the greater Balance that ye can't see.

Trust in the love that brought us together, you, Koda, and me...."

His head tilted to one side. "Now, what do ye say, Indigenous holiday?" His charm was inviting. "It's up to you, my most beautiful granddaughter." She was his only granddaughter, but still she liked it when he would say that to her. "Those answers you need," he said again, "are just beyond ... here," and his arms made another sweeping motion through the doorway.

Her eyes looked beyond the screen door, then gazed down at the floor. How old and worn and familiar the wood. How smooth and soft beneath her bare feet. How pretty its glow in the morning light. Her mother walked on this floor. So did her grandma.

It really does come down to this. But what about school? What if I miss something important? She scoffed at her own thoughts.

If she declined her grandfather's alternative, she would be late now anyway, and Dr. Lawson would no doubt choose just that moment to be peering through the blinds of her office window, and there she would watch Grandpa's mustang pull in front of the circular drive, and stop....

She would meet her in the hallway and ask her why she was late. Rainy would have to tell her something to keep her grandfather out of trouble. She'd still probably get detention. Then she'll walk alone into Mr. Kline's class, and he will look up from his textbook over his black framed glasses at her coming through the door, book and notebook pressed against her chest like a shield, and require her to stand there under the American flag above her head before taking her seat (his rule for coming to his class late), and, disgruntled at her tardiness and equally disappointed she was there, since no test or quiz was assigned, Mr. Kline, the Colonel, would release a frustrated sigh loudly at the interruption of his reading about the Mexican War and how the United States of America reclaimed its territory after much sacrifice and heroism and, of course, got to be the great country that it is today, despite the obstacles, he would say, and very lucky that no one had showed up late for the war. Then he would point to her seat, and she would sit down at her desk, catch her breath, and open her book....

Slowly, her eyes rose to her grandfather. Leaning a bit forward, her head tilted to one side, she peered past him, again looking beyond the door, and then, she lowered her arms and clasped her hands, once more glancing down at the floor, and then up at Grandpa.

"Okay," she said, her hands repositioned on her hips, "Indigenous Holiday," and she went into her bedroom.

In a few minutes she stood in blue flip flops in the hallway dressed in her blue drawstring knit shorts and matching blue and white tank top.

Her grandfather was sitting on the porch step, facing the direction of the water. The wolf lay alongside of him.

Taking a deep breath, she exhaled, and then stepped through the door, and into another painted page of her life story, a life story that was still unfolding....

THE BEACH AFTER A STORM

The freedom of a mind being opened is what you feel....

At the beach on a weekday morning after a big storm, the world can seem especially clear and the air especially clean with only the big blue of Father Sky between you and the rising mighty Sun. There's no whiff of chemicals you can smell, no apparent trace of toxins or exhaust fumes that you're breathing. No car noises. No traffic. No tourists. Maybe no planes whining overhead, advertising some beach bar's Ladies Drink Free night.... No Jet Ski rentals ripping through the water, or parasails. No sirens. No bells signaling the beginning or ending of class. Not even teachers talking. No changing classes and muddled conversations of moving crowds. No computer key boards clicking. No alarms on your cell phone because you shut it off. Just the sound of the waves up ahead. Just the freedom of a quiet mind being opened....

CHAPTER THIRTY-FIVE

THE DOOR

Koda walked alongside Rainy as they headed for the beach, weaving occasionally from one side to the other, his powerful body brushing her long legs, the warmth of his long hair, luxurious and powerful on her skin, a sense of security accompanying always his presence. And along the trail he stopped and sniffed at survey wooden stakes with plastic orange flags sticking out of the sand all along the back of the dunes, marking areas in squares, of what was coming.

Time is running out....

An old wolf and a Native American girl, a rare sight on any day that could alter the perception of the world for most people for just an instant before they would reverse that mind alteration and see only what they can allow themselves to see, a dog and girl, and the girl not in school. But, who could be looking? Folks were on their way to work, or already working. Kids were in school.

Nobody's around.

She turned one way then another. It's like she was the only human being in the world. And, for that brief a moment, she imagined it really was just her and Koda, here in this amazing place she loved.

A crow cawed from a nearby palm, and the sounds of excited sea gulls from the beach ahead echoed into her consciousness.

"Can you feel it, Koda? Somethin's different."

There was something different, something out of the ordinary she didn't know, something urging her forward....

As they approached the dunes, she stopped again. Gazing down, she observed these long wrinkles in the sand that reminded her of ripples the ocean makes on the beach when the tide recedes. These ripples, though, were on the other side of the dunes. But, the tide did not come that far. Even in the storm last night. She reasoned that they must have been made by the wind. She removed her flip flops and carried them in one hand as she walked over rippling lines. It felt to her like she was stepping into waves of energy, currents undulating beneath her feet into a sensation of time-shifting. She thought that maybe it was her imagination, but she could really feel the energy. It tingled from the bottoms of her feet and up her legs. She could actually feel something extraordinary, something electric in the air.

Koda took the lead, and she followed in the direction he was headed over the dunes.

With the slight limp of his rear leg becoming more noticeable, he, never-the-less, remained protectively ahead, making his way through the sea grass and sea oats. Already, his senses revealing the unexpected....

Now sometimes, dreams can cross over into this reality, when something you dreamed all of a sudden starts coming true right before your eyes. The sensation can become so strong, you might even have to remind yourself that you're not dreaming. But then, if you think about it, this whole life can be a dream. The Mystery's dream. Who can really know? The world really can be a place of magic, and that's what magical realism is, not the kind where illusionists entertain us with tricks and cameras and sleight of hand, but magic in the spiritual sense; life is magic. Dreams are magic....

Descending the hills of sand onto the beach, the great wolf stood, his long bushy tail slightly wagging, brushing over the sand, his black nose sniffing what it was that lay upon the shore. When Rainy arrived, he looked at her staring in awe....

It was the door.

Part of it clung to the beach, but most of it swayed with the small incoming waves. She didn't question how a door from something that happened that was more than a dream could be there. She just pushed it off the sand and walked in the water alongside it to see how it floated. She pressed her hands on it using all her weight. Its buoyancy caused her to smile. Then, with total confidence, she simply hopped on and looked back at Koda.

"Don't worry," she said sitting on her door. "Tell Granpa where I'm headed...."

Then she turned and saw the island that they had talked about and where she realized at that moment is where she always wanted to be, and started paddling out across a turquoise sea.

CHAPTER THIRTY-SIX

THE ISLAND ACROSS THE WATER

Koda did not leave with her. Instead, he remained on the beach. Though he stood with his head bowed and concerned as she paddled away on the door, he knew that this was Rainy's journey. When the silver dolphin emerged alongside of Rainy and the door, then dove again, Koda turned, and headed home.

As the island rose just before her, she stopped paddling. Staring ahead at the patches of white sandy beach, she couldn't know that Koda had made it up the porch steps where Grandpa was waiting. At that exact moment he greeted Koda, placing his hand on the gray wolf's head, her fingers had touched her necklace, and she was wondering about Grandpa, for he had strung the shells together that he had collected from that same island months before her birth and where she was headed now.

The feeling of the pretty shells against her fingertips suddenly made Rainy aware that the necklace was a pledge of some kind from her grandfather, to everything they loved. It made an attachment too, one she could touch when he would no longer be there....

Grandpa ran his fingers through Koda's mane, and seeing Rainy in his mind and smiling, and Rainy stroked the shells on her necklace, wondering how he had already known that she would one day be heading for this place she had never been.

There exists this synchronicity that occurs when you're living in the wheel of life. It's the stuff of magical realism, a conscious awareness, and that what we see goes even beyond this world, and we can actually become in sync with everything.... Ever since she could remember, the little island had always imparted a yearning for Rainy, sometimes accompanied with a child's curiosity. Because sometimes it would not be there.

Though her and Grandpa had fished together and explored other islands out in his small boat, he always skirted around this one. He said it was because it belonged to the sacred ones, and that a human being should only go there under certain conditions.

They would see other boats pass the tiny island by and speed towards the larger islands because the boats usually carried a lot of people and their dogs in them, and the beach was too small and shallow for fishing nets or to stake out fishing poles, and for a grill and folding chairs and coolers filled with soda and beer that the boaters often brought with them. Besides, you had to catch the tide just right to not get grounded on the sand bars. A lot of times, because the boats were moving so fast, the people in the boats didn't see the little island to begin with or maybe were just not paying attention or maybe the island was simply not visible to them at all.

It was an island where only birds and turtles and other sea life could find anytime. It was a place where they often found mates and procreated. A lot of water birds, like the pelicans and gulls and herons, had nested in the mangroves that edged the shore on one side, but some, like crows, chose the palms while the splendid terns nested in the sand among the tall grasses that grew up on the other side of the island.

Green sea turtles weighing hundreds of pounds would emerge from the water, making the arduous journey to the base of the dunes where the small beach was the highest and widest and facing the great water, to lay their eggs, and then it would take up to two full moons later for the eggs to hatch.

"The newborns often head for the water at night," Grandpa said, "under the cover of darkness. They're the strongest little creatures," he said. "It's their wisdom that guides them to the light of the horizon, which can often times be when the moon's in one of her waxin' or wanin'phases."

He told Rainy that the baby sea turtles' chances of making it to the water were real slim, often heading in the wrong direction because of city lights, and of course there are a lot of people who refuse to turn off the lights of their beach houses and condos during the turtle nesting cycles, even if they're asked to, and the poor babies emerging from the sand for the first time, head the wrong way, for wisdom has its challenges in a Koyaanisqatsi world. Often the birds wind up grabbing them at the first light of day, and the little ones that do make it into the water, the predator fish are waiting.

He said that even without human interference, it's hard for them. Only a very small number of the babies could live through all that, and then survive a full year in the ocean. He said the chances of those that made it into the water were about one in a thousand.

"Grandmother Turtle gives all that life to the world," he once said, "for the life of one." He said it was the greatest expression of gratitude and sacrifice he'd ever known.

Those turtles that did survive, though, could live a real long time, and get to be older than a lot of humans. A retired marine scientist had told Grandpa once when he was a boy that he knew of turtles living over a hundred years, if human beings didn't do something to hurt them. Grandpa said the ancestors used to say that such a struggle over millions of years on this earth had made a turtle's heart so strong that sometimes it would continue to beat even after the turtle died.

"Rainy," he said, "a human being with a strong heart was said to have a turtle's heart."

As her hands stroked the shallow water, pulling her closer to the island's shore, the silver dolphin suddenly appeared again, moving on the water's surface alongside of Rainy and the door. The energy that the dolphin brought seemed to help her move faster.

As she paddled closer towards the island, her sharp eyes scanned its beach. Drifting quietly, she searched up and down the shore for evidence of turtle nests, but she could not spot a single one. Grandpa had said this could be the beginning of their nesting cycles.

She grew troubled.

Where are they? Why aren't they here? What happened?

It felt as though her life force had all at once escaped her chest, leaving her with an emptiness that actually felt heavy, a weightiness of realization, unwelcomed and unkind.

Without the turtles, there's no more running out of time....

As she struggled to breathe, a wave of relief washed over her, and joy quickly filled her heart at the instant she finally sighted a nest, and yet she grew almost simultaneously uneasy again. There was only one. One lone turtle's nest at the bottom of a small dune when her grandfather had described a line of many, and then, with her hands opened and outstretched, as she floated on her door, her own voice asked in the way you might coming home one day and your house was burned down, or not even there, but gone. Disappeared.

"What happened?"

Alongside of her, the dolphin's breath interjected; bursting again, sea spray blowing skyward, the mist raining down on her, it diverted momentarily, her attention, and even caused her worried face to calm in relief, the gentle mist of dolphin magic still working in a world where an indigenous girl could quickly lose her sense of balance in a dying world becoming more and more out of balance.

Then the dolphin submerged in a direction away from the shallows of the island, not emerging again until further away, and then further, and further away, until that most extraordinary silver dolphin had disappeared in the deepening turquoise of the sea.

As the door slid up to the unspoiled shore, Rainy slid off and stood in sugary sand, in crystal clear water, her fingers feeling her necklace, her eyes gazing down at the diverse shades of pretty coquinas moving beneath and around her feet: grey, white, rusty brown, purple, and pink, all the colors of her necklace, and then her gaze rose up, following the mangroves and then over the patches of sea oats and grass, to the sabal palms.

She was, at last, standing in that sublime space, on the tiny island that was, like Grandpa had said, no ordinary place.

FIRE AND ICE

Some say the world will end in fire.
Some say in ice.
From what I've tasted of desire
I hold with those who favor fire.
But if it had to perish twice,
I think I know enough of hate
To say that for destruction ice
Is also great
And would suffice.

ROBERT FROST

CHAPTER THIRTY-SEVEN

THE END OF THE WORLD?

Sometimes you can't see it from the shore. Other times, you could be looking right at it, and then you turn your head; the island's not there anymore. Grandpa had explained that some islands floated in the sea like stars in the Milky Way, and that sometimes they were visible, and sometimes they were not. He had always said that such a particular island was a sacred place that nature especially wanted to protect....

Turning back from where she had come, Rainy Peek was seeing how far she had traveled. She caught sight of Koda and her grandfather, who was waving to her from the other shore. He told her with his waving hand, and with his mind, that it was alright, for he too had once long ago followed something that was more than a dream.

The door. The dolphin. The place where Rainy was now. It was all the way that it should be. She was a human being living her destiny....

Dragging her door onto the beach, she turned to wave once more to Koda and her grandfather, but they were gone as though they were never there at all. She shook her head to clear it, remembered trust, and turned. It was entrancing. It seemed as though no other human being had ever been here before. Leaving the door, she started walking, but after only taking a few steps, she paused. Something black and sticky stuck to the bottoms of her feet. It got between her toes.

Alarmed, she sat immediately on the sand, and horrorstruck, she glared at this thick tar-like goo that had now gotten stuck on her hands too. She quickly reached for a stick of driftwood, and snatching it up, she used it to try and scrape the black stuff off. It wouldn't come off! No matter how hard she scraped, the hideous gunk clung to the bottoms of her feet, and between her toes, and then her fingers, and now it got stuck on the ends of her long hair. It was on her knitted blue shorts, and now her white tank top. Her arms and legs. Heaving a sigh, she stopped, examining the filthy driftwood stick, wondering what she would do with it, when she heard a terrifying sound like a moan so grave she was afraid to turn around, but she did....

And gasped.

A green sea turtle was crawling with great effort up the beach, stressed and laboring towards her nest. The back of her shell was on fire. She was burning to death. Rainy's face turned from horror to terror, and her stomach grimaced with an anguish she had never known. Instinctively, she grabbed two handfuls of sand, pouring them and more handfuls over the back of the large shell, smothering the flames as the turtle dragging herself up as far as she could, maneuvered herself near the top of the beach, turned, and stopped, and Rainy, gritty black sand fixed to her hands and feet and hair and just about everywhere, fell to her knees before the great Mother Being.

Tears dripping from the corners of the turtle's eyes became Rainy's tears. Her labored breathing, became Rainy's breath. Her pounding heart in synchronicity with Rainy's heart.

The ancient eyes of the Turtle Mother, and the young eyes of the Indian girl, weeping; their lives together besieged. But, life must continue, the great mother being said. We are created to help life continue. To perpetuate life. To maintain the beauty of the Great Mystery.... I need to lay my eggs.

And, the great Turtle Mother, like she has been doing for more years than Rainy had lived, managed to dig out the sand from beneath her painful body, and give birth covered in that hideous black horror, her precious green shell burnt and now almost black itself.

Rainy staggered to her feet, her once long hair streaked by the sun, now blackened too, her fingers and hands; her legs and her clothes covered in it. As she stood unsteadily in the tarry sand, her eyes wide opened, set again in that same repulsion and terror that had first gripped her sight, the shore where she had just landed on her door, now saturated too in the black hideous goo.

Then she saw the fish, that moments earlier streaked colorfully beneath her, bloated and floating in the same oily mess and its staining away too the colors of all the shells and shellfish. A tiny sea horse, gasping his last breath. A blue crab barely moving, his one outstretched claw unable to help him reach the opening in the sand where he had lived. And the fine sugary sand itself, once glistening white and welcoming, now black as mire and frightening.

Who said, it would never come to this. Who said, it was all perfectly safe. Who said these things? They're always gone from what they do.

It was all around her. Could it be what she had feared? Could this be the end of our world?

Then she heard the struggling of ten thousand feathers, the sounds of wings that can't take flight. It was coming from the water birds in the mangroves dripping with the heavy black goo; others tangled in fishermen lines left on the ground where the egrets and storks and herons walked, or caught in the plastic beer and soda can wrappers that boaters tossed over their boats and beach goers had left on the beach, or others who had thrown them out the windows of cars, the sewers dragging the plastic wrappers with dirty rainwater and flushing them into the bays and the oceans, and now all snarled in the claws and talons and feet of pelicans and skimmers and terns; sea gulls and cormorants and king fishers, all the flocks of beautiful birds struggling for life on the mangrove branches, each one bound in his and her own slow and gruesome death.

Dark energy was everywhere. Dark matter was everywhere, and when she turned again to the sea and saw the most exquisite dolphin's body tossing in the small black murky waves breaking towards the shore, Rainy fell to her knees, and with her eyes closed, she cried like she had never cried before.

"Enough! Enough!" she wept; her body quaking, her small fists pounding the tar stained sand, tears covering her smudged face. "Don't do this anymore," she cried, and collapsed. "Don't do this anymore...."

And then, she heard a child's voice.

CHAPTER THIRTY-EIGHT

THE EXTRAORDINARY ENCOUNTER

"Rainy," the voice called from somewhere.

She opened her weepy eyes, and lifted her face. Wiping her nose with the back of her hand, she sniffled and shivered, like an infant who has cried herself to sleep. Then, looking real slow, she saw that the dreadful black gunge was gone from her hands and her feet. She pushed herself up and sat staring at a healthy turtle withdrawn into her nest doing what her kind has been doing for more than 200 million years.

She rubbed her eyes and wiped her face. She gazed at the water, and the water was still as amazing as ever. Turning quickly, she saw in the mangroves, the birds perched and preening quietly in the trees. Then she stood and saw a dolphin breach way out past the sandbars.

It must've been a dream. But she had never fallen asleep.

"Rainy," the voice called again.

She craned her neck in all directions, but she couldn't see anyone. She turned one way but saw only mangroves and palms.

"Rainy, over here," the voice called again. "Over here."

She headed with an urging that she didn't understand, to where she thought the voice had called her name. And, it did not take her long to cross the small island to the other side.

"Over here," the voice called again, this time much closer. "Rainy, over here."

She made her way along the narrow shore to where it curved, and there, in the shade of the palms sat a little girl. She appeared to be about three years old. It seemed to Rainy that she had seen this girl before, but did not know where or when.

"Over here, Rainy," the little girl motioned with a gesture of her arm, and waving hand. "Sit here with me."

Her senses keened like a wolf, she stepped warily now, drawing closer to the little girl, but as she did, the little girl had changed into an older girl, a teenager with long brown hair, highlighted with golden streaks that framed a kind and full face and brown shining eyes. Rainy hesitated, aware that she had stepped into a reality unlike the one from where she had come. Something mysterious had happened. This she knew for certain, but strangely, she did not feel afraid. Instead, she saw how pretty the older girl was.

"Come, Rainy Peek," a young woman said and smiled where the teenage girl had been.

Still cautious, her curiosity and courage urged her even closer. "How do you know my name?"

"All things in time, my dear. Now come," the old woman with long silver hair replied. "Sit with me awhile, and we will talk of the world."

It has been said...
In the very earliest of times,
When both people and animals lived on earth,
A person could become an animal if he wanted
to
And an animal could become a human being
Sometimes they were people
And sometimes they were animals
And there was no difference.
All spoke the same language.
That was the time when words were like magic.
The human mind had mysterious powers.
A word spoken by chance
Might have strange consequences.
It would suddenly come alive
And what people said wanted to happen could
happen –
All you had to do was say it.
Nobody could explain this;
That's the way it was.

TRIBAL SONG

CHAPTER THIRTY-NINE

THE AH-NUH'S MESSAGE

She sank to the sand alongside the old woman whose hair was now the color of sunlight on the silver dolphin's skin. Even as the old one sat, her elongated back made her seem especially tall. For a reason of which Rainy was not fully conscious, she was imagining the woman the size of a large bottle-nose dolphin.

They sat near the top of a sand dune, together in the shade of palms, within a cluster of swaying sea oats, and faced the shore. It was the old woman who began speaking, one eye fixed forward, and like a dolphin, the other looking at the girl.

"It has been said that a long time ago, the only people to live here were the Indians. They had tribal names then," she said, "names they called themselves." And then as in a rapid clicking, she spoke their names in words: "Tocobago. Calusa. Tequesta. Timucua. Yamasee.... *Human Beings of the Land Where the Wind is Born.*"

She motioned with her arm which spanned it seemed to the girl the whole shoreline and beyond.

"They loved the Ocean. They called her name and bestowed offerings and prayers to the spiritual beings who dwell within her, and care for her.

"You mean, the Ah-nuh?"

"I am Ah-nuh...."

The eye of the shape shifter that was scanning the shoreline momentarily refocused and joined her other eye looking at the pretty Indian girl sitting next to her.

"Your mother discovered me in a dream when she was a young girl. She took on the pain from the barb of Ah-nuh and gave her blood. Later, she gave offerings of flowers she had planted in gratitude so that Ah-nuh would know her daughter. Even your grandfather's mother held him in her arms and had called out to the Ah-nuh. She too gave offerings, these of her own creation, the beauty of her art, that the Ah-nuh would help guide him in his greatest time of need. Your grandmother offered her pain and her blood to Ah-Nuh. She did this for your mother. Your grandfather's sacrifice was one of great emotional pain that also emanated out of great love. That energy he offered to help sustain Ah-nuh.

"You would have a destiny, your grandfather said.... In gratitude, he allowed you to help him renew his house and make it "pretty". All the energy of love and creativity he offered to Ah-nuh."

Then both of the old one's eyes searched in opposite directions up and down the beach, and she smiled at the memory of something that was not there anymore, something her imagination would enable her to see, like looking through energy waves of heat, but now she couldn't. Nuclear bomb testing in the oceans and recent naval sonar blasts had damaged her ancient memory power. For the violent behavior of humans had no limitations.

Still she sat inhaling what she could only now pretend to imagine the remembered scent of burning cedar drifting in the air, and the pretty maidens with their mothers and grandmothers outside the thatched lodges, and the feathered and painted young men and their fathers and their grandfathers heading out in their canoes.

"It was a time of peace," she said. *"They took only what they needed, used with respect what was available. Expressed always their gratitude."* She spoke rapidly, in pulsing bursts, but fluently. Each annunciation, a pulse beat, a word, and Rainy could make out every one:

"They lived always to keep the balance with the sea that sustained them. They cherished the gift of life and accepted the necessity of death. They affirmed and celebrated the Great Mystery that is the source of all life. And when it came to hunting and fishing, they never aimed an arrow or tossed a net for the biggest. Always honored the spirit of what was killed. They were healthy, and their environment was healthy. They were grateful and fulfilled."

Rainy tilted her head upward and looked at the dolphin woman, the Ah-nuh. She was, indeed, something more than human. Everything that was happening was something more than human. Something greater. The old one's hair hung long and silvery white concealing a pale and ashen color in naked human-like form. Nothing about her seemed in proportion and yet everything was....

Triangular tattoos marked her ancient face, and spirals and circles, and lines of geometric configurations that painted her arms and legs were more than decorations. They recorded acquired powers and passages from one world into the next, perhaps, one form into another, and her kind and intelligent eyes, almost human in appearance, were obviously not human eyes at all. While one remained focused on the water, the other moved independently, glancing down from time to time at Rainy. The girl could see in that one eye, its black center was encircled by a cerulean blue with flecks of brown and no white where humans would have it. She saw too in its deepest and darkest space that the essence of ancient wisdom dwelled in a soul much older than one in an ordinary human life. "This world of sky and water and land was their home, Rainy Peek. Turtle Island is your home too."

"Turtle Island," Rainy said. Where and when had she heard those words, Turtle Island? Turtle Island....

The age-old Ah-nuh reached for a long piece of driftwood that lay half concealed alongside her in the sand. Placing the tip down, she pulled herself up with surprising little effort, for someone as tall and large and who seemed so really old, in a single fluid motion, and stood.

One eye remained gazing at the water, the other contemplating the young girl at her side, she asked, "Do you see your Mother, Rainy Peek?"

"I don't understand...."

"Your Mother. Do you see her?"

The unexpected question startled the girl, but the idea in this unusual instance had seemed strangely plausible. Why wouldn't it be? She was not in ordinary time. Not in anything ordinary anymore. The girl rose to her feet, blinked, and searched, scanning the area all around as far beyond as she could, expecting in this extraordinary moment to see her. Maggie. Her mother. Mommy.... But she saw no one. She turned to the old woman, her head slowly shaking once, twice.

"I don't understand."

"But you hear her ...still ... in your memory."

Rainy's face became a pensive reflection; her eyes squinted; her lips pursed. Her head slowly nodding, again, once, twice. She was saying without speaking...Yes. She's in my memory.... "'Turtle Island,' she said it to me.... I was in the ocean of her womb, but it was me who just spoke the words."

"Do you see your Father?"

No longer off guard, the girl's eyes welled up as emotions rose inside of her like a moon-strong tide. Even so, she searched the beach for him, and still in some unexplainable way, expecting to see him – her father–somewhere. Maybe. Daddy? She saw no one.

Now, as if the tide had all at once receded, she looked up desperately at the old woman whose both eyes were fixed on her.

"And yet, you feel his love...."

"My parents are dead, Grandmother. They were killed."

"Yes," the Ah-nuh said, raising her head. "Yes, the mother who gave birth to you, and the father who loved his daughter, have died. And I am sorry. For such is the nature of destiny.... It is indifferent."

"I still don't understand."

"Some things need not be understood because they are of the Mystery." She returned her gaze to the expanse of the shimmering sea. "We accept what we cannot comprehend. It gives us peace. But, surely, you've already learned this."

"But why did you ask me about my parents if you knew...?"

"Because you still have parents.... And they are very much alive. They are very much with you."

The attention of the old woman's dark and blue eyes focused again on the turquoise water, and her ears, unlike human ears, unseen beneath her silver hair, were listening. The tide was returning. She smiled, the waves breaking into small white crystals of foam, hissing and rolling over the sand bars towards the shore, the palms behind her rattling in the gusty salt air, the sea gulls squawking and squealing all around her. The song of the beach everywhere ....

As she stood holding onto her walking stick with one hand, she gestured with the other, extending her arm again in a sweeping motion that seemed to the girl that was Rainy to include the whole world.

"The Mother whose elements and essences created the life blood within you, is within all things around you. She is all around you, Rainy Peek....

"She is the warm sand between your toes. She is the mangroves. She is the Ocean before you, the Ocean that gave you the door. She is the Mother who holds you now. She is the Earth. You have never been without a Mother."

Like a spider finding completion in the center of her web, Rainy felt herself in the center of everything, the threads of the Ah-nuh's words connecting all the girl's life experiences to the center of the universe within her own center, her relationship to all things of the Mother threaded and extending out into the Mystery, and she was sensing in a way she had never known, her interconnectedness to all things, great and small, past and present and future.

"All that you see and can't see above you: the heat of the Sun, and the Sun, the blue air, the stars at night, the distant clouds, their promise of rain, and the falling rain that is your namesake.... All of this," she said, "is your Father.

"You are a child of the Earth. You are a child of the Sky.... That is what makes you human. And who you really are."

"Then this is what it means to be a

real Indian."

The very old woman closed her eyes, and again, raising her head slightly, she blew this time through her lips a puff of breath into the air like a prayer. Then her gaze fell on that place where sky and ocean intersect. And, with a single slight tap of her walking stick in the sand, she left the dune and moved light as air towards the shore before she paused at the water's edge .... The young girl behind her, now sliding alone half way down the dune in the sun-dappled shade under the shadows of the palms.

"You can spend your whole life learning what it means to be an Indian, Rainy Peek," the old one said, turning back towards the girl, "and it will be an astounding and humbling journey. For being Indian, for being a HUMAN BEING, means many things....

"But," she said, lifting her face to the girl, "there is none more important, for it is the one that you have come to know now. To love the Earth as your Mother...."

>>·<< >>·<< >>·<<

She leaned on the long stick of driftwood and spun in the direction of the sea. Both eyes returned to the horizon.

"It is true," she said, of a young girl's questions cried out in a stormy night. The wind was growing stronger, lifting her words to the girl on the dune. "Some people are cruel," the Ah-nuh continued, her language of rapid clicking and words merging and making sense. "And some may not even mean to be. They have said and done things that have hurt you, and have hurt the world, but often because it was the way they had learned how to be, or didn't learn how to be–human."

Contemplating the tip of the driftwood, she rubbed her fingers over it, enchanted by its smoothness, a silkiness that only time in the cycles of life could create of wood, or bone, or shell, with wind and sun and sea. It was everything that life has in common.

She turned again to face the girl. "Many humans have forgotten how to live. Over generations, in their minds, they have detached themselves from our Mother. Detached from nurturing, unguided by their natal mothers, they have detached themselves from empathy. They have detached themselves from respect. They have detached themselves from gratitude.

"Unlike you, they cannot feel, nor allow themselves to imagine that Earth is their mother too, that all life is related," she said. "Such ancient wisdom dwells no place in their childhoods, no place in their governments. No place in their sciences. Nor in their religions. And the absence of this wisdom, can make them cruel. Now, even the notion of loving Earth as Mother contradicts the very ways they have chosen to live.

"Unlike you, when their birth mothers abandon them, when their birth mothers can't fit their children into their own lives, when their birth mothers ultimately experience death, such children they have left behind can only live in the delusions of all those who have become like them, motherless."

Without conscious thought, Rainy had sketched a circle in the sand, her finger cutting a straight line across the bottom. The bottom line.... The Ah-nuh observed the sand drawing. Then without speaking, she bent and left the walking stick of driftwood behind. Turning to the sea once more, graceful and elegant, she elevated like a tall heron taking wing, gliding from the spot on the beach where she had been standing to another at the shoreline.

Her silvery white hair covered her back, but Rainy could see her shoulders rise and fall with long deep breaths.

"Our Mother's heart beats once every year," the Ah-nuh's voice transported in wind to the girl who remained half way down the dune in the flickering of sunlight and shade.

Now, one eye shut, the old one stood facing the horizon, as though asleep and awake, and soon, she was grimacing. Her mind flooded with the images ending our world: giant smoke stacks burning coal spewing out carbon and toxins and the towers of nuclear reactors leaking radiation that poisons but you cannot see, and the smog from industries and factories and trucks and cars of too many people; the oil wells pumping; oil rigs sucking; tunnels blasting; machines cutting and gouging and grinding. Pipe lines leaking. Fracking and fracturing. Dumping. Drilling.

"They are lost!" she cried, then squealed and shuddered, as her shut eye opened to the loud, flapping wings of scattering, startled gulls. "They have severed their kinship with their Mother, and they are lost!"

Once more, with one eye opened, she closed the other, and could see into the darkness behind the one: fleets of fishing boats casting nets as long as football fields, trawlers scooping in everything they contact. Countless sea life suffocating in air. Oil platforms fastened to the Ocean's secret places bleeding black from their lines of hoses and tubes. Islands of garbage, floating land masses of filth. Sewer runoff. Agricultural runoff. Red tide. Dead zones....

"They take and they take and they take,"

she spoke in a broken voice of pulsating and squawk-like sounds and words so besieged it caused a young girl and maybe even the whole world at that moment to tremble. "And what do they give back...?"

In an instantaneous second, somehow seeing in her own mind the death images of a world out of balance, Rainy jolted to her feet.

"I don't want to be like that!" she cried. "I don't want our world to be like that.... "

The Ah-nuh turned her head halfway to the beleaguered girl. Both of her eyes now tiny ponds of tears, one remained staring in the direction of the sea, the other at the girl.

"They have acquired untested knowledge," she said, her voice clear and suddenly unmoved and indifferent, the rapid clicking hardly evident. "They have sacrificed the ancestral wisdom already proven. That is where the danger lies ... for them, for us, and for Earth. The spirit of the island has shown you the consequences."

With her back to the water, her silvery grey hair framing her human-like face, both eyes of the old woman concentrated on the girl, and then she motioned with her long arm to a particular place up the beach at the base of another dune. It was a turtle's nest.

"For more than two hundred million years. More time than any human can imagine, Mother Turtles have laid their eggs in such a way.... Now, because of the behavior of the motherless, maybe soon the great mothers will be all gone too."

Rainy stumbled down the dune, stopping at the base where she stood, her shoulders drawn in, the fingers of her hands interlocked, her thumbs pressed together against her chin, her toes digging beneath the warm sand.

"But the cycles of the Earth?" she said in a voice as soft as a whisper in the air.

First the rapid sequential clicking, then the words.... "They will change.... They are changing now. The Circle of Life is breaking.... It is breaking now."

The old one could not suppress her quivering lips, and again she turned, seeking comfort and consolation and composure from the sunlight shimmering on the water like a million suns in a celestial sea.

"If they don't stop their behavior soon, if they don't stop violating her body and learn to respect her, and they don't stop taking from her without love, and without gratitude, then the energies of all that they have destroyed will return.... And all their anger; their greed; their violence; their prejudices and intolerances. The carbon. The plastic. The toxins. And the spirits of all the innocent. All these and more will manifest in drought. They will summon as storms of dry wind and dust; storms of torrential rains and heavy snows. Storms of cold and ice and storms of heat and fire. Storms born of the Sun for what they've done. Storms born of the Ocean. The whirlwinds. They will manifest. The Ah-nuh must protect the water.... It is what we must do. It is the purpose of our existence." There was of burst pulse, like another soft squawk, and another whistle ....

"Maybe then they will listen...."

And another whistle followed.

>>•<< >>•<< >>•<<

The old shape shifter remained looking at the sea, but again, she raised her outstretched arms, and as a great blue heron elevates with the motion of her wings, she glided wingless along the wet shore. With her tail-like dolphin feet leaving no imprints, she slipped into the liquid energy of the blue-green sea.

"Ahhh-nuuhh...," she sighed, the sound a breath of soft wind caressing Rainy's ear just as it had her grandfather's long ago.

Then the deeper water beckoned, and with the ocean at her waist, she paused, her eyes following a line of pelicans swooping in long high arcs, a young turtle paddling beyond where the waves were breaking, his head just above the surface. A rainbow fish circled her changing form. A school of mullet splashed and vanished. A manta, poised just above the sandy bottom, watched her, loving her.

"Ahhh-nuuhh...," she sighed again.... "I worry so much for them."

With the breeze lifting the strands of her wispy white and silver hair, her whispered words traveled like ghosts in the salty air, "They are the innocent."

Then, another piercing whistle, penetrating time and distance as if this one was meant for all to hear.

In a moment, she was passing over the sandbars now as a dolphin on her tail can skim erect across the surface of the water, she moved deeper from where she had emerged, and she had aged even more.

Rainy climbed, hands and feet gripping the sand, pulling and pushing her back to the top of the dune.

"Where are you going?" she cried out. "Will I see you again?"

Great grandmother turned, the water embracing her shoulders, and for the last time, in a faraway voice, she spoke in rapid clicks of pulsating bursts to the young girl being standing among the swaying stalks of sea oats.

"Rainy Peek," she said, her voice of dolphin sounds and words ancient and raspy, "with the turtle power bestowed upon you today, you will help save some of this Earth as we have come to know her.... You will help save some of her children. Never surrender her, Rainy Peek! Just as you will never forget the beauty of your birth mother, never forget the beauty you see in your Earth Mother, for one day, you can tell your child, and then he too will know what it means to be an Indian, and a human being. And, like you, he will never be without a mother."

The sea winds gusted.

"Wait!" the girl cried, and leapt the decline from the dune, nearly falling. With long strides, her feet kicking up sand, her long hair in flight, she ran to the shore, and into the water, thrusting her way through the blowing foam towards the sandbar, through the churning of currents around her legs, and into the incoming set of breaking waves, she dove, and surfaced. "How will I help save the world?" She was treading water and alternately bobbing on her toes as the sea rolled, and a distant figure ahead shimmered in the trail of sunlight. "Ah-nuh! Wait! Ah-nuh!"

A sudden consciousness, an abrupt awareness, had without warning, caused Rainy's whole body to shiver. A chill everywhere, up and down her submerged swaying arms, her legs, the spine of her back. She could even feel it in her hair. The water seemed electric.

"Are you...?" Rainy faltered, tottering in the motion of the deeper water beyond the sandbar and breaking waves... the fragmented memory of loving arms and a soft shoulder in the chaos of a kindergarten classroom.... Another worldly form standing behind her and Grandpa at the cemetery; the silver dolphin that freed the door.

"Are you her...?" Nearly breathless, she struggled to tread water and keep her head up, her feet slipping in the sand beneath the surface....

She stumbled and fought to remain upright as the water reached her lips. Breaking behind her, the waves, their strong currents tugging her legs, and she, trying to find her balance.

Then, overcome with the recollection, she settled in the calm between the sets, her wet brown and sun-streaked hair down her back and her shoulders, drifting in the water, her sight never leaving the ancient and mysterious being who had turned to her for the last time, and closing her one eye while the other fixed on the girl, sent another puff of breath into the air.

With her toes bouncing on the sand below, her arms moving, the water enveloping all but her head, the tips of Rainy's fingers brushed along her face the breath of a kiss, and where a dolphin's silky silver skin had once touched her spirit in a dream that was more than a dream....

Into the horizon, where Earth and Sky meet one another and embrace the world, the very old woman arced above the water as a dolphin and dove with a great splash, sea spray appearing, a silver dorsal rising sharply and disappearing....

CHAPTER FORTY

THE REUNION

Koda's surprising low pitched howl filtered into Rainy's consciousness and caused her head to turn toward the direction from where it came. Pulling away the loose strands of wet hair from her eyes, she caught sight of Grandpa and Koda, who were in Grandpa's little boat, coasting up to the beach where Rainy had left her door.

The door was gone.

As he came over the dunes, he was smiling and waving as happy grandfathers will do, and Koda's long bushy tail was swaying as a happy wolf's tail will do, and the very old woman had disappeared as a magical being will do....

Beyond the shore where the sky meets the sea, and the worlds of sleeping and awake and of dreaming and not dreaming all come together, there exists another world, a world of change and endless possibilities. A world that is magical and real all at once.

As a grandfather embraced his granddaughter, and a wolf named Koda sniffed along the shore, they all looked up at the moment that a lone silver dolphin splashed in the distance, sending forth a powerful burst of sea spray and all the hope of the world that resounded in her breath.

You must remember the gentleness of time

You are struggling to be who you are

You say you want to learn the old ways

Struggling to learn when all you must do

Is remember...

JOHN TRUDELL

CHAPTER FORTY-ONE

SOUTHERN BREEZE....

During Rainy's sixth grade certificate ceremony, Mrs. Kingsley sat alongside Grandpa on a foldout chair set up under the flag pole, both wearing curious expressions when Mr. Kline stood at the podium with his award in hand, telling everyone how hard it was being a good teacher, and that if it weren't for his teaching history, their children might never really know how great America is.

A few days later, Mrs. Kingsley would move to the Atlantic coast in order to be closer with her aging mother who needed special care and company. The first years of her retirement, she had been driving the five-hour distance between the two coasts, staying for longer stretches with her mother each trip. She finally had to decide to move because her mother's health was failing, and Mrs. Kingsley couldn't make the drive anymore....

They had nearly two complete cycles of the seasons together. Daughter caring for mother. Mrs. Kingsley had arranged the funeral, thanked the folks who helped, and had seen to any of her mother's accounting that needed to be done. Then Mrs. Kingsley fell asleep one night on the second full Moon after her mother's death, on the couch in her mother's apartment, and never woke up. She was 74 years old.

Grandpa had said that he could recognize a weary heart. Mrs. Kingsley was tired, and hers wore out, as hearts can do. He said that he didn't know if Mrs. Kingsley believed in heaven, or how she felt about death, but he figured that wherever her spirit journeyed, would be a good place to be.

He said that the kind of energy she put back into the energy of nature was needed.

Irene Glassman, the elderly lady who owned and operated the beach store, told Grandpa when he was shopping for a new wind chime for the front porch, that she had known Mrs. Kingsley, "...quite well," she said. "Since she first started teaching, we became friends....

"One stormy morning," she said to Grandpa, "while no one else was in the store, she told me that she was a Buddhist." Irene said Mrs. Kingsley chose to keep it low key as "...some folks might've not understood."

Irene also told Grandpa that Mrs. Kingsley had been cremated. "A few Buddhists had come by," she said, "to claim what Mrs. Kingsley had left in storage, for she'd willed her possessions to the Buddhist Tao Center in the town where her mother lived." When they stopped in the store, one of the monks held a small, plain wooden box that they asked her to give Rainy or her grandfather. "And, oh, yes, I almost forgot," she said, after she had handed it to Grandpa. "They asked me to tell the young girl they liked the story of the red bead very much."

Rainy was just completing eighth grade at the time, and had taken the news of Mrs. Kingsley's passing hard. Sadie couldn't seem to console her, nor Koda, nor Grandpa. After weeks had past, finally, one day Grandpa and Rainy sat together on the porch steps after school. Koda sat behind them, sensing something in the air. The bamboo wind chime Grandpa had bought at the beach store was playing it seemed its first music in the sudden arrival of a tropical breeze from the South.

"Rain," Grandpa began, "we've each known grief. It's a part of the human condition.

It's a terrible feelin'. But it's a necessary part of healin'."

She was looking down and running her fingers over the turquois edge of the step. Before the renewal she might've gotten a splinter from the rough wood, but Grandpa had sure smoothed it out.

"I know," she said.

"I know ye know. But please hear me out... as I love ye, and I understand you're hurtin'." He paused and settled alongside her, and like always, trying to find the right the words. The bamboo chime played above them and the brown oak leaves rustled on the ground and bird sounds permeated the air. "Grief can cling to ye, Granddaughter. It can stick to you like the sap of an oak in winter. Stay stuck with ye all day. You can't wash it off. You sleep with it at night. You wake up and it's still there in the mornin'."

"I know, Granpa. I'm sorry," she said, a warm soft breeze lifting her hair. "I've been sad too long for my own good."

"You got nothin' to be sorry for, sweetheart. I'd been more worried if ye didn't hurt. The world lost a great teacher. You lost a special friend."

She shrugged and nodded and smiled just a little.... "I've not been a pleasant person to be around," she said, turning her head to face the wolf.

"I'm sorry to you too, Koda." He acknowledged the sentiment, but was still tuned to the air. And to the spirit that had arrived.

Rainy stared ahead at the rutted driveway, snaking towards the road, the mailbox at the end. She saw that the lilies were blooming. After the shadow man had run them over, they came back.... After all these years, she thought.

But some things don't come back.... Yet she was learning that they can, just not in ways we might expect....

"It's only that Mrs. Kingsley's dying raised up all these feelings I used to have, Granpa, and I feel bad she doesn't get to teach anymore."

"Grief can trigger those kinda memories and feelin's, Rainy. But ye got a young heart, and it's a strong heart. As ye get older in life, you'll need a strong heart because you care so much and love so much. Those ye love get older too, and they die. It hurts every time, but just be certain that you're grievin' Mrs. Kingsley's absence in your life, and not grievin' for her. You can even grieve for the children who will never know her, but do not grieve for her. She's in the Mystery."

Rainy didn't want to think beyond the moment, couldn't think beyond it, but Grandpa's words played in the notes of the bamboo wind chime. And he glanced up at it, his eyes gleaming, and then looked at Rainy who was also looking up at the hollow bamboo tubes of different lengths playing music in the gentle southern breeze.

"Mrs. Kingsley was pretty like that, and her words played in your ear, gentle like that too."

"They did, indeed," Grandpa said. Then he stood and stretched and put his face closer to the wind chime. "The road never gets easier, Granddaughter," he said, speaking as much to himself as to her. "You just learn to cope better... understand a little more."

Sitting back down on the step, he glanced up again at the music of the chime, and he smiled.

He took two fingers of his hand, the forefinger and the middle finger, and he touched Rainy's heart. "All those ye loved, Rainy, are inside... here," he said. Then he touched her forehead. "And in here.... In your memories. In your stories." Then he kissed the top of her head.

The bamboo tubes played above them in a warm southern gust of salty air. "They're a part of everything."

He leaned his back against the steps, gazing with more than his eyes past the driveway, past the jungle of trees, across the road construction, and the steel and concrete support beams of new development. His vision sailed over the remaining dunes and last of endangered sea oats, and out to the turquoise sea.

"We have to let go at some point, as their spirit must continue the great change," he said, "not hindered by our grief....

"As for the livin'," he said, gazing back prophetically into the soft brown eyes of his granddaughter, and taking her hand, "the living must carry on for all those beings we love in this life who are still here."

"Where there is love, there is life...."

MAHATMA GHANDI

CHAPTER FORTY-TWO

TWO OF HEART

Outside the sleek modern building, a beautiful young woman sat on a bench in the warm sun, enjoying the mixture of the heat and cool autumn air. With a nervous patience she awaited her appointed time, and her turn to walk through the big metal door of the University Conference Room at exactly two minutes before the old clock on the Science Building wall across the concrete walkway read, 3:15.

The sky above her was intense blue, but in the east, piling high, were the great mountains of cumulous clouds, and she was thinking that the wind will be coming first, then the Thunder Beings, and of course, the rain. She had not noticed just ahead of the storm, a small scout cloud was passing over, eclipsing the sun. The cloud's shadow had caused her to suddenly shiver, a sensation she had over the years understood came with the approach of the unexpected.

It was at that moment, a man had stepped out of the shadow the cloud had cast and walked towards her. He wore his dark hair in several long braids, his skin the hue of copper in the sunlight. He held a book and a folder in one hand tucked close to a flowered shirt. As he drew near, the small cloud had sailed on, and the sun reappeared above and slightly behind the man, making him appear, for an instant, luminescent.

"Hello," he said, in a friendly and kind voice, and stopped at the bench where the young woman sat. Guarded.

"My name is Tom Brightman," he said, and smiled shyly. "I hope it's okay I say hello."

Her shield lowered.

"I'm a graduate teaching assistant in the English Department."

He looked over at the entrance of the Conference Room Building. "It has a nickname," he said, and gestured in the direction of its metal door. The young woman looking up had to use her hand to shade the sunlight from her eyes. "What has?"

"The door," he said. "Doctorial students call it Heavy Metal."

He watched her perfect lips smile. "I've heard that," she said.

As her sight adjusted, even in shadow, she could see his face. He was handsome and pleasant, open and intelligent. Several braids draped his shoulders, tucked behind his ears where they showed premature hints of white spider thread strands of hair. Early wisdom. A trace of lines from the corners of his eyes. Time in the Sun, struggles overcome, pain outlasted, and often intense focus, and the eyes themselves an unusual brown with flecks of hazel green, almost star-like, caused her to feel her heart beating.

He noticed her discomfort at his position before the sun, apologized, and asked if he could join her on the bench. He noticed something more: this electric feeling. It was surging through his body, the sensation making him aware of himself in ways he never had.

She dropped the hand above her eyes, and moved over, allowing him room, a small space between them.

"Don't be too nervous," he said, sitting down. "I went through it last week. I've a masters in English. I'm trying for a doctorate in Tribal literature. I'd be the first." He sighed, and shrugged, some of it frustration, some fatigue, both an unintentional reaction resulting from the long battle he had waged to get this far.

She looked at him with an inquisitive gaze that she did not mean to linger in his eyes.

"Anyway, my committee shot so many questions at me, I knew why students have called them the firing squad. I know one thing for certain. Next time I won't even mention the tribal creation accounts that contradict the Bering Strait theory. I'll save it for the classroom." He shrugged his shoulders again, more an expression of humility at the defeat this time. "Otherwise, I guess I handled myself well enough, but in the end, they agreed to give me six weeks to resubmit."

"I'm sorry," the young woman said. "Tribal literature holds the wisdom of our preservation."

His eyebrows raised. "Change isn't easy." He glanced at her apologetically. "But, of course, you know this...." His eyes shined. He really liked her. Everything about her. He wanted to be with her forever. How can that be? "I still have two classes to teach this semester. They help pay for my education here."

They sat loving each other and never wanting to leave. They sat smiling inside about how wonderful life could be together. How can this be?

"You mustn't be too nervous," he said, noticing her soft and deep brown eyes, glancing in the direction of the door called Heavy Metal, not knowing about the door she had ridden as a girl to a secret island. "Your committee will be different than mine," he said. "I'm certain you'll do... fine. More than fine."

"I'minthesciences,"shesaid."Specifically, marine science, but also environmental. My studies have concentrated mostly on water and rescue. We've got our issues too...."

He loved to hear her talk. Her voice, the energy resonating in every word. The long braid descending past her shoulder....The sacred feather tied to it....

"But I too have a feeling you'll succeed as well," she said. "You'll show them," and then she paused, taking a breath. "And thank you," she added, her heart feeling the true depth of those words that suddenly sprang from her lips. "Your confidence in me...." And a smile had to complete what she couldn't put into words.

Trying not to appear obvious or rude, he forced himself to restrain his keen awareness of the young woman's beauty. He made every effort to not let his gaze be too apparent, or linger too long, as she again checked the time on the old clock across the way on the Science Building wall.

Such beauty must emanate from inner beauty. It was something he understood.

Her sun-streaked, dark auburn hair. The single braid, and feather that was not simply a decoration. She had earned it.... He knew that in the way you know things about someone you just met, someone you just fell in love with.... And her brown eyes! Oh my! So warm and mysterious. Her face, exquisite and smooth and sun colored. Her full lips. The turquoise turtle earrings. The silver turtle necklace. Her small wrists. She's wearing no watch. A coral bracelet. The skin of her arms and her legs, taut and strong. The body of a swimmer, he thought. The sound of her voice like nothing he's ever heard. Nor could ever not hear again. And her heart... her heart is for certain, Indigenous. He could feel its strength. Her soul, her spirit.... She was everything to him.

He had fallen completely in love.

She saw him blink, as though he were startled. Self-conscious, he glanced up at the clock as well.

"They got the design right," he said, in a nervous stutter, trying to draw attention away from himself.

Her expression at once was curious.

"Its design...," he repeated. "The clock. They made them in circles."

She laughed aloud, surprising herself how his irony and perception unexpectedly tugged at her heart strings and couldn't have belated her reaction.

She glanced down. Her cheeks flushed. Then she looked at him. "But it's the only time they know," she said, and smiled.

Again, she shifted her focus to the building she would be entering, and he sighed again, hoping he had held it in, trying to capture a momentary glimpse of her so as not to be intrusive. She is so beautiful. Beautiful, he thought. What is this word that should be used as sparingly as love, that to him suddenly seems to be everywhere and in everything: the intense blue sky, the salt tang in the air, the tall palms clustered along the sidewalk, birds of paradise flowers, and the bed of orchids! Even their two shadows on the grass behind the bench. The mockingbird singing from an old oak, the tree's huge twisting limbs dressed in Spanish moss near the entrance of the building. Beautiful. The word itself.... The idea summoning the ancient incantation, All is beautiful. All is beautiful!

"I...," he said, pausing, not wanting to finish what he felt he needed to say, but understood he must.... "I appreciate you needing a moment to yourself." His voice once again clear and kind. Then he stood, preparing to leave.

"Rainy Peek," she said, looking up, not concealing the concern in her eyes that she could lose him forever.

He pressed the folder and the book he was carrying to his body, but was holding her in his gaze. "A good name," he said, "Rainy Peek."

In truth, there was a powerful familiarity when he spoke her name, a vibration, when what seemed ages ago he had heard in a dream planted like a seed in his mind, her name, waiting for this time....

He shuffled his book and folder from one arm to the other. "Would you like to meet afterwards, Rainy Peek? Maybe go for some coffee or herbal tea even? There's a nice coffee house just off campus. Not too far. We can walk...."

Coffee. Herbal tea.

It only took an instant for her response, but it seemed to travel the distance between stars.

"Yes," she said, before realizing that she had said, yes. "That would be nice, Tom Brightman."

She was watching him walk away, every movement was moving her. Then she became anxious and more aware of that ever persistent artificial time again, and had glanced up at the old relic clock. When her eyes went back to where he had been, he was gone.

It was already 3:08, but now, out of the blue, there was something more special about the sun's heat on her face, the fall breeze keeping her cool, and the salty trace of the water on her lips, the hint of moisture on her skin. It all seemed to hold the young woman in a new kind of unfamiliar, yet comforting embrace, like Koda pressing at her side for the first time, and she was no longer feeling anxious or alone. She felt grateful, as she reached into her dress pocket, her fingertips brailing the coquina shell necklace her grandfather had made for her, and the small medicine bag that contained a lock of wolf hair.

And she looked once more at the exact spot where Thomas Brightman had appeared....

CHAPTER FORTY-THREE

A Phone Call in the Night...

She had left late in the evening after the call from Sadie.

Since the sixth grade, when the two girls had shared stories of family lost and family found, when they understood how cultures can touch us and intertwine us, they had formed a bond between them that would stay strong for the rest of their lives. You know, it's been said that when you're old, if you can look back and count the number of real friends you've had in your life on the fingers of one hand, you've been blessed.

In ninth grade when Sadie got real sick and had to stay in bed for days, Rainy would go by their house and help her grandmother with the chores, and her exercises. Seeing how Sadie was a year older and a grade higher than Rainy, her helping Sadie with her studies when she was sick, helped Rainy too, as she could get an edge up on what she had to learn for the next year.

Grandpa would pitch in and often with a list in his pocket, go grocery shopping, but on a few occasions Mrs. Willis went along.... She said in her broken and slurred speech that her first boyfriend owned a mustang like Grandpa's, and sometimes on their way to the store or heading home, Grandpa would glimpse her sitting low in the passenger's seat next to him, hunched over towards the dash board, holding a big brown paper bag of groceries with her one arm that was still working, and showing half a crooked smile that seemed bigger than most folks could know.

He had felt especially grateful to Granny Willis, and to Sadie, because they supported him, teaching his granddaughter about the cycles and changes of being a woman that Grandpa just couldn't. Not to mention the recipes that diversified their meals. And, whenever she could, Mrs. Willis would save a fat marrow bone for Koda.

In eleventh grade, Rainy and Grandpa had been at Sadie's side at the gravesite. And Rainy held onto Sadie who was crying at the words the minister was saying at how the angels came and took her grandmother up to heaven. He also spoke about love and caring for our children, and grandchildren, and how everything returns to dust and ashes as souls returned to God. Grandpa stood alongside the two girls, rubbing the tobacco leaves in his hand with his fingers and making his own silent prayers of love and gratitude that he would sprinkle on the earth by the grave with few people ever noticing. Sadie would live with Rainy and her grandfather for the rest of that school year, and when her mother was released from rehab, Sadie left to be with her, to take care of her.

With Rainy and Grandpa's help, Sadie made it through high school, despite her mother's struggle with addiction, and another six months in jail for shoplifting and a year more in drug rehab. Despite all that, the girls excelled through their junior and senior years. In her junior year, Rainy learned to drive her grandfather's mustang and could shift and downshift a stick that even most high school boys couldn't do. They would occasionally talk Grandpa into letting his mustang out, so the girls could see a movie at the new multiplex or shop at the new fully air conditioned mall or park at the beach at sunset, which is what they liked to do most, listen to music, and talk. They dated boys occasionally, doubled dated, but never committed to any of them, losing interest in them as fast as they had lost interest in malls.

After graduation, Sadie went to a college nearby on a scholarship, then nursing school.

Now, it was Sadie, assistant director at the new rehab center across the bridge, who would be there for Rainy....

She would stop by to check on her grandfather's house during the week, do any straightening up or go through Grandpa's mail that he might have overlooked, removing the important matter for Rainy to see when she got home, or helping him to read it when he couldn't. She also checked the daily pill box she would fill once a week to make certain he had not missed any doses of his heart medication, even though Rainy would call often to remind him.

Sitting on the porch steps of Grandpa's house, Sadie held her cell phone up to her ear.

"Granpa refused to leave with the paramedics tonight, Rain. He chose to stay home.... It appears his time's coming.... It won't be long."

CHAPTER FORTY-FOUR

SPIRITS LIFTING

She drove through what seemed like a dark eternity to be with him. At other moments, though, the trip home was going to end too fast because she knew what awaited.

She thought she was prepared.... How could you be ready for such a thing? But maybe preparation isn't always a deliberate act. Maybe we get ready for our loved ones passing all along, especially by loving them more as the end draws nearer. By squeezing hours out of a day or minutes out of a conversation. Consciously, deliberately, remembering the sound of their voices.

I'm comin', Granpa! she wept. Don't die, Granpa. Not yet....

Then, further towards the edge of night, a scattering of headlights would pass by under the blur and twinkle of the Interstate lamps, giving way to the thicker darkness of the back roads, and she would grip the steering wheel, focus on the double yellow lines, and hear herself questioning time....

...Why does it have to be so short? But, what is it? This thing called time? Damn! Where does it go? And then she heard herself answer, "Time is of the Mystery...."

She drove on and on into the wee hours before dawn. When she came to the entrance of their house, she had to cross the extra lanes that now served the new condo and storefront traffic. The creek alongside the school bus stop was gone, paved over black with asphalt for extra lanes; a sewer line ran its course parallel to the newly named Beach Boulevard to the bay. A four way traffic light, complete with arrows for turning lanes hung over the intersection.

As the tires of her car landed on the crushed shells and sand of the driveway, the mists of memory spirits had already gathered. They drifted in between the lilies that were still there, near the mailbox, and still pretty. They hung in the air around Sea Pony, the mustang parked under the palms, not far from the house, a car cover tied over him. They floated near the Jasmine in front of the old house.

She sat for a moment, spellbound, observing a hazy glimmer of orange and pink appearing just below the tree line in the backyard. Turning the engine off, she breathed heavily in silence. A dim light glowed from the kitchen. Smiling, she gazed at the rusty red and turquoise steps. As her eyes adjusted to the early light, she smiled again at the prettiness of the steps and the porch posts, recalling the Sunday morning they painted them, and the turquoise blue door, and the black Dakota and Mayan symbols framing it. Dakota/ Mayan fusion, he had called it.

The mists of memory spirits settled closer, drifting around her car...

With the window down, she could hear the cicadas' electric singing suddenly start, and the crickets chirping, the fronds of the palms rustling when the fingers of the offshore wind brushed over them. She thought she heard a tree frog. Her senses keened on everything. But something big was missing. Her protector, Koda. He was not waiting for her at the top step of the front porch, expecting her, and he never would again. Yet, over the years, she would look for him there, even see him briefly as a silhouette in the doorway... then not.

The presence of death had taken a seat alongside her; an unwanted passenger, an

260

unwanted companion. She thought about her parents and found herself remembering a very old Indian woman, a gentle stranger with long silver hair wearing a necklace of small shells, who was holding her close while her pre-school teacher and other people she didn't know tried to explain to a little girl that her parents were not coming to get her because there'd been a terrible accident. How do you explain to a five and a half year old, the death of her parents? How does a child understand it? With her head turned away from excited voices, she shielded herself from the horror of the truth, pressing her small face to the softness of the old woman's shoulder, slightly covered in her silver hair.

There was no shoulder to place her cheek on now. While sitting inside her car, she stared at the emptiness where Koda was.... She was in tenth grade. She could see herself through the opened window of the car and the misty mind clouds, even as the faint light in the kitchen blurred and twinkled, blurred and twinkled.... She and Grandpa on the floor sitting on either side of the old wolf, as Dr. Anne slowly injected the medicine that would free Koda from his worn-out body and from the relentless pain of his wounded legs....

The last days had gotten bad for Koda quickly. Once, his hind leg, where the bullet had broken the bone, gave out on him, and he collapsed. But, with Grandpa's help he willed himself up because he knew if he didn't Grandpa would fall down from trying. Next day, a more severe limp developed than the one he already had. A painful looking limp. Days later, both rear legs could no longer support him, and when he tried to squat and go to the bathroom, he fell, and he couldn't get up.

"We must allow him his dignity," Grandpa had said shaking as he lifted Koda for the last time, and together they carried him up the porch steps and into the house, Grandpa holding Koda under his once broad white chest and powerful head; Rainy lifting his back legs that always seemed so long, even now as they fell limp across her arms.

"His mind's still sharp," Grandpa had said. "His spirit's strong as ever.... We won't let ye down, Koda."

Grandpa looked at Rainy. "His loyalty's to us, his pack, and he'll do whatever it takes, suffer whatever he has to, in order to be with us. We'd be selfish to allow it, Rainy. We have to help Koda.... Could ye please call Dr. Anne."

Rainy stroked behind Koda's ear and along his thick mane, and with tears falling, was telling Koda how much she loved him and how thankful she was to him, while Grandpa sat and rocked back and forth, back and forth, chanting an Indian song to the Great Mystery, letting the Mystery know a special being would be coming, and clasping onto Koda's white front paw and trying not to cry, for the wolf he had saved and loved had taught him many things, taught him to find purpose and to live again, and that now he was teaching Grandpa how to die. And how to let go.... That is was alright to let go.... After Koda's last whimper came with his final breath, Grandpa said that Koda had made the jump. He stood and hugged Dr. Anne, and thanked her. He had a good death....

Grandpa was right. Koda had made his Great Change knowing for certain that he was loved, and that he had left love behind, and that nothing Granpa could think of in the whole world was more important.

Then Grandpa turned his head, dropped slowly to his knees, and leaned over Koda's body. Placing his face in his hands, he wept. Outside, a sudden crack of lightning shook the small house and the entire world, and then almost simultaneous, the thunder boomed, and it rained. All at once. It rained heavy, and the winds blew wild and powerful all night until morning....

As Rainy sat behind the steering wheel, looking through her opened car window, it seemed that the little house itself was getting more and more empty. So was the world that she had known for most her life.

Despite Grandpa's heart growing too tired and now beginning to beat too many times out of rhythm, he chose to stay living in his small house near the beach, refusing any amounts of money from developers for it and the small spot of land where he had lived for much of his life, and he still kept Rainy's room available the years she had been away at college for her to come home and stay when she could. His weak pulse would beat faster and stronger with each visit, and with the news of her accomplishments, his chest filled with pride. Whenever he would see this graceful and elegant young woman that was his granddaughter heading through the front door, his eyes would shine, and he would smile a happy, joyful smile.

His eyes teary when she couldn't see them whenever she had to leave; but, if she did manage on occasion to see her grandfather's emotions begin to leak out, he would explain that it was simply the feelings of life going through him living in the Wheel, living in the Balance. And it was okay.

On this sacred early light before dawn, Rainy sat alongside of her grandfather on the bed, her head pressed lightly on his chest. She strained to hear his heart still beating, but she could only barely feel it. She could imagine his smile, though, as the tips of his fingers touched her hair for the last time.

"Rain," he whispered, and then he took a shallow breath and seemed to drift off into that place in between life and death.

"It's okay, Granpa," she said, trying to make her voice sound strong, that it really was okay. "You've left lots of love, Granpa.... We've lots of memories. And stories, Granpa. We've so many stories.... You can go. I'll be alright.... Koda's waitin', Granpa. I can feel him."

Only once did Sadie come into the room and place her hand on her friend's shoulder, but she could glimpse them occasionally through the opened door, keeping a watchful eye, respecting the moment that was taking place, keeping a special loving strength available that only a friend could at such a time. She would offer Rainy an opportunity to step outside, but Rainy just stayed with her head lightly resting on her grandfather's chest the whole time he was passing from this world into the Great Mystery of the next, and she held his hand.

She was crying, silently, her tears dripping down her cheeks, not unlike the rain outside when she was born nor the first time when she stood on the front porch, looking up at the rain drop forming at the edge of Grandpa's eye, trailing water down his cheek, and then falling onto her arm....

She kept listening to his breath becoming more distant and fainter. Then, as the white heron plume had occasionally brushed against her ear when she was a girl, his spirit, in a whisper almost too soft to imagine, had lifted with his last body breath. His energy went into the Mystery where it was needed, where Koda was, lingering for a while in the dawn mist as memory-spirits at the edge of space and time will do....

And everything was quiet.

Even if it's a handful of earth.

Hold on to what you believe,

Even if it's a tree that stands by itself.

Hold on to what you must do,

Even if it's a long way from here.

Hold on to your life,

Even if it's easier to let go.

Hold on to my hand,

Even if someday I'll be gone away from you.

TRIBAL SONG

CHAPTER FORTY-FIVE

THE UNFORESEEN REQUEST

Dr. Ramirez stood behind the podium at the edge of the crescent table.

"Rainy Peek?" he said.

The young women sat in the chair, her grandpa's eagle feather graced a single braid of her long hair, the color of cedar wood at dawn, streaks of sunlight woven into a single braid hanging down her shoulder, passed the turquoise and silver turtle earring. Her pleasant smile radiated a kindness and strength that made the panel of professors proud, and even humbled, in her presence, for they had served her as teachers. Her back straight, knees slightly spaced, and her hands clasped loosely in her lap. Only for an instant did she glance directly at the eyes of the grey haired, mustached man who had addressed her from behind the podium, then quickly scanned the faces of his colleagues, a strong sense of self, complimenting her own sense of humility.

"Yes, Professor," she said. "I am Rainy Peek."

"Ms. Peek, I know I speak for all of the teachers present here today when I state that you have been an exceptional student at this university, and in the program of environmental science. Your internship with our marine staff and your fellow students, and your work with them after the Deep Horizon platform exploded and the subsequent oil spill that followed was highly praised. Your rescue of endangered sea turtles, and other marine life, at the risk of your own, was nothing less than heroic."

The faculty seated in their swivel chairs, and in their sympathetic civility, could not hear the terror in primal voices on that blazing dark night in the Gulf. They could not hear the honking of great herons and egrets, the squealing of the gulls, the terrified panic of pelicans flapping wings too heavy with oil to fly. They could not hear the turtles in their screaming silence burning in water that was on fire. Coastal fishing and shrimp trawlers had used tubes and buoys to make another burn box, encircling a large area of the water, and trapping the oil. The bird and animal rescue crew shouting back from their smaller vessel that there were birds and dolphins and turtles trapped inside. The BP ship's captain yelling at the rescue crews to "get out!" and then shouting the orders to the trawlers, "Light it up!" The faculty could not hear in that horror of flaming darkness, the warnings of the other rescuers and the crew for her not to dive in; "Rainy!" they cried. They could not know what had mysteriously protected her as she rescued the turtles, drawn together desperate for refuge, until a rescue net tossed from the bow of the boat began dragging her own body back as she rolled in near unconsciousness over a dead dolphin towards the desperate and outstretched hands of her anxious sea mates and friends. They could not know why her skin hadn't charred beneath her wet suit, why her beautiful hair did not singe in the searing water, why her heart remained still beating....

Dr. Ramirez lifted a paper from the podium and began to read, often lifting his eyes from the words on the page to the courageous young woman at her seat: "Everything regarding the evidence and records of that night and the subsequent days and nights that immediately followed, Ms. Peek, you handled in an extremely professional and even heroic manner under great duress. You saved marine life, risking your own. No other student of this university has ever been invited as a special guest to the White House.

"And because of your heroism, our marine rescue and environmental departments have been awarded significant funding to support our continued efforts in rescue and research.

"Ms. Peek," the professor continued, "the thesis you submitted for your dissertation was not only an exemplary paper in its research and scholarship, but showed a passion for your topic rarely achieved and acceptable in academic, nor scientific writing, writing that too often separates the mind from the heart, scholarship from compassion, science from empathy. We are proud to award you two doctoral degrees: the first in Marine Biology; the second for Wildlife Rescue and Management."

The other professors at the crescent table agreed with gestures, and convincing nods, their approval.

"But," the professor who was speaking at the podium resumed, "at the request of your esteemed teachers before you, we would like to put aside routine inquiry regarding your chosen fields of study, in lieu of this one final question, and then you may be excused to begin your new life." He shuffled to another sheet of paper and read.

The young woman listened with all her senses, like a handsome wolf had taught her, at the unforeseen request.

"Of all that you have learned at this university, having some of the best minds of science as your teachers, and having some of the greatest literature in the world at your fingertips, and having been schooled in humanity's finest artistic and cultural accomplishments, what do you consider to be the most relevant scientific knowledge that you have acquired?"

Then he paused, and not satisfied with himself, placed the papers down, and gripped the edges of the podium, leaning forward, pushing against it, needing to say again what he had just said using different, less formal, words, not as much from his academic mind as from his own heart.

"Ms. Peek," he asked. "We would like to know, what is the most important lesson that you have learned that can be applied to your chosen field of science ... learned, not just here at the university, but in your life? And, please, take a moment to reflect...."

"No one saves us from ourselves.

No one can, and no one may.

We ourselves must walk the path."

- BUDDHA

CHAPTER FORTY-SIX

ONE CYCLE ENDS, ANOTHER BEGINS

In that precise instant in the University Conference Room, poised and confident before her teachers, Rainy Peek found herself in a moment of reflection, giving appropriate respect to a question that warranted it. Strange, she thought, puzzled at her muted melancholy when she read Terrance Walcott's name on the list released to the media after the platform explosion, "...men killed...."

She could still hear the distant echo of those words, "... real Indians are all dead." She could still remember wishing him off the planet for his joking in class about making money shooting wolves from airplanes. Then she wondered about the kid who called when he saw she was in danger.... She never knew about the bracelet.

As Rainy Peek sat in that hardback wooden chair in the climate controlled room with no breezes, the plumes of the eagle feather fastened to her single braid started to dance ever so slightly in the still air, stirred by the energies gathering around her, and of the imaginings racing through her mind: Grandpa in a wolf hug with Koda watching her leave for school.... The sound of his voice when he shared a story or a wisdom.... The special feeling she always got running her fingers, or her toes through Koda's mane, or scratching his belly; and then she remembered Mrs. Kingsley... her sweet smile and her sweeter southern words sliding into her brain, like water drops on a banana leaf, her delicious cookies, and reaching out to a third grade girl in a passing darkness....

Rainy blinked and looked attentively at the committee members, her mind flashing in the lightning of the storm that took her on a spirit journey to find the door... the little sacred island... and Earth in the immensity of endless space... how resplendent it all was ... how fragile it all became ... when the oil washed ashore, and everything changed....

With her eyes fully opened and engaged, she could see Dr. Ramirez standing at the podium patiently awaiting her reply. She could see more, though. She could see deeper inward, her thoughts speeding through memory and this thing we call time, her lips forming the whisper of words spoken long ago.... "Memba mi tell yuh dis, Child.... Everydey buck-it go a well....Wan day de battam drap out...."

She saw with clarity Mother Turtle struggling towards the dunes with the back of her shell on fire. Only suddenly dimensions split apart, and the water is burning, and she shook back and forth in that swiftly passing recollection... desperate birds grasping at life, entangled in fishermen lines and the shreds of their discarded nets, and the plastic grocery bags and plastic soda and beer can wrappers people had left behind. Wings that will never fly again suffocating in oil. Then, among the dunes, the little girl that all little girls of her people once were, and then the teenager she would become. She sees the woman she is now and the old woman, in her, all the great grandmothers that ever were and are to come, and she sees the silver dolphin. Ah-nuh....

"Ms. Peek?" the professor at the podium quietly and politely asked again, he and the other teachers awaiting their student's response.

"Yes, Dr. Ramirez, and members of the committee," she said, "I apologize for my extended moment of reflection. Your question is quite profound."

"It's okay, Ms. Peek," he said calmly. "It is an unusual question. Take another minute or two if you need."

She smiled gratefully and nodded, Thank you.

A few of the faculty wriggled in the big chairs. Impatience. A civilized disorder, it seems. They looked around. Some looked at their watches. One flipped opened her laptop.

She was sitting with her back still straight but not leaning against the chair, the receding overhead lights glistening on the silver of her earrings, her feet comfortable in her simple black pumps, still planted firmly on the tiled floor.

"Thank you, Professors, for sharing your knowledge with me," she said, "and now I can share with you what I consider the most valuable wisdom that I have thus far learned regarding science in my brief existence."

She inhaled deeply, deliberate and slow; and exhaled, mindful and calm, a breath....

>>•‹‹ >>•‹‹ >>•‹‹

Her mind speeding closer to the moment at the end of this cycle of her life when everything meaningful from the past manifests; she sees her mom and dad as they were when she was five years old. She feels them with her now. And Grandpa. How could she begin to grasp at all the love he gave to her? She feels it all around her and inside of her now.

Thoughts, faster the speed of light, faster than her breathing, she reflects on her ancestors, and all the people who love and respect this land. And those who are not people, like Koda, the wolf she had loved, her protector and companion, and all the wolves shot for no good reason. She thinks about the eagles and pelicans and hawks and gulls and egrets and wood storks and herons. The turtles. The whales. The orcas, and dolphins. She thinks about the tiny rare sea horse whose species may soon be nonexistent. She thinks about panthers and jaguars stalking life on the brink of their own extinction. Her thoughts come faster than light and breath, she sees the lions and elephants and Bengal tigers and all the animals denied their freedom in amusement parks and zoos, and polar bears falling through the ice. She sees in her mind what was and what may never be again, the magical forests and the emerald jungles and the great snow-capped mountains and the creeks and the rivers all running free and clear into the beautiful womb of our incredible ocean.

>>·<< >>·<< >>·<<

At that juncture, the instant before she offered the answer that would speak for them all, her reflections slowed, and she took a deeper breath. Something she had almost completely forgotten had appeared. Something her grandfather had alluded to a long time ago when they were discussing her purpose in life, had manifested at this moment; something she couldn't recollect back then about destiny, the guilt of a little kindergartener who had abandoned the lifeless body of a tree frog on a toxic rusty oil drum. What had once seemed like the fragment of a child's nightmare suspended in the mists of a young woman's distant memory suddenly leapt up and into her consciousness ....

This had been her destiny all along. The purpose and driving force of her life: To give dignity, find balance in the death of that tiny creature.

"May I stand, Dr. Ramirez?" she asked.

"Of course, Ms. Peek," he said, welcoming her request. "Por favor," he said in Spanish, "Please..." and then he sat at the table with the other professors.

She rose from her chair in a single fluid motion, her dark auburn and sun-streaked hair cascading over her shoulders and down her back. Grandpa's eagle feather tied to the single braid that hung along her right ear, lightly brushing the turtle earring that once belonged to her grandmother Jewel. They became his gift for his granddaughter's sixteenth birthday. Turquoise for the sky, he said; silver, for the earth. Together... equal...Sky and Earth...male and female.

With her hands now folded in front of her, she looked at the panel of professors and said that she was grateful for this opportunity and for all the opportunities the university had provided her, and again thanked them for their patience. She had tapped into that part of herself that was a part of all things, that voice, no longer having to be silent, her voice, choosing and chosen to speak for all voices not invited. She was the orator. The one who finds the words....

"Nature is alive," she said, her tone assertive, clear, captivating, the eagle feather stirring as if a breeze had caught its plumes. "The

276 universe is alive," she said. "We are more than atoms and molecules and neurons and neuron receptors and electrons and carbon, and the universe is more than planets and moons and stars and solar systems and galaxies. We are life. We are related to all life and all things. We share an incomprehensible Totality that always was, and will always be, the Great Holy Mystery, the origin of all life and all things. Western science, in all its departments and scholarship, with all its inventive terminology and technology, research and explorations, and for whatever rationalizations it deems necessary, will never prove otherwise.

"The Sky is our father," she said. "It's as simple as that, and yet more complex and sacred than many of us can allow ourselves to envision. The Air and Clouds and Falling Rain, and even what we so coldly call the ozone is our Father, the Sky."

She held open her hands, and suspended just above them, appeared an image about the size of a Mayan ball, a holograph of some mysterious nature, of the slowly spinning blue and beautiful Earth. In the unexpected, when minds had crossed boundaries for the committee of esteemed teachers who were seeing in that instant–magic, when thought and words manifest and imagination transcends realities, Rainy Peek took on a beauty that could only emanate from the wisdom of which she spoke, and from the image suspended before her.

"The Earth is alive," she said, her eyes glowing in the blue spectral world formed from her imagination into the aura of her opened hands, embracing the image like holding mist. "The Earth is our Mother," she continued, eloquence and a sense of urgency resonating in her voice. "All beings born of the union of Sky and Earth deserve the wisdom and compassion of our intelligence, but most importantly, they deserve the respect that all love needs and affirms – they deserve our gratitude–nothing less."

When the shape she held dispersed into strands of sea fog warmed in a tide pool, she looked up unobtrusively at the esteemed panel of teachers, placing her hands over her abdomen, interlocking her fingers.

The humanities professor blinked, and shaking her head, she could not cause the image of the Earth she had just beheld suspended above the hands of this young woman to vanish from her mind, and she took on a kind of confused humility and sorrow all at once. The ancients understood this magic. Their accounts of creation and the forces that moved in the universe and influenced our world, are not simply myths.

Next to her, the English professor sank bewildered in his chair glancing to either side, searching other faces for signs affirming what he had just seen. Merlin must've had the magic. Fiction is born out of it.... Where had he read that? Or was it something he heard? Why can't I remember?

One of the scientists fussed at the table. This isn't science, his eyes were saying, examining the area around the student's chair. What is this? He scanned the ceiling and stared with a sullen annoyance at the booth where the visual aid equipment was stored for Power Point presentations. Where's the computer? Where's the device? Where is the mechanism?

One of the older scientists, captivated as he had not been since he was a boy looking at the rings of Saturn through the lenses of his first telescope, had placed his hand on his middle-

278 aged colleague's arm. It's okay. Not everything can be explained.

Dr. Ramirez was sitting up in his chair, leaning forward, his hand pressed against his mouth, his eyes narrow and focused, something in his Peruvian blood stirred, something in his old soul became energized, observing the beautiful young woman, knowing for certain she was not like any student who had ever come before them.

"In this way," she continued, "the Sky and Earth need to know, they are loved by their children, and we, no matter how civilized we have become... no matter how sophisticated we believe we are... no matter how big our bank accounts may be. How fast our cars can speed. No matter the 4G coverage of our smart phones or how many Apps we download.... No matter how tall our buildings... how big and ruthless our armies or powerful our bombs. No matter how many probes we send into space, we are still their children. Earth and Sky.

"Every chemical and cell that is in us was born of her. And none of us, whether we love and respect the Earth, or we do not feel at all for her, none of us will be exempt from the consequences of irresponsible and greed driven human behavior.

"We are living in a state of Koyaanisqatsi," she said. "We are living out of balance, and sooner, than later, that will be our end."

Outside, a clap of thunder trembled the walls of the conference room and caused the lights to blink. The storm traveling east across the bay had arrived.

When the beautiful young woman with the eagle feather tied to a single sun-streaked braid stepped through the metal door into the presence and powerful force of her namesake, she sighed and smiled.

A handsome man with starlight in his eyes was standing under the overhang of the doorway, partially shielded from the downpour....

"I have something for you," he said, as the sound of rain fell everywhere. "A graduation gift of sorts." He handed her something wrapped in a red cloth. "I came across it on the beach some time ago.... I understand they're rarely ever found.... I've held onto it for a long time because I didn't feel it belonged to me, but that one day I would know...."

When she opened the cloth, she gasped.

It can't be, but it was. How does love find its way in this Koyaanisqatsi world? How does love know?

Her quivering fingers traced ever so lightly the length of the bone-like barb of a ray, feather brushing along its sharp pointed edges. She stared teary-eyed and amazed at the sacred object and at the spec of blood that suddenly appeared on her fingertip. Gazing up at this man that she already loved, she couldn't find the words. She couldn't speak.

With deep felt tenderness, he lifted her hand, and together they watched as raindrops washed the spec of blood away, and he smiled, and she smiled, streams of water trickling from the corners of their eyes.

And the sound of rain grew stronger and more powerful....

ACKNOWLEDGMENTS

MOTHERLESS would not have been possible without the loving encouragement, insight, and wisdom of those who read various drafts and excerpts of the manuscript and provided a writer's greatest gift: Barbara Schoenbeck and her grandchildren; MariJo Moore and her grandchildren; Trace A DeMeyer; Ellyn Kingsley; and Cynthia Vandehoef; Debra Morrow; Linda La Pointe and Chic Atkinson; Jason Schoenbeck; Shimmering Horse Woman in Moonlight; Richard Smith and his daughter Arianna; And Sam Gilliland, National Poet Treasure of Scotland, my deepest gratitude; Chris Stone for photography, and Calusa Horn for your courage and inspiration; Carises and Debbie Horn, for the precious art and the medicine of the stones; Ihasha and Alexis Horn (also for photo), the love and pride I feel for you. And thank you to an incredible editor, Beth Wareham; heartfelt and soulful designer Kimberley Heurlin; quiet-force and designer, Katherine Phelps. And thank you, Paul DeLucia AP, DOM; and Martin Keane AP, CCH, MMQ, for helping to keep my life in balance during the journey; thank you to those great minds whose brief passages grace the pages between chapters; And, of course, the one who writes alongside me nearly every day, who listens and advises and inspires me, whose intelligence and gift of words that are as profound as her beauty and courage, my life companion and bff, award-winning author, Amy Krout-Horn. And to the one who believed in MOTHERLESS, the one who is a special human being devoted to helping make the world a loving place, agent extraordinaire, and publisher, Lisa Hagan, I am now and forever grateful.

ABOUT THE AUTHOR

GABRIEL HORN
WHITE DEER OF AUTUMN

Gabriel Horn's publications span across four decades, and include the novel he co-authored with his life companion Amy Krout-Horn, the 2012 National Indie Excellence Book Award winner for visionary fiction, Transcendence.

Selected Who's Who Among America's Teachers, he has received the University of South Florida's Distinguished Alumni Award for Outstanding Professional Achievement, and has been awarded Faculty Emeritus at St. Petersburg College.

For over 40 years, from reservation schools, to American Indian Movement (AIM) Survival Schools, to public schools, colleges, and universities, he has unwaveringly advocated the academic respect due the history, literature, and philosophy of Native America, and has been an outspoken defender of the natural world.

Readers Guide and Discussion
Questions for Motherless

Before the discussion, try and look up on the internet if there really are such islands documented that have appeared, then disappeared such as the one in the book.

(1) When the bus driver says to the kindergartner, "**Everydey buck-it go a well....Wan day de battam drap out**...." (a Jamaican expression also found in a Bob Marley song). What do we feel the bus driver **foreshadows**?

(2) The Jamaican bus driver helps take us a bit out of our comfort zone as the language he uses is an unfamiliar version of English, but also because he uses profanity when language and frustration overwhelm him. Would some people think negatively of him because of the way he speaks English, or his use of profanity? Do we feel his profanity is understandable under the circumstances? What words would you use that are not profane to describe what the children are experiencing, and what has been dumped in the ditch?

(3) The narrator shows that one does not have to be of a particular age, race, religion, or ethnicity, to care for the natural environment that sustains all life that sustains human beings.

a. How does a person know, or learn, to respect the environment?

b. Are most people born with this **innate wisdom**?

c. If so, how is it possible to destroy this **innate wisdom**?

d. Is compassion and care for the natural environment something human beings can **still** be taught?

e. Though it is possible to teach young children to respect the natural environment, how would you suggest teaching older kids, and even adults, to respect the environment?

(4) Describe a scene from a time in your own life when you have experienced some kind of pollution. In one word, how did this make you feel?

(5) Why does Grandpa think it's important to know when the summer and winter solstices occur, or the spring and autumn equinoxes, or the phases of the moon? What can happen to human beings when they no longer are aware of natural time?

(6) How do you feel about Grandpa sharing the Indigenous perspective of American history with Rainy?

(7) The story provides different examples of what it means to be a mother, and a father. What are examples that are not being a mother and father, and ways that are?

(8) How would the world change if people

regarded the Earth as a living being they called **Mother** and all forms of life, even rocks, on this planet as alive, and therefore, relatives? Why does this world view threaten some people of industrial nations, and how can it change what is now called the American way of life?

(9) What do you feel is a healthier world view: the earth *is not* alive, but a resource put here for human use and consumption? Or, the Earth *is* alive, and she is the Mother of all life on the planet? Why do you feel this way? How would you support the way you feel?

(10) Who **benefits** from the belief that Earth is a resource for unlimited human consumption and use? Who suffers?

(11) Grandpa struggled with himself when it came to answering Rainy's questions about history. He was concerned that maybe she was too young to learn an Indigenous view. Feeling that it was something her mother and father would have wanted her to know, however, he decided to share with her a history of America that is "not a good history," and one that is rarely ever taught in school. In what ways do you feel knowing this history can help you to be a better person, and America to become a better country?

(12) Where should energy corporations, including nuclear energy, be allowed to drill, mine, or frack?

(13) Why do you feel that water is, or is not, sacred to you?

(14) Native Americans are responsible for over half the world's food staples, and much of the food we eat here in the United States has its origins in Native America. Even the US Constitution is rooted in Native America as are so many other contributions. **Why do you think that none of this, in most schools and classes, is taught**?

(15) When Grandpa discusses dark energy and dark matter, he tells Rainy that scientists do not know what they are, but that they do exist. Grandpa uses their ritual of the "star talk" to use metaphor to teach Rainy. Describe an encounter you've had with dark energy, or dark matter, as a metaphor for a negative feeling that made you uncomfortable or frightened.

(16) Recall a class (history, English, math, science, physical education, foreign language, etc) where you felt the teacher didn't like you. How did you deal with the situation? What was it like? What did you learn from the experience, and did the experience affect your attitude about the subject?

(17) Neither Grandpa nor Rainy, nor the narrator of the story, ever used the pronoun "it" to describe or refer to something that was alive...? How does that word "it" reflect a person's understanding (world view) of life? Can you think of a time when someone

you knew, or even you, had called a tree, or a bird, or an animal, an IT?

(18) What examples in religion or history does the idea of sacrifice play an important role? Can you describe a time that you **sacrificed**, given up something, for a good reason?

(19) When Tom Brightman gives Rainy the sting ray barb at the end of the novel, she realized immediately the object's connection to her mother. What kinds of objects do you have that hold a special connection to another person, animal, or even a specific experience?

(20) Do you feel hopeful when you think about the future of the Earth?